BLOOD AUTUMN

*A novel of historical horror with
erotic overtones*

"What a wonderful, scary writer Kathryn Ptacek is!"
—John Coyne

"Kathryn Ptacek is already better than many famous horror writers I could name."

—Peter Straub

Look for this other TOR book by Kathryn Ptacek

SHADOWEYES

BLOOD AUTUMN

KATHRYN PTACEK

TOR

A TOM DOHERTY ASSOCIATES BOOK

This is a work of fiction. All the characters and events portrayed in this book are fictional, and any resemblance to real people or incidents is purely coincidental.

BLOOD AUTUMN

Copyright © 1985 by Kathryn Ptacek

All rights reserved, including the right to reproduce this book or portions thereof in any form.

First Printing: January 1985

A TOR Book

Published by Tom Doherty Associates
8-10 West 36 Street
New York, N.Y. 10018

ISBN: 0-812-52447-0
CAN. ED.: 0-812-52448-9

Printed in the United States of America

*To
Andrea Minasian
for the first year of her new life*

Thanks to

—the Georgia Historical Society of Savannah, Georgia, and the Savannah Public Library, who answered all of my questions,

—as well as to the city of Savannah, which proved hospitable while I was there,

—Reverend Geoffrey Marsh for answering several questions of a theological nature,

—Ashley McConnell for her long-standing patience in regard to Ireland and matters Irish,

and, of course,

—thanks most of all to Charlie for his support and love, his terrible jokes (escargot, eh?), and for being there this past year.

Where youth grows pale, and spectre-thin, and dies.
—John Keats,
"Ode to a Nightingale"

Prologue

Savannah, Georgia: 1889

"I didn't think you priests were supposed to gaze unabashedly at beautiful women, Uncle," the older man's nephew drawled slightly, his brown eyes following the direction the other man's had taken.

"Really, Guy," Father Daniel protested, "we are human, after all." The Church, for all its spiritual ways, as he well knew, had a history of the appreciation of beauty, ranging at times to the point of hedonism.

"But aren't priests supposed to be beyond reproach?" Guy continued.

"You mean above suspicion, and you are referring to Caesar's wife. The reference is commonly believed to be derived from Plutarch."

"Ah."

Guy Maxwell, while intelligent and a well-trained and talented physician, had never claimed to be a classical scholar and had already lost interest in their conversation, although not the reason for it. Almost involuntarily his eyes strayed to the woman across the room who commanded his and his uncle's attention, as well the admiring glances of the other men present at the Parkers' party.

Father Daniel had been one of the first of many arrivals on this hot September evening. Joseph and Celeste Parker were not members of his parish, but previously the couple had expressed interest in helping orphaned and abandoned boys. The Parkers had thus invited Father O'Neil of St. Mary's Orphan Home to the party, knowing that some of the wealthiest and most influential citizens in Savannah would be there. Father O'Neil, however, had developed a persistent cough two days ago and had insisted that his assistant Father Daniel attend in his place.

Once at the Parker home the priest had looked around with unabashed interest, for his duties did not often take him inside the town's mansions. A two-story Federal with an exterior of the celebrated Savannah grey brick, the Parker house was impeccably furnished with furniture handed down through the family for many generations. Proudly, Mrs. Parker had exhaustively detailed the lengthy history of each notable piece, and Father Daniel had smiled faintly, remembering that at one time he, too, had owned handiwork by Chippendale, Hepplewhite, and Sheraton. The sin of pride, he had admonished himself unsuccessfully.

For a while longer they had chatted; then she had excused herself to greet other guests, and shortly afterward Guy Maxwell and his colleague, Rose O'Shaunessey, also a physician at the Savannah Hospital, had arrived together and joined the priest.

A colleague as well as his nephew's lover, or so Father Daniel suspected. As a priest of the Catholic faith, he was supposed to frown on such behavior; as the man he had once been, he approved heartily, for the woman doctor displayed a sensibility not often found among those her age, and she was witty with a quick smile and ready humor, had capable hands that looked gentle as well, and no doubt possessed a fiercesome temper if her bright red hair were interpreted correctly. Too, Father Daniel enjoyed talking with her, and had since Guy had introduced him to her several months before. Unlike many of his vocation, Daniel did not shun women. Indeed, all his life he had enjoyed being with them and had often found his empathy being repaid with trust. He did not think that Guy could have chosen a better woman than Rose.

The three had chatted, the doctors about their work at the hospital, the priest about his boys at St. Mary's, until Rose had entrusted Guy to his uncle's care and had wandered off to chat with an acquaintance. Gradually Guy's and Daniel's conversation had shifted to the woman who had entered the large salon minutes before. While the new arrival's worshipful cortege shepherded her out to the flagstone terrace where the air was cooler, Guy and his uncle applied themselves to the pleasant task of studying her.

From head to toe the newcomer wore black, and the priest wondered if she was in mourning, although he saw no crêpe. The décolletage of her simply cut evening gown dared much, delving lower than those of any other lady in the room, and many eyes strayed to that shadowy valley revealed. Upon her head perched a dainty hat with a half veil that tantalizingly shaded the upper portion of her face, a veil unnecessary, for the hotly burning southern sun had set several hours ago. Long kid gloves, opera slippers, and a double strand of jet completed her severe costume. Her black hair trailed in long curls that caressed her shapely shoulders.

Neither tall nor short, she was perfectly proportioned with an hourglass figure the priest did not think was achieved through the use of deforming corsets and stays worn by so many other women. Her skin glowed with the

luminescence of an Oriental pearl. He couldn't be sure of
the color of her eyes, although from time to time he caught
a glint of them from behind the veil. Her face—that portion he could see: the full red lips, the pointed chin, the
wide cheekbones, the straight, finely formed nose—he
would have described as beautiful, although that seemed
woefully inadequate.

There was a *presence* about her, a grace; no, an
impression of unrivaled loveliness. Was this the face that
launched a thousand ships, as Marlowe had asked three
centuries before, Father Daniel wondered? Or the face of a
nymph, a naiad, a Grace, as Scott would have claimed, or
was it merely the face of a woman, but one who seemed
more than the sum of every woman he had ever met, ever
envisioned?

Father Daniel blinked, and found himself leaning forward,
breath caught, as she spoke to the men surrounding her.
He was unable to hear her, but he found he was being
sucked into a vortex deeper and deeper, the swirling sides
rising around him; he was losing himself within the lovely
depths of the glittering eyes he imagined and the luminous-
ness of her skin and wetly shining lips, and remotely he
heard a voice, and knew it was Guy still talking to him,
and with great reluctance the priest pulled himself out of
the attractive vortex and breathed deeply. Guy's voice was
no longer faint.

"It's really all the same period, after all. Isn't it?" he
asked.

"What?" Slightly startled, the priest glanced at the
young man.

"Caesar and the Romans and Jesus Christ. It's all about
the same time, isn't it?"

"Good God, Guy, I haven't the faintest idea of what
you mean!"

"That makes two of us," he admitted, somewhat ruefully, as he grinned.

Daniel chuckled, and the younger man joined him. After a moment he lifted his crystal goblet and indicated the beautiful woman. "Why aren't you over there with the rest of those young gadabouts instead of staying with a feeble old man like me?"

"Because I am chaperoning my uncle."

"A foul business for someone so young as yourself, and certainly not the most exciting of tasks. Go on." He waved his hand. "I know you want to meet her."

"There's time."

" 'Do not squander time, for that's the stuff life is made of.' "

"Quoting the Bible again, Uncle?"

Daniel sighed. "Franklin, not the Bible."

Guy lit one of those long cigars, which he knew his uncle detested and which he still insisted upon smoking nonetheless, and the priest sipped his wine as the smoke whirled in a blue-grey cloud above their heads and drifted in sinuous tendrils toward the French windows.

For the occasion the Parkers' servants had hung gaily hued paper Chinese lanterns upon the lower branches of the trees in the garden, and now in the darkness insects buzzed and darted, circled and droned in the bright orbits of light. The priest could clearly see the long delicate form of a dragonfly bumping against the lantern closest to the doors.

The woman watched the dragonfly, then smiled faintly as she stretched out a hand to brush the insect away, or so Daniel expected. Instead, in one fluid motion she had caught it, then flung her hapless prisoner inside the lantern. The dragonfly fluttered frantically around the paper prison until its wings brushed against the candle flame. Instantly the insect ignited, the paper caught fire, and one of the men leaped forward, pulling her away just as burning embers showered downward.

Incredibly, no one appeared to have witnessed the dragonfly incident. No one, except the priest. Perhaps it had been enacted entirely for his benefit. After a moment he dismissed that as a nonsensical notion.

Momentarily something inside Father Daniel fluttered like the poor dragonfly, and he frowned. A fleeting memory. Gone. Almost there again. Almost a recognition. Of what? This woman? Had he previously met her? Before he lived in Savannah? Surely he had. She was from his long past, but for some reason the priest couldn't determine the occasion or place, and that greatly troubled him, for his mind was not generally—he thanked God—given to such unfortunate lapses.

He relayed as much to his nephew.

"What's that, Uncle?" Guy sounded distracted, his voice almost dreamy, as his eyes remained fixed on the woman. The priest wondered what Rose must think of her beau's fascination, for surely she saw Guy had eyes only for this other woman. Daniel glanced at the woman doctor, but she stood with her back to them as she conversed with several women.

The bough where the paper lantern had hung was now dark.

"That woman."

"What about her?"

"She reminds me of someone. Someone from my younger days. Back when I was in England, I think."

"A passing resemblance, no doubt." Guy dismissed it, licked his lips.

"No, no. It's more than that, Guy. She looks just like the woman. I think." His nephew did not notice his confusion. "It's been so many years, though," Daniel mused. So many years . . . too many. Try as he might, he was unable to recall under what circumstances he could have met the woman. Before he could even speculate further, he saw Rose strolling toward them. She caught the tail end of the conversation.

"What's been so many years?" she asked, her voice containing the slightest trace of a northern accent. Her bright blue eyes were alert, filled with intelligence and compassion, and Daniel thought it would be an excellent idea for Guy and Rose to marry. Tonight, though, he feared, might put a strain between them.

"I was saying, my dear, that I believe I've met that woman before."

" 'That woman' is named August Justinian, and she's the widow of a planter," Rose replied.

The priest blinked in surprise. "How did you . . ."

Her lips twitched. "I asked."

"I should have known," he said, chuckling.

"I had to know." Her eyes strayed to Guy.

True, the priest thought, she had to learn the identity of this mesmerizing woman. Too much was at stake for her tonight.

Apparently Guy hadn't listened to their exchange. Daniel didn't think his nephew was aware of anything but the other woman. For a few minutes longer Guy continued to watch silently, then stubbed out his expensive cigar, and left them without a word.

Pain in her eyes, Rose looked after him as he walked across the room. "She's like a flame, and the men are moths."

"Yes." And the priest remembered all too clearly the burning dragonfly. " 'Shall I, wasting in despair, Die because a woman's fair?' " Rose raised a slender eyebrow, and he shook his head. "An old poet, dust for two centuries now."

Guy had reached the terrace and was introducing himself to the widow. Too far away to actually hear Guy's words, Rose and Daniel found it wasn't necessary. The expression on the young man's face was sufficient. Momentarily the conversation in the room lulled, and they heard the echo of the other woman's laugh as she edged closer to Guy and smiled up at him.

The shade of a half-forgotten memory stirred as Daniel tried to peer into the past, but a thick fog had enveloped his mind and all the forms were ghostly and surreal, vague, as though they hadn't been his own memories.

Guy was lost, too, the priest thought sadly, and wondered why he thought that.

"I'm surprised you aren't over there, Father Daniel." Rose's tone was ironic.

He shook his head. "Not I. No, I am content to assume the role of watcher, but that's all. I leave flirting to others far younger—and some older." He noted that some of the woman's—she had a name, he had to remind himself—admirers were far older than he.

"You said that she seemed familiar."

"Yes," he said slowly. "It's as though I know her from sometime . . . someplace . . . but not recently."

"An old flame?" she teased.

"Hardly," he replied dryly. "I think I would have remembered that, after all, and yet that's the strange part of this puzzle, my dear, for you see, I cannot recall where or when or how I might have met her. Usually I don't forget names and faces—I can't, as a priest. And I've been unable to stir a single memory."

Apparently Rose took his lapse of memory far more

seriously than did Guy, for she frowned. "It is odd. Very odd, don't you think?"

He nodded, unable to erase the image of the burning dragonfly from his mind. "The whole evening has been odd." He paused, then murmured, half to himself, " 'Fair is foul, and foul is fair.' "

"I beg your pardon, Father?"

"Nothing important, my dear."

They fell silent, companionably so, while the priest sipped his wine and Rose watched Guy. More and more male laughter came from the terrace, and every so often Father Daniel heard the sultry voice of the woman. Of August Justinian, he corrected, reminding himself of her name. *The woman*.

Some twenty male admirers now clustered around her, each one listening intently to her every word, and in their midst was poor lost Guy. Poor Rose, Daniel thought, and glanced at the woman doctor.

She gave him a brief smile with just the smallest hint of sadness.

"I think I must be going, Father. I've a long day tomorrow."

"Of course, my dear. If you wish me to escort you . . ." he began.

"No," she replied quickly, "that won't be necessary, Father; I don't have far to go."

He held her hand in his for a second, squeezed it; then she nodded and left. She did not glance back at Guy, nor did he notice her departure.

Daniel sighed heavily and moved his chair a little closer to the terrace so that he could give his full attention to the woman. To August Justinian.

". . . am just returned from Paris," he heard her saying. She received general approval from her admirers. "I had wanted to travel to Rome this past summer, but now I will wait until next year."

"Jasper's just back from there," one tall balding man rasped loudly, nodding to a middle-aged man by his side. "Damned unsafe over there, ma'am. In my opinion, it wouldn't be a good place for a woman to travel alone. Not at all."

"I never travel alone," she replied, and the others all laughed.

Unabashedly the priest eavesdropped—listened, as he preferred to term it—and learned that the woman had traveled widely throughout Europe and Asia. She had an education of sorts, that much was obvious, although he did not think it formal. But she seemed very learned in numerous subjects, being able to hold an intelligent conversation with the men on any topic they chose, and she was facile in many tongues, which she amply demonstrated at the requests of her companions. All of the men surrounding her were utterly charmed by her, and the more they fell captive to her, the more Father Daniel grew suspicious.

Or perhaps suspicious was too strong a word, he thought. Perhaps he was simply displaying caution in his immediate acceptance of her. Normally he wasn't overly circumspect, though, for from the first moment he had met Rose he had liked her and had known she would be good for his nephew. So why was he now proving so reluctant when all the other men were the widow's adoring devotees? It didn't make sense.

The men were enchanted by her, Daniel thought as he finished his drink, as though she were— He looked up to see her staring at him. Or so he thought, but almost immediately she spoke to Guy, and he dismissed it as a coincidence.

Or had it been?

The hours passed, the darkness growing more complete outside the Parkers' home, and slowly those attending slipped away to return to their own homes. When no more than a handful of guests remained and the priest was drowsing from the effects of the wine, a slight noise roused him. He glanced up to see the beautiful widow gliding through the French doors and across the marble floor toward him. He scrambled to sit up.

She stopped a few feet away as he clambered awkwardly to his feet. Still he could not see her eyes because of the veil. She did not move for a minute, then spoke in a husky voice. "You have been watching me, Father."

It was teasingly offered, and yet Father Daniel felt as though he had been jolted to his inner core, for at that precise moment he knew why the widow was familiar. It was as though the remark had unlocked the gates to his memory. She *was* the same woman. He knew this, yet could scarcely credit it, for their acquaintance dated back some thirty years. Over thirty years. It was she: the very woman he had known, who had not aged, who had not changed at all, not as he had.

How was it that after all those years she remained the same outwardly? Surely, this must be her daughter, a cousin, a sister.

No. He knew as he looked at her that was the woman he had known.

The woman's moist lips smiled, as if she sensed his dilemma, and she laughed, a low sound that curled about him, caressing his face, his spine. It sought entrance to him. And found it. He grew aware of a most alien sensation, a tingling in his arms that crept to his chest, withdrew to his midsection, then seeped downward to his groin, and he ached as he had not in all the years since his first difficult days at the seminary.

Her head was tilted slightly to one side, although not in a particularly coquettish manner but more in the way that a bird cocks its head at a worm. Her eyes were bright and never blinked as she watched him. Father Daniel licked his dry lips, and as he stared into those eyes of dusk he remembered how it had been long ago, in that time in London just after the mutiny in India, and he knew, too, that his lifelong flight had ended.

August had come to claim her prize.

PART I

London, England: 1859

"Beastly! Whole damned lot of 'em ought to be shot. Bloody ignorant wogs."

Wyndham Terris tossed the newspaper down and sloshed the brandy around in its snifter, and striving to forget the unhappy memories his words had stirred, stared morosely into flickering flames in the nearby fireplace.

"Damned right," Henry Montchalmers said calmly. "Thieving rascals, the whole bunch. Can't see that we've done a bit of good over there."

Lyttleton glanced at the front page of the newspaper to see what had caused Terris' agitation. The first article detailed a journalist's eyewitness account of the execution some five and a half months ago of Tatya Tope, one of the Indian Mutiny's most well-known rebel leaders. A summary of the entire mutiny followed.

As if anyone had to be reminded, Lyttleton thought wryly, for after all, hadn't everyone followed the dramatic events of the past years, the two years that it took for the British army to quell the rebellious Indians? He scanned the article, and while he found it fairly bloody in description, he couldn't understand why Terris was taking it so to heart until he recalled that Terris had lost a brother in battle there. He glanced sympathetically at Terris, but refrained from saying anything, for he didn't wish to further upset his friend. Instead, he shifted subjects.

"Oh, that reminds me. This morning I received a note, which I warrant both of you will find of some interest." Lyttleton paused dramatically to light one of the thin cigars he affected. He inhaled, and leaning back in the leather chair, he smoothed the ends of his dark moustache with two fingers. "Tommy's just returned from abroad."

"Tommy Hamilton? By Jove, now that's welcome news!" Montchalmers exclaimed delightedly. He sipped the amber brandy and cocked an eyebrow at Lyttleton. "Gone to India, hadn't he?"

"Yes," Lyttleton replied, sitting forward. His cigar had gone out, and he toyed with it for several moments until it was burning once more, then continued. "Made a bloody fortune over there, I hear."

"Rubies," grunted the third man.

"What's that, Wyndy?"

"Said he's made a fortune in rubies, no doubt. The wogs are bloody rich with them, y'know. Practically pave their streets with 'em. Put 'em in their scurvy navels. Dirty heathens."

"Diamonds, too, I don't doubt, and sapphires. Emeralds, even." Montchalmers ignored Terris' last comments and sighed deeply as he contemplated the vastness of another man's wealth. "Damn, if some fellows don't have the luck."

Lyttleton smiled slightly, knowing that Montchalmers was far from being destitute. His friend had been left a sizeable fortune by his late father, although most of the money had been put into a trust for Henry. The senior Montchalmers had only been too aware of his scion's spendthrift ways.

"Diamonds and rubies, sapphires and emeralds might well be part of it, I shouldn't doubt, but there's a tidbit you'll find even more intriguing," Lyttleton said craftily. He sucked wetly at the cigar and blew an ill-formed smoke ring that wavered for a few seconds above Terris' head before it dissolved.

"More intriguing than gemstones?" asked Montchalmers, plainly incredulous. "By God, what could that be?"

"Tommy's brought back a wife," Lyttleton announced triumphantly. He continued stroking his moustache.

"Good God!" Montchalmers drained his brandy. "You can't mean it! By Jove, I'm uncommonly glad for the ol' fellow!"

Terris merely stared, his mouth agape.

Several other members of the club sitting within the same room frowned deeply at this indecorous outburst, and Montchalmers hastily lowered his voice.

"Brought back a wife, you say? Old Tommy tied the knot, eh?" Lyttleton nodded vigorously. Montchalmers looked around, then whispered: "Is she a bloody wog?"

"Don't know a thing about her, or about how they met, old boy. All I know is he's got this wife now." A second smoke ring proved more successful.

"Can't be a beastly wog woman," declared Terris. "Couldn't hold his head up in society if he brought one back. He'd be cut by everyone. Besides, she'd be some bloody sort of pagan. They worship cows and monkeys, I hear."

"Hindu," corrected Montchalmers. "Good God, you don't think—I mean, whatever was old Tommy thinking of? He must have been suffering from some sort of a brain fever if he's done this."

"I suspect we'll find out soon enough." Lyttleton inhaled deeply on the cigar and breathed out. The third ring was perfect. The three men watched as it drifted upward and finally dissolved just short of the plastered ceiling.

"How's that?" Montchalmers demanded, pouring more brandy.

"The three of us are invited to dinner tomorrow evening at eight. Formal attire, please, lads," Lyttleton drawled. "At which time we shall have the distinct pleasure of making the acquaintance of the new Mrs. Hamilton."

The three men arrived at the house in the fashionable street early the following evening, eager to hear Thomas Hamilton's exciting tales of a turbulent India and to view the army officer's bride, although not precisely in that order.

The elderly butler bade the gentlemen come in at once and ushered them into the front parlor, which he left without further conversation.

Soft light from the several ornate gas lamps spread across the spacious room which was diminished greatly in size by too many pieces of dark heavy furniture. The jumbled styles displayed Hamilton's eclectic taste, and while several pieces were fairly good, Lyttleton noted that none was of any great value.

Oval portraits of slender, fair-haired Hamilton ancestors, all bearing a remarkable resemblance to Tommy and in gilt frames of varying sizes, cluttered the tops of tables and cabinets and the wallpapered walls.

An Oriental carpet of faded maroon and Hessian blue muffled their footsteps, while a painted clock on the mantel opposite ticked briskly in the room's silence. The thick velvet draperies had been drawn against the unusual heat of the early October night and the noises of the street, and Lyttleton found the room airless and altogether too warm, and not a little dusty.

An unusual odor lingered in the air as well, almost a musky scent, he thought. While he couldn't identify it, he did not find it unpleasant.

"Such a dismal place." Absently searching through his pockets for a cigar, Lyttleton stared at an ornate china figure on the top shelf of a whatnot. An elaborately dressed shepherdess tended her tiny flock, and the goat god Pan, with pipes to his slyly painted mouth, sprawled at the innocent's feet and stared lewdly up at her. He found it a particularly repulsive piece. "Never have liked the way Tommy did his place."

"Done for him, old boy," replied Montchalmers somewhat matter-of-factly. He had known Hamilton the longest of the three men, and had in fact been in school with him from the very first, for they were the same age. Terris and Lyttleton were also long-term friends of Hamilton's, but had met after they had gone on to Oxford. "Inherited it all from his mother, a pretty but tasteless soul. She died about five years ago."

"Looks it," said Terris dourly. He stared down at the red velvet of the mirror-back parlor sofa. "Maybe *she*'ll redo it, now she's living here."

She being, of course, Tommy's wife. Lyttleton had to admit that after he had bade his friends good evening the day before, he had returned home and thought much of the impending dinner engagement. What would this woman look like? What sort of woman had married their dashing friend? Speculation had led nowhere, and so he had eagerly waited for this evening and had dressed with particular care, as he knew the others had.

"Good evening, gentlemen."

Lyttleton hadn't heard the door open, and neither had the others. As one, they turned, and gaped as they beheld Tommy Hamilton's bride.

She was not an Indian woman, as they had almost begun to anticipate, even though she spoke with a slight trace of accent. What her nationality was, they could not tell; indeed, they could only stare.

Her jet-black hair was neither drawn loosely into a chignon, nor was it primly pinned under a frilly cap as was the current fashion, but rather the gleaming tresses hung loose. The sleek hair shifted as she walked toward them, almost as if it had a life of its own. Her chin was slightly pointed, her cheekbones wide, and her high forehead bespoke of intelligence. Her flawless skin was a delicate shade of alabaster-white. Her rich mouth possessed a full lower lip, the upper slightly pouted, and her lips glistened as if she had licked them just a moment before. Elegant dark eyebrows arched over her black eyes which sparkled like the brilliants set in a ring. Thick lush lashes fringed those eyes, which had been outlined with a deft hand, and Lyttleton was reminded of the kohl used by the ancient Egyptian queens.

She wore a puff-sleeved gown of black muslin. The wide skirt, draped over a crinoline, was decorated with dozens of tiny flounces, and ribbon bows tied back the overskirt. The gown only served to emphasize her hourglass figure. The off-the-shoulder neckline was cut very low and wide over flawless full breasts. On her feet were silk slippers.

The only color that broke the sombreness of her costume

was the strand of highly polished rubies clasped around her throat. Rubies as red as her full lips.

Montchalmers stared hungrily at her ripe breasts, so white and soft-looking and inviting, and envied his old friend for being able to pillow his head between their fragrant warmth. At his side his fingers convulsively curled and uncurled as he envisioned kneading the pliant flesh. He wanted to kiss them, fondle them tenderly, lick their rosy buds that would stiffen with the pleasure he gave her.

Terris thought her waist was the tiniest he'd ever seen, and knew no corset had bound it ever. He wondered if his hands could encircle it. Below, her hips curved out, hips that guarded the secret gate to this woman, and he could feel her warm thighs clasping him so tightly. White thighs that promised incredible passion, a passion he would never receive from this woman, a passion that only Hamilton would savor, and at that moment Terris, because of his loss, hated his friend.

Mesmerized by her eyes, Lyttleton found himself in those darkly glittering depths that promised sultry secrets; he ached for the mysterious and wonderful shadows that beckoned to him and to his soul, for the wonder that waited for him and his love, and the cigar in his hand, which he had located just before the woman had entered, dropped, forgotten, on the carpet.

"I am August Hamilton." Her low voice sent a thrill through the three men, and she stepped toward them, offering her slim hand. The friends crowded forward immediately, bumped into one another in their confusion as each tried to reach her first.

Lyttleton won, and clasped her hand in his, and pronounced his name. Her hand was cool to the touch, almost icy. He bent from the waist, and the heat in his lips more than made up for that cold skin as he dropped a kiss upon the top of her hand. He was reluctant to release it; he wanted to keep holding it, to keep touching her, to keep in contact with her. Her fingers lay limply in his.

Finally Lyttleton remembered his manners and stepped back, allowing his two friends to have their chance to introduce themselves. Terris muttered his name, while Montchalmers continued grinning inanely at her.

Her long lashes swept down as she studied them each in turn.

"My husband will be along in a moment, gentlemen, and until that time I am commanded to entertain you. I have heard so much about the three of you and your exploits, but I wish to hear all of these tales from your lips as well."

Wonderful lips, Lyttleton thought wildly, beautifully formed lips, so very kissable, so wet and glistening, and he wanted to seize those alabaster shoulders so that he could cover her mouth with his and gently blow the warmth of his body into her. Acutely aware that his body was responding eagerly, he glanced down and blushed.

None of the men spoke, but rather, grown shy and tongue-tied, they shifted from one foot to another and continued to gaze at her. Lyttleton had so many questions poised on his tongue, and yet he couldn't speak, couldn't tell her what he wanted to tell her.

"Wine?" she asked, moving away with a faint whisper of her skirts.

"Yes," they answered as one voice, the spell of silence broken.

She tugged at a velvet bellpull. When the elderly servant answered, she ordered wine for all of them; he bowed and left.

"Do you mind if I sit, gentlemen?"

"No, please!"

"Please allow me!"

"Here, Mrs. Hamilton."

August Hamilton bestowed a gracious smile upon them, but managed to dodge each man's zealous attempt to have her sit next to him. Instead, she chose a high-backed ebony chair, sat and clasped her hands in her lap, and leaned forward a little. Light from the gas lamps gleamed on the smooth skin of her breasts. Montchalmers licked his lips. Lyttleton dropped his eyes. She waved to them to sit, and they did so, bringing their chairs close to make a ring around her.

The butler returned with a teakwood tray laden with a decanter and four glasses. He set it down and bowed out, while August Hamilton poured wine. Lyttleton was the first to receive his; as he took it, their fingers brushed briefly and he nearly dropped the glass.

Quickly Lyttleton brought the wine to his lips and took a long swallow. The liquor burned all the way down his throat, yet it felt good, steadying the dizziness he had been experiencing ever since August Hamilton had entered the room. He blinked and passed a hand across his face. What had happened to him? To his friends? They still stared silently at the woman, while she was in turn gazing at him. Once more he looked into her dark eyes, and saw . . . Saw what? He frowned, and sipped his wine, and listened to her speak.

". . . said he so enjoyed your summers together, Mr. Montchalmers. He told me often how you two would sneak out of the house to go fishing in the pond on your uncle's estate."

"Ah yes, the pond." Montchalmers laughed, an embarrassed sound as he recalled boyhood memories. He grinned foolishly at her.

"And you, Mr. Terris," she said, lowering her lashes,

"Tommy had so much to tell me about you as well that I feel as though I know you, too."

Terris beamed as though she'd said the most wondrous thing about him. Again August was watching Lyttleton, and he was waiting for her to speak to him, and in that moment the others fell away, leaving them alone, just Lyttleton and the beautiful woman, the two in the golden light, and once again he could smell that odd yet compelling odor, and the scent wafted around him, caressing him, beguiling him, and he lost himself within the depths of her dark eyes as he kissed her lips and breasts, her warm flesh against his, and it was warm, warmer, warming—

"Lyttleton, Terris, Montchalmers—how good it is to see you chaps again."

The tremulous voice cut through the warm darkness and jerked Lyttleton back into the room. Momentarily unsettled, Lyttleton shook himself and prepared to greet his longtime friend. He turned, and the cheerful words died in his throat as he stared in shock at what he saw.

Thomas Hamilton huddled in a cane-back wheelchair, a plaid rug laid across his knees.

Prior to his being sent to India two years earlier, Hamilton, a tall and vigorous man in his mid-twenties, had enjoyed excellent health. Now he looked like an old man, a man faded into his seventies. Or even older, Lyttleton thought, horrified.

Hamilton's once-muscular body was wasted, the flesh hanging loosely upon him, and he shook constantly, as though in the throes of some tropical fever. His guinea-gold hair was shot through with streaks of white and grey and was long and unkempt. Deep ugly lines ravaged his once-boyish face, and his hand—claw, Lyttleton thought wildly—trembled as he held it out. Its back was mottled, as though the man suffered from some skin disease.

The eyes were the worst, for despite all the other changes in the man, they were just as blue—though somewhat rheumy—as Lyttleton remembered, but no longer were they youthful eyes filled with good humor. Hamilton's eyes darted wildly, never lingering long on any single object. From time to time he closed them momentarily as he stifled a moan. He acts trapped, Lyttleton thought, and shuddered at this unbelievable transformation.

Swallowing quickly, he forced himself to bury his shock for the moment, and in the stunned silence that seemed to echo through the room, Lyttleton leaped to his feet and hurried forward.

"Good to see you, old man," he declared jauntily, not feeling particularly lighthearted and wishing that he could be anywhere but here now. He vigorously pumped Hamilton's hand, then released it, reluctant to touch the skin any longer than necessary, for it was hot, and dry, unhealthy, and he was totally repelled.

Hamilton's eyes shifted to his wife, then back to Lyttleton, and as his withered lips lifted, a thin line of saliva drooled out of the corner of his mouth. The blue eyes seeped a white discharge. Quickly Lyttleton stepped back to allow the others to greet Hamilton.

Hamilton glanced again at August, who stood most attentively by his side, and momentarily Lyttleton thought he saw fear in his friend's ruined face. Surely, though, he must be mistaken.

Still stunned by this dreadful decay in his friend, he wondered what terrible thing had happened to Hamilton while he served in India. Perhaps, as Montchalmers had suggested the previous day, Tommy had suffered from a brain fever. Surely, not even that would do it. Lyttleton was no doctor, but he knew it took more than a fever to ravage a man in this manner. Or might Hamilton have fallen prey to some lingering tropical disease? God knew, the barbaric country was practically rotten with them. Whatever it had been, had it occurred after the couple were wed? Or before? If the latter, Lyttleton thought, then

August was a veritable saint to marry this ruined man and to care for his infirmities.

Admiration for the beautiful woman's courage and dedication filled Lyttleton. How tragic that such a young and vitally alive woman was burdened by this invalid. He shook himself and frowned slightly, displeased with his uncharitable thought, and reminded himself that this pitiful invalid was his good friend. He saw the outline of shrunken legs beneath the plaid blanket. Surely, Hamilton could not serve as a proper husband to his wife. Lyttleton ran his tongue across his dry lips.

August took out a daintily embroidered handkerchief and, unconscious of the men's stares, dabbed at the damp sides of Tommy's mouth. She was murmuring something to her husband, and while Lyttleton couldn't hear the words, he could distinguish the tone, and it was loving and concerned, and that further saddened him.

With great effort Tommy jerked his clawlike hand up in one palsied motion, and knocking the handkerchief aside, he shrieked, "No, no, don't!"

A moment of embarrassed silence followed, then Lyttleton cleared his throat.

"Well, old man"—and he winced inwardly as he realized he'd used the unfortunate phrase twice now—"Henry claims you must have made a bloody—beg pardon, ma'am—fortune in diamonds and rubies over there. Come now, you must tell us all about your time in India, Tommy, for you must know we're eager to hear each and every tale." He spoke in a cheerful tone and suspected it sounded forced. His friends looked just as dazed as he felt, and neither had spoken since they'd greeted Hamilton.

"Er, yes, do tell us, Tommy." Montchalmers tried to smile, but failed.

Terris' skin had a slightly greyish cast to it, as though he were ill. He would not look at the man in the chair.

Tommy shifted his eyes to the woman, then back to Lyttleton. "I have diamonds." He nodded, his head seeming to wobble on his neck. "Rubies. Oh yes." His voice rose like a querulous old man's. "Blood rubies they are." He peered at August, then cackled, the sound rising higher and higher. It faintly resembled a laugh, but became more maddening with every moment until Lyttleton wanted to put his hands over his ears to shut the revolting sound out.

He was spared that by the entrance of the elderly servant, who announced that dinner was served.

August leaned over to whisper in her husband's ear, and his laughter abruptly cut off. The ensuing silence was almost worse. Montchalmers stepped forward to help push Hamilton's wheelchair into the next room.

"Please permit me, ma'am, to assist you." His voice was as sombre as his face.

She raised a hand slightly and shook her head. "Thank you, Mr. Montchalmers," she murmured, "but I always help my husband. I think it helps to calm him." Hamilton shuddered.

Wineglasses in hand, the three friends glanced at one another, then followed the Hamiltons into the spacious dining salon, and once they were seated with Hamilton at one end of the long table, his wife next to him so that she could assist him, Lyttleton across from her, Terris seated to his left, and Montchalmers to her right, the three men started talking at once.

"So much has happened in the past two years, old man"—that phrase again, Lyttleton thought sorrowfully—"that frankly I don't know where to begin to bring you up to date. Of course, you had my letters, Tommy, although I must confess yours were rather sparse."

"I had a few," Montchalmers added quickly, "but then, Tommy was never much of a faithful correspondent. Too, I'm sure Tommy was quite busy with whatever it is that soldiers do." His smile this time proved more successful.

Again silent, Terris looked as though he would begin weeping any moment.

"Well, at least we had those to keep us in touch, right?" Montchalmers nodded eagerly, while Lyttleton cleared his throat. Lyttleton had to keep talking, as did Montchalmers; he had to fill the damning silence. He drained his wine, filled the glass with more, and knew that they were all drinking too much, far too much, but he didn't care.

While Lyttleton and Montchalmers chattily brought their friend up to present on all the gossip and news of the past two years, the servant brought in the first course, a beef broth.

Lyttleton noticed that August sipped a little of her soup, then set her spoon down to watch her husband, who was idly tracing circles in his bowl with his spoon. Tommy Hamilton caught her watching him, and his face clouded over, and he looked as though he wanted to shriek.

Other courses were brought, and August ate little. She had to be upset, Lyttleton told himself, for this was no doubt the first time she had presented her husband to his friends. What a strain it must be on her, and once again he found himself admiring her courage.

Finally, the main course was set before them and Lyttleton applied himself hungrily to it. So far his appetite had not suffered. Hamilton stared at the cut of rare beef on his plate, and suddenly the emaciated man began weeping.

It was quiet, unlike the wild laughter earlier, and because of that it was all the more pathetic. His thin shoulders shook, yet he made no noise.

"I am sorry, gentlemen," August Hamilton said, rising gracefully and setting her linen napkin down, "but my husband is greatly fatigued and should go to bed now. Please, excuse us."

The three men rose as one and silently watched as she went around to Hamilton and pulled his chair away from the table. His face buried in his hands, Hamilton did not look up.

Without being summoned, the butler appeared and opened the door for them. It closed quietly behind the Hamiltons, and the three friends sank slowly into their respective chairs as they stared at one another.

"We should leave now," Lyttleton suggested, half rising from his chair.

Montchalmers waved him down. "I don't think so. After all, we were invited for dinner, and while things have been a little . . . unpleasant, it would be rude of us to run out on her now. And that's precisely why we should stay. She needs the support now."

"Besides, we have to find out," Terris' quiet voice added. "We have to know what happened to Tommy." His voice broke, and he glanced away.

Lyttleton nodded silently. Question after question flitted through his mind, and he dismissed them, one by one, as being unsuitable. He couldn't press this woman for details when she had suffered already. Too, he truly wanted to go home. He was emotionally drained from this evening, and wanted to rest and try to forget some of it, at least for a few hours.

Before the men could speak further, August entered with a rustle of her skirts. She smiled apologetically at her guests.

"My husband is resting comfortably now. Would you care to retire to the library?"

The three men nodded, for their appetites had fled with the ruins of the dinner, and followed her down the hallway to the library, where they settled into comfortable chairs and sipped after-dinner drinks. Or rather, Lyttleton corrected wryly, the drinks that would serve as their dinners tonight.

For some minutes each man remained silent, lost in his own thoughts, but Lyttleton knew what was uppermost in his mind, just as he knew the thoughts of the others. What in God's name had happened to Tommy to reduce him to this pitiable state?

Still, they were gentlemen, and embarrassed, and didn't know what to say or how to broach it to this poor woman who had endured so much. Someone has to, Lyttleton thought, after he'd listened to Montchalmers clear his throat for the fifth time. Someone has to speak, has to be the first.

Unable to stand the suspense any longer, Lyttleton set his empty glass down on the table next to him and shifted slightly in his chair.

"August—Mrs. Hamilton—"

"Yes?" she responded, her voice so soft.

Soft as black velvet, and the image it brought was warm and fragrant, and desirable. Sternly Lyttleton forced his mind back to what he had to say.

"How did your husband, that is, how did Tommy come to . . ." Lyttleton stumbled to a lame halt, and cursed himself for bungling it so. She must think him an absolute fool.

"How did Tommy have his health ruined?" she supplied for him. Her dark eyes were so compassionate, he knew she did not think him a fool.

"Yes."

"Please," said Terris hoarsely, "how did you meet him, and when?"

Montchalmers merely smiled at her.

August pushed back a strand of black hair that had fallen over her forehead, a gesture watched intently by the three men. She breathed deeply, and Lyttleton could see the pain these memories brought her. She folded her hands in her lap, and with other women the gesture might have been prim, but with her the flexing of her fingers, the angle of her hands seemed almost provocative. He shook his head at the absurd notion.

"It is somewhat of a long story. I don't know if you would wish to listen to it, for I'm sure you will find it quite boring."

"Not at all!" Montchalmers said. "We would love to hear it. Please, do go on."

She nodded, and indicated that they should refill their wineglasses. When August began speaking, her voice was calm in what had to be a supreme effort in keeping emotion from coloring it.

"I am the daughter of a British colonial, gentlemen," she said. "My father lived in India most of his adult life, and India is where I was born. We lived in the northern regions of the country and moved to Delhi in December of 1856. A few months later I attended a party given by a friend of my father's, and there I was introduced to Lieutenant Hamilton." She paused, her face relaxing as the memories returned.

"He was so handsome and dashing in his uniform, more so than any of the other officers, and all the women there were in love with him. I did not have an opportunity to speak with him before we dined, but later, as I went out onto the verandah, I heard someone behind me and found that Tommy had followed me outside. We talked much in the next few hours, he of his life in England, me of my life in India. As we talked I knew I wanted to see him again, and I hoped that he felt the same away. But when the evening was finished, he said nothing and my spirits were dashed. My father and I returned home, and I believed I would see the handsome lieutenant no more.

"I was wrong."

Lyttleton glanced at her and saw that the darkness of her eyes had shifted subtly. Suddenly a chill ran through him, and he realized that he felt slightly uneasy, though, he told himself, perhaps that was because of what had happened with Tommy earlier. It was the only explanation, wasn't it?

She continued in her narrative.

She did not see him for many weeks, and then they met again at a concert. She invited him home, and once he was at her house, they rediscovered their attraction for one another. As he was leaving, Hamilton asked her father if he could call again, to which the older man readily agreed.

Thereafter, Tommy and she devoted much time to each other, having discovered they shared a mutual attraction. They attended various parties given by the other colonials, went to the theater, and strolled hand-in-hand along moonlit walks.

But all the while their affection was blossoming, something much more unpleasant was growing. For months an undercurrent of unrest had rumbled through the country, vague with half-whispers of uneasiness between the native Indians and their British overlords. There were reports of isolated incidents, unpleasant stories that were quickly hushed whenever an Englishwoman entered the room. Tommy listened to the reports and rumors, and growing concerned, he urged August and her father to leave the country for their own safety. He told August he would miss her, but he didn't wish anything to happen to her.

Her father stoutly refused to leave, claiming that he and his daughter would be fine, and no matter how much Tommy Hamilton argued, the old colonial just shook his head.

A few months later, in May, the Sepoy Rebellion began when the Indian soldiers revolted against their British officers.

"I will spare you the details of that terrible struggle," August said, "for I'm sure you are already acquainted with them."

Terris nodded, his face dark with renewed grief over his brother; Montchalmers only bit his lip and closed his eyes as he recalled what he had heard. Lyttleton, like his friends, was familiar with the details, for he had read the horrifying accounts in the British newspapers, had heard the gruesome tales of those travelers and colonials who had managed to leave the country before they were caught up in the deadly maelstrom. Others were not so fortunate, and from them came tales of torture and mutilation of British men, as well as women and children, tales of appalling murders that demonstrated too late to the British the long-suppressed resentment and hatred of the Indians.

The survivors who had returned to England had told their fellow countrymen of the hells they had faced in that far-off country. The hells that August had faced, Lyttleton reminded himself.

This elegant and beautiful woman sitting before them had survived the terrors of the mutiny, and he was filled with wonder. Quickly he searched her face, as though believing he could see scars of that hideous ordeal, but it was unblemished and any she might possess were hidden inside. He forced his attention back to her lest he miss any of her tale.

She had paused to take a sip of her wine. When she next spoke, her voice was scarcely above a whisper. "My first thoughts were with Tommy, but I could not discover if he lived, for he was quartered in Meerut, forty miles away, while I was still in Delhi. I lived in a blackness for days, not knowing his fate. That was far worse. It was later that I discovered from Tommy's fellow officers what had happened. As you might expect, gentlemen, Tommy fought gallantly.

"My father and I did not suffer as others did. While our house was attacked the day after the mutiny began, we managed to repel the invaders, and thereafter we hid in the cellar until help arrived. Others—our friends and acquaintances, the other Europeans who did not flee—met a different fate. All died, many in the most gruesome ways." She closed her eyes, and Lyttleton could well imagine the sufferings she had witnessed. Curiously, though, a faint expression, almost like a smile, lingered on her lips.

"When my father and I were forced upon occasion to leave the cellar for food, we dressed as Indians and went out only at night, and thus did we live until the British assault upon Delhi in mid-September and the city's subsequent fall. The rebels were hunted down, and the streets were filled with the dead and the dying, both Indian and English. It was a terrible sight, for the dogs and vultures scavenged among the bodies bloated from the sun and heat." She touched her tongue to a drop of wine glistening on her lower lips. "Some order was restored by the British, and after we were rescued, I asked after Tommy. I had not seen him for months and feared the worst. No one seemed to know what had happened to him, and my hope of ever seeing him alive diminished. But one night some weeks later I saw him stumbling down our street. I called for my father, and we brought Tommy back to our house. He was suffering from various wounds received in battle and running a high fever, and he did not seem to know us."

August said that she nursed Tommy through his long illness, never leaving his side and often going without food or rest. Her father was concerned about her own health, but she refused to leave the wounded man. Slowly Tommy improved, and as he convalesced they rediscovered one another, and the deep attraction that had existed between them earlier now blossomed into love. When Tommy was once again well, he and August talked of marriage. The couple settled on a short engagement, and within a few months they were married.

Their happiness, however, proved too to be short-lived. Only a few weeks after their marriage Tommy's illness returned, and it was further compounded by a fever which was then spreading throughout the country. She went from doctor to doctor, seeking help, but none of them could offer hope, and slowly, agonizingly, her husband wasted away until he became what they saw that night. Her sorrow was twofold, for her father died from the same fever.

"I knew then that the only hope of saving Tommy's life was to return him to his homeland where he could be treated by the excellent English doctors and where he would be removed from the ill effects of the tropical climate. Thus, when he was strong enough to travel, we came to England." Finished with her tale, August closed her eyes and leaned her head back.

Shadows lay smudged under her eyes, and her skin was even paler than earlier, and while Lyttleton thought she looked exhausted, she still had the strange twist to her lips. Puzzled, he glanced at his companions. Terris and Montchalmers had listened rapt to her narrative, never speaking, never moving. Now they stirred, Montchalmers being the first to speak.

"It's an incredible story, Mrs. Hamilton," he said, deeply affected, "and I commend you highly upon your immense courage and strength. How terrible it must have been for you, ma'am!" He shuddered dramatically.

"My dear Mrs. Hamilton," exclaimed Terris almost immediately, his voice slightly breathless, "is there anything that I—we—can do for you? There is no need for you to struggle with this burden by yourself. Please! Allow us to help!"

Lyttleton, alone of the three men, remained silent. Her tale had affected him, too. But something had made him uneasy, and he didn't know what it was. In one way her story seemed as though it had been recited from memory, and yet that couldn't be what bothered him. He did not have long to reflect upon it, however, for Terris stood almost at once and nodded to his friends.

He raised his glass high. "A toast to a courageous woman."

"Hear, hear," Montchalmers said.

Lyttleton nodded but did not speak. He glanced at August and found her gazing at him. He smiled, and the corners of her mouth lifted slightly.

"Thank you for sharing your experiences with us, ma'am," Montchalmers said, "and if you should ever need help, please feel free to call upon us."

"Thank you," she murmured.

"I think we should be going, Mrs. Hamilton," Terris said. "It has been a long and emotional evening for you, and we don't wish to tire you."

"Yes, yes," Montchalmers said. "We must go so that you may rest."

Lyttleton bowed over her hand, as the others had, but did not speak. Her eyes met his and locked as a wave of warmth rushed over him, almost as though he were blushing. He knew, though, that he was not. With an effort he broke the contact and stepped back to the others.

They departed the house and climbed into Montchalmers' carriage. Lyttleton glanced back and thought he saw a slight movement by one of the drapes upstairs, but he must have been mistaken. He leaned back.

"Where are you off to now?" he asked, his voice quiet. He was feeling oddly subdued, and he didn't know why. Perhaps he was tired from the strain of the evening, the horror of seeing his old friend.

"Henry says he'd like to return to the club for a while," Terris said, "and so would I. Care to join us?"

Lyttleton shook his head. "I think not, although thank you for the offer. I'm tired, and I think I'll return home."

"Extraordinary," Terris murmured from the other side of the coach.

"What is, Wyndy?" Lyttleton asked.

"That woman."

"Indeed she is!" Montchalmers agreed enthusiastically. "Damned fine looker. Bit of a waste for ol' Tommy, I would guess. Not," he added hastily, "that I'm sayin', that is, I mean . . ."

Terris rescued his friend. "We know, Henry, what you mean."

"Don't you agree, old boy?" Montchalmers asked.

Lyttleton, frowning and preoccupied with his own musings, was staring out into the darkness of the London streets.

"What's that?"

"Your mind is far away tonight. Or," Montchalmers

added slyly, "is it a few streets behind us, eh? Certainly I wouldn't blame you."

"Don't be ridiculous," he snapped. He was more curt than he'd intended. Still, Montchalmers seemed more than unusually lewd and insinuating tonight. "I'm sorry, Henry. I'm a little distressed by what I saw and heard tonight. I can't get it out of mind . . . that wreck of a man."

"None of us can." Montchalmers' voice was serious now. "It must have been one hell of an illness. Thank God, Tommy had Mrs. Hamilton to tend to him so devotedly."

"Yes, thank God," Ferris echoed. "She's an absolute angel."

"Hear, hear," Montchalmers said.

"You can let me out ahead," Lyttleton said. "I'll walk the rest of the way." Once the carriage stopped, he grasped his walking stick in hand, bid his friends farewell, and strolled away. For a while he could hear the clopping of the carriage horse's hooves on the cobblestones; then the sound receded, and he was left alone with his thoughts.

Lyttleton recalled the curve of August's white bosom. Montchalmers and Terris thought she was an angel? No. What she was, he could not say; but she was not an angel.

That night Lyttleton did not sleep well; strange dreams interrupted his rest. Upon waking, he could not remember the nature of the dreams, and only a sense of uneasiness remained with him.

A few days after he'd met Tommy's wife, Lyttleton was again reminded of the Hamiltons when right after breakfast his servant Edgar brought in a note.

Lyttleton opened the note and stared at the palsied, barely readable script; then his gaze dropped down the page to the signature. Tommy Hamilton. Tommy wrote that he wanted to see his old friend—privately. His wife would be out all that afternoon, and he asked Lyttleton to come to him while he was alone, for the matter was urgent. Lyttleton frowned, wondering what Tommy wanted. He thrust the note into his coat pocket, finished his tea, and fully intending to go see Tommy in the afternoon, left the house.

But on his way there he encountered friends, and they fell into discussion. One thing followed another, and he completely forgot about the note until starting to change for dinner, he put his hand in his pocket and found the slip of paper. All at once he remembered what he had meant to do, and he was horrified that he'd forgotten.

"I won't be having supper," Lyttleton informed a surprised Edgar as he rushed out of the house.

With a growing sense of urgency, Lyttleton hailed a hansom cab and set out for Tommy's house. Unfortunately, the evening traffic was heavy and sluggish, and just ahead in the street a vegetable wagon had overturned, bringing all traffic to a standstill.

Lyttleton drummed his fingers impatiently on the padded leather seat as he waited for the wagons and horses and vendors to untangle. The air inside the cab was hot and close. He opened the blinds and stuck his head out the window and gulped deeply. That wasn't much better, for the street smelled of rotting vegetables, horse manure, and dust, all made worse by the heat, but at least a slight breeze blew and stirred the odors.

The sense of urgency was growing stronger, making him more impatient by the second, and just as he was preparing to leave the cab and strike out on foot, the cart ahead rolled out of the way. After a few false starts and more wasted time, the cab finally moved ahead. As soon as he reached the Hamilton house, Lyttleton paid the driver and took the steps up to the house two at a time. He rapped on the front door and was admitted by the butler.

"I've come to see Lieutenant Hamilton."

"One moment, sir."

The butler left him in the front parlor, and again Lyttleton noted the unusual odor that he had noticed on his earlier visit. Before he had time to think any more about it, he heard the whisper of material behind him and turned.

August Hamilton stood in the doorway and looked just as beautiful and just as compelling, and her eyes glimmered.

Tears, he realized, and took an involuntary step toward her.

"August—Mrs. Hamilton—" Lyttleton began.

"It's Tommy." She spoke in a muffled voice. One tear crept down her cheek, and she quickly brushed it away. "Poor Tommy." Her shoulders shook.

"What happened? He isn't . . ." Lyttleton was unable to finish, for an invisible hand tightened around his chest, squeezing the breath out of him.

She bent her head, her jet hair swinging forward to shield her cheek. "I'm sorry, Mr. Lyttleton, but I must tell you that I have ill news. Tommy died this afternoon. I wasn't here at the time, and when I came home, the servants told me . . . It was so sudden!"

Lyttleton was shocked into speechlessness.

If only he had come earlier, he might have seen Tommy while he still lived. He might have known why Tommy wanted to see him. Lyttleton opened his mouth to ask if August knew the reason, but something inside him kept him from speaking, and he shook his head sympathetically instead. Self-consciously he set his arm loosely around the woman's shoulders and patted her somewhat awkwardly. As her head shifted to rest on his shoulder a distinct and pleasurable tingle passed through Lyttleton.

"I'm so sorry, Mrs. Hamilton, so frightfully sorry about Tommy. It's such a shock—certainly he wasn't in good health, but I never expected . . . I cannot believe he is— We were good friends, you know. I'm so sorry, Mrs. Hamilton." She nodded against him but did not answer. "Here, please sit." Gently he guided her to a chair, and she sank into it.

"Thank you so much, Mr. Lyttleton," she murmured.

Closing her eyes, August rested her head against the back of the chair.

She looked so frail and vulnerable, and Lyttleton's heart ached for her loss. He cleared his throat and took a deep breath.

"If there is anything that I may do or that my friends may do now, please let us know."

"Thank you."

They were silent for a few minutes; then he spoke again. "What will you do now, Mrs. Hamilton? I know it cannot be pleasant for you to contemplate, but I—that is, my friends and I—are concerned about you."

"You mustn't worry really about my plight, Mr. Lyttleton. While it is true that I have no family and friends left in India and that I am new to this country, I think I have little choice other than to stay here."

He thought he detected some irony in her tone, and something more. But surely not at this time. He glanced at her and found her face as composed in its grief as a few moments before.

Again there was silence between them, the only sound coming from the ticking of the clock across the room. He was to blame, Lyttleton knew. Events might have gone differently today if he had only called upon Tommy earlier. If only he had come, then Tommy would not have had to die alone. How terrible she must feel, Lyttleton thought, not to have been with her husband when he needed her so.

"How did Tommy die, Mrs. Hamilton? Had I realized he was quite so ill, I would have visited him before this."

"I believe it was his heart."

"Had you called a doctor?"

She nodded, mute.

Lyttleton's eyes narrowed thoughtfully. "The doctor confirmed this?"

"Mr. Lyttleton—please, I cannot go on," August whispered, a sob catching in her throat. "My husband has just—just . . ."

Immediately he felt a surge of remorse. "Forgive me, Mrs. Hamilton! Please forgive my rudeness! I would like to pay my final respects to Tommy while I am here, if this is not an inconvenient time."

"I'm sorry, Mr. Lyttleton, but there will be no viewing of the body."

At first he thought she meant there would be none at the present, and then he realized she meant no viewing at all. "No viewing! But, Mrs. Hamilton, I'm a friend of Tommy's!"

"Mr. Lyttleton, please believe me when I say that I quite understand your desire to see Tommy, but I do not think you should, for it was a most unpleasant death and apparently he suffered toward the end. I wish to spare you this ordeal." August gazed at him, a beseeching expression in the dark depths of her eyes. "Please understand, Mr. Lyttleton, I am not being contrary." A shudder passed through her.

"Very well, Mrs. Hamilton. I understand." The truth was that he didn't understand her denial, which he found strange. It didn't matter how terrible Tommy's appearance was; he still wanted to say good-bye one last time. She should have known that wouldn't have mattered; he could have borne however Tommy looked.

The elderly butler entered at that moment and spoke in an undertone to his mistress for a few minutes. "I'm sorry, Mr. Lyttleton, but a household matter demands my immediate attention. Do you mind sitting here alone for a few minutes? I am sorry."

Lyttleton had the feeling that she expected him to leave. He was determined not to. "I don't mind waiting at all."

"Thank you," she murmured and swept out, the servant following.

Lyttleton paced the length of the parlor, sat on a sofa, then stood. He couldn't wait. He was going to find Tommy. Curiously, he felt furtive, as though he might be punished if he were found outside the room.

Outside the parlor Lyttleton hesitated as he listened for voices or footsteps, but he heard nothing. He proceeded to the next room, another salon duplicating the first in style and furnishings, and equally gloomy. It was empty. He had visited Tommy here many times before his friend left for India, so he was fairly familiar with the house. The library, kitchen, and dining room were the only rooms left on the first floor, and he doubted Tommy was in any of those. His friend must be upstairs.

Carefully he advanced up the stairs, his breathing surging and pounding, and thunderously loud to him, and more than once he caught himself holding it so he would be quiet. When he was at the top of the carpeted staircase, he paused to get his bearings.

The hallway swung left around a corner and led to the master suite of a bedroom, small parlor, dressing room, and bathroom; to his right the hallway crooked to the right and three guest bedrooms.

Which way? Doubtless, Tommy's wife would remain in the master suite. Lyttleton closed his eyes as the images surged into his mind. August reclining, naked, upon a silk coverlet, her legs spread open, her hand trailing down her stomach to caress her—

No! For a moment he thought he shouted it, and he listened, waiting for someone to discover him on the landing, but no one did and he realized that he hadn't spoken aloud.

What was wrong? he asked himself as he headed to the

right. Why had he thought that? He shook his head and entered the first bedroom.

As it happened, Lyttleton found his friend in the first bedroom.

Heavy draperies had been tightly pulled against the evening, and no lamps were lit, and at first he almost missed the bed and what was in it. Then he saw. He stepped inside, found a long taper nearby, lit it, and walking over to the bed, held the flickering candle aloft.

It was Tommy, but a Tommy who looked far worse in death than he had in life. August had not been exaggerating about her husband's appearance, and his hope that Tommy might have found some release, some repose, was shattered.

Life had not ended peacefully in sleep for Tommy. Far from it.

In death, Tommy's face was severely contorted. The glazed eyes gaped open, and the ashen face wore an expression of such horror that Lyttleton involuntarily stepped back. His friend's mouth hung open, as if he had screamed even as he was dying, Lyttleton thought. Tommy's withered limbs remained twisted, as though he had strained against something that held him down, as though he had writhed in agony. It was as though Tommy had faced demons in the last moments of his life, and as he confronted the other world he had found it populated, too, with demons. Lyttleton could only hope that his friend had now found some rest.

For a long moment Lyttleton stared at the dead man and relived the many memories of their long friendship and he wished that there had been more years. Finally, he blew out the flame and left the room.

It was still important, he thought as he went down the stairway just as stealthily as he had ascended, that no one catch him abovestairs. At the foot he paused and heard voices coming from the back of the house. He returned quickly to the parlor and had no sooner caught his breath than the door opened.

"I am sorry to have left you so long, Mr. Lyttleton. Were you able to amuse yourself?"

Again the irony, he thought, although this time it seemed almost a taunt.

"Yes, thank you. I'm sorry again, Mrs. Hamilton, about your loss, and I know that I shouldn't take up any more of your time, for no doubt you have arrangements to make. If you would like, I will inform Terris and Montchalmers." She nodded. "I would appreciate it, too, if you would notify us of the service."

"Of course, Mr. Lyttleton. How kind of you to come this evening." She paused, and her lips parted, and he found himself staring at their redness, their fullness. Thoughts of Tommy fled until he forced himself to recall what had happened today. "May I ask, Mr. Lyttleton, what brought you here tonight?"

"Certainly. I was concerned about Tommy, so I thought I'd come for a visit. I was too late, though." His voice was bitter.

"Yes, that is a shame, for last night Tommy called for you several times."

Lyttleton winced. "Good evening, Mrs. Hamilton. Until we meet again."

"Yes."

She gave him her hand, and it was icy, like the cold of a grave.

As he suspected he would, Lyttleton found Montchalmers and Terris at the club. They called for him to join them, which he did.

"What brings you out on this hot evening?" Montchalmers demanded. "I'd have thought you'd be staying home, reading some book or the other." He peered at his friend. "What's the matter? You look gloomy."

"I'm afraid that I am gloomy, and I have gloomy news for you both."

Terris sat up. "What is it?"

"I've just been to see August Hamilton."

"You sly dog!"

"Henry!" Lyttleton said, his tone admonitory. Montchalmers' smile faded. "There is no easy way of telling you— Tommy died today."

"My God!" Montchalmers said.

"No!" said Terris. "It can't be. I know he was ill, but he wasn't *that* ill, surely."

Lyttleton shook his head. "I don't understand it myself,

Wyndy. Perhaps the journey from India weakened him. Perhaps he was worse than we thought. Mrs. Hamilton informed me that he died this afternoon while she was out. I'm afraid it wasn't an easy death, either."

"Poor Tommy," Montchalmers said. He swallowed quickly and looked away.

Terris would not look up, but Lyttleton could see tears in his eyes.

"I told her that I would tell you, and she'll notify us of further arrangements."

"Dead," Terris whispered. Lyttleton nodded. "But how? How did Tommy die?"

"Mrs. Hamilton thought it was his heart," Lyttleton replied in a neutral tone.

"What did the doctor say?" Montchalmers asked. He still looked stunned.

"I really don't know, Henry," Lyttleton said. "We did not discuss that." He did not want to relate that part of his conversation with August Hamilton, for he was still uneasy about it. Too, he had decided on his way to the club that he would say nothing to them about the note he had received from Tommy that morning—nor the expression of horror on Tommy's face. It was sufficient that he had told them of their friend's death.

They talked for some time of Tommy and of their memories, and as other friends and acquaintances drifted into the club, Lyttleton informed them as well. All of the men shook their heads ruefully over the loss of such a good and upstanding man.

When the three friends were once more alone, Montchalmers said in an innocent tone, "I suppose she's bearing up quite well, all things considered, what?"

"Yes." That wasn't precisely an accurate description of

August's state, but Lyttleton didn't know what was. He frowned thoughtfully as he stroked his moustache.

"Damned brave woman if you ask me," said Terris, shaking his head admiringly.

"Yes," Lyttleton murmured. The others, too engrossed in their own grief, would not notice if he answered strangely, and for that he was thankful. Suddenly he was very weary and wanted to go home. "I'm sorry, gentlemen, but I can't linger tonight. Tommy's death has shaken me, you know."

"Quite understand." Montchalmers heaved a gusty sigh. "I'm sorry, old fellow, that you had to be the bearer of bad news. Damned unlucky for you, though it could have been any one of the three of us. I was planning to drop by this evening to see Tommy."

And his young attractive wife, Lyttleton thought, then pushed the unworthy thought away.

After a few minutes more, Lyttleton left. Outside the club he paused and breathed deeply. There had been too much smoke in the hot rooms of the club, and out on the street it felt much cooler, although he knew the temperature couldn't have dropped much since he went in. Still, it did feel good.

He started walking, and once more his thoughts turned to the unusual events of the day.

Behind him a shadow slipped out of a doorway and began following him.

Why had Tommy sent the note to him? Or had it just been chance? Surely, it could have been Henry or Wyndy who had received the note. No, for Lyttleton remembered that August had said her husband had called for him the night before. For him. He frowned. None of this made sense.

It was close to midnight now, and the streets were less

crowded than earlier. Lyttleton was nearly halfway home when he realized he was being followed. He glanced behind him quickly, but he saw no one and nothing out of the ordinary, and yet the sense persisted that he was not alone. The hairs along his neck prickled, and he cleared his throat noisily. It could have been a cat or a dog . . . or a pickpocket. Or worse.

He listened; still nothing. He began walking again, faster this time, and a chill of fear ran down his spine. A cat or dog would have made noise; this was too silent, too intent. His pace quickened, and he sensed the thing behind him matching his speed.

There was *something* back there, something that was following him and wanted him, something that was terrible.

He looked around for a cab but didn't see one, and that's when he broke into a run. He wanted to get home as quickly as possible.

It was drawing closer, Lyttleton sensed, closer, until he thought he felt its breath on his back, chill and deadly. Odd, he thought, that he should think of his pursuer as an "it." It could be anyone . . . anything. Gradually he drew away from the pursuer, and as he turned a corner he could see the familiar lines of his house. He breathed deeply with relief, and behind him, ever so faintly, he thought he heard laughter.

The wind, he told himself, even though the wind was still. He ran across the street, finishing with a final burst of speed that brought him right up to the door. Lyttleton fumbled for his key, found it, and unlocked the door. He slipped inside, closed the door, and leaned against it, feeling relief that he had made it to his house. And he was safe here. He knew that. He sighed with relief.

"Sir?"

It was Edgar, his usual aplomb shaken by his employer's

rather hasty entrance. He looked at his employer expectantly.

Lyttleton nodded pleasantly, realizing how odd it must look to his servant. "Good evening, Edgar. I'm home for the evening now." His voice was calm. "I'm retiring to the study and don't wish to be disturbed."

He had caught his breath and started toward the study. Once he was there, he sank down in his favorite chair. The shelves filled with familiar books on three sides of the room made him feel comfortable. Already the fear he had experienced on his way home tonight was fading.

Lyttleton closed his eyes and leaned back. Too much had happened lately, and all of it was more than a little strange.

Here he'd met up with Tommy again, and then a few days later the man dies. There had been the disastrous dinner, the devastation of seeing the wreck that was their friend, the mysterious note, and then Tommy's sudden death.

And August.

He could not neglect adding her to the list of oddities. He well remembered the half-smile playing across her lips earlier. Almost as if she had been mocking him. Almost.

But none of this made sense. Or did it? No, he told himself firmly, and so he would wait before saying anything to the others. That was a prudent course. But how long would he wait? What could he say, after all? He had only suspicions, and as for that, he didn't know why he was suspicious.

Lyttleton sighed and closed his eyes. He tried to keep the painful memories of his friend away and found success only when he finally drifted off to sleep.

Outside the house in Eaton Square the shadow waited and watched.

The lights in the house went out one by one until it stood dark like the other houses on the street.

And still the shadow watched.

Watched, and made a sound, a sound almost like a low laugh.

Funerals are so damned depressing, Lyttleton thought as he stood in the cemetery near the freshly dug grave and listened to the minister's words. He found the Anglican service somehow less reassuring than the Roman Catholic one, and realized that today he felt worse than he had since he'd seen Tommy again.

It was just two days before that Tommy had died. Such a short time, Lyttleton thought, and yet somehow it seemed longer. The day after his visit to August Hamilton he had received a note from her about the funeral.

Montchalmers and Terris had attended with him, and they stood to one side, their heads bowed as they listened to the service. The widow had been so overcome by grief that her physician recommended she stay home and rest rather than face this further strain.

Lyttleton glanced at the faces of the mourners. He knew some of them, not all, and all wore expressions of sorrow. He looked back at the coffin, its polished wood gleaming in the sunshine. It wasn't right for the sun to shine today.

It should have been overcast, damp, raining, but instead blue sky showed above them and the birds sang in the trees towering over the graves, and it looked like a bright spring day.

Not a day for death. There had been much of that in his family and among his friends. Both his parents were dead, as well as a brother in his infancy. A fiancée had died only weeks before a wedding; friends had died in service of their country or from some damnable disease. Or as Tommy had. From whatever had killed him.

For some reason Lyttleton thought about his mother. He could recall neither her face nor her voice, for he had been only four years old, and his sister a mere infant, when his mother had left their house one night. She had never returned. The next day his father had announced that their mother was dead. Lyttleton frowned now as he realized that he could only remember a faint echo of her laughter, and he thought she had dark hair, but he couldn't be sure.

His father had destroyed all existing portraits of her so that the children grew up without a concrete image of her. Too, the elder Lyttleton refused to talk about their mother after her death, and shortly after the funeral he had begun drinking. In the months after, he grew increasingly morose, neglected himself and the children, and died within two years.

The brother and sister had gone to live with their father's younger brother, and there they had learned about their mother from their grandmother. The old woman was Irish, and Roman Catholic, although her husband had been a nonpractitioner. She had remained faithful all her life, retaining her rosary, liturgy, and saints to pray to.

She had talked to the children about their mother; though she'd never liked the woman much, she hadn't wished her dead, but what was done was done. And she had talked of her religion, too. Lyttleton's uncle had found no objection as long as his mother didn't try to raise the boy as a Catholic.

His grandmother died when he was fifteen, leaving him her rosary, its finely carved beads and cross of rosewood, and a crucifix that had hung in her room above her bed. For years he had treasured them, for he had greatly loved his grandmother, and even now he kept them in his bedroom. The minister finished the service, and the three men turned to leave. As they walked away from the grave they kept their silence, none of them feeling like talking. Once they were outside the high walls of the cemetery, they paused to chat.

"Are you planning to go by and see Mrs. Hamilton?" Montchalmers asked Lyttleton.

"Not today, Henry. I'll give her a day and then drop in."

"Well, old man, I think I'll go later." Montchalmers' expression looked slightly furtive; it puzzled Lyttleton.

"I think I will, too," Terris said, his tone faintly challenging, and for a moment he and Montchalmers glared at each other.

Lyttleton said good-bye and left, returning home. His low spirits continued, and he found he could not visit August Hamilton the next day. He was still a little uneasy from the last time he had seen her. Perhaps, if given time, the feeling would ease somewhat.

Montchalmers and Terris, though, proved extremely diligent, for they found time to call upon the widow several times together, as well as separately, after the funeral. Lyttleton said nothing, although he thought the frequency of their visits was rather extreme. And not quite proper, either. If he thought they were simply going to console her, that would be quite all right, but remembering how they had looked at her, he doubted that consolation was their reason for being there.

A few days later the three friends met up at the club. Lyttleton had not yet been to see the widow, although he had sent a bouquet of flowers to her. No doubt Montchalmers and Terris had more than made up for his absence, he thought wryly.

Once settled with drinks and lit cigars, Montchalmers and Terris reported that August Hamilton was observing complete mourning, but they declared she was too young to shut herself completely away, and so they had finally persuaded her to attend a quiet soirée that night.

"You mean Lady Brightstone's?" Lyttleton asked, raising one eyebrow.

"The very same," Montchalmers replied lightly. He had already downed two glasses of brandy, although he hadn't been there above half an hour, and was now making some headway on a third. His face was red, as though he'd run a great distance or drunk a great deal. Lyttleton would have wagered on the latter.

"It's all right," Terris said. "I expect it'll be quiet enough, if not downright sedate. Those sorts of things always are. Probably it'll be jolly boring, if you want to know the truth."

Lyttleton frowned slightly. "Tommy died scarcely five days ago. Don't you think you're both being precipitate? Shouldn't she stay secluded for somewhat longer?"

"No," Terris said shortly.

Montchalmers didn't answer, but as Lyttleton studied his face he saw that the other man felt the same. Certainly Lyttleton didn't want to see the young woman buried alive, as it were, by the convention of formal mourning, and God knew, he didn't observe all the rules all the time, but it seemed downright indecent for Montchalmers and Terris to rush her out of her extremely short bereavement.

Perhaps he was mistaken, though. It would be a quiet evening with good conversation, and no dancing or music. Surely no harm would come of his two friends inviting her to lady Brightstone's soirée. After all, they were simply thinking of her. Or perhaps, one cynical part of him pointed out, Montchalmers and Terris acted out of their own selfishness. It would be most improper if they continued to call frequently upon the young widow. It would be an altogether different matter if they met her at various social functions.

If only they had waited a little longer, a month or so, he would have felt more comfortable.

"Good God, man," said Montchalmers, finishing another glass of brandy, "I can't see her shutting herself away for all her life, y'know."

"A few weeks would hardly have been a lifetime," Lyttleton said quietly.

"It is if you're young and beautiful like Aug—Mrs. Hamilton."

"You might remember that she *is* in mourning and isn't to be courted," Lyttleton pointed out more sharply than he had intended.

Terris said nothing. Montchalmers applied himself to his brandy.

Now was the time to mention the note, Lyttleton thought. Both men should know that Tommy had wanted to see him alone that day—when his wife was not present. He should tell them because for some reason Tommy must not have trusted August. That had to be it, he told himself, and he remembered the look of fear on Tommy's face that night at dinner as he looked at August. Instead, he remained silent, and the moment passed.

He wondered what he would find at Lady Brightstone's.

In the few days since the funeral August Hamilton had grown even more beautiful than she had been. It seemed to Lyttleton that her skin glowed more luminously, that her eyes were lovelier and her smile more captivating. He grew aware of his body's response, and blushing a little, he half turned away from her. It would never do to be seen lusting for the widow of one's friend, particularly when he had been condemning the others for it.

"How are you, Mrs. Hamilton?" He had just arrived at Lady Brightstone's soirée and had found that the others—Montchalmers, Terris and August Hamilton—had all preceded him. Somehow, he hadn't been surprised.

"I am fine, thank you, Mr. Lyttleton," she murmured. "I haven't seen you in a while."

"I've been busy."

"Oh."

She made it sound as if he'd deliberately stayed away from her, and of course, he hadn't. Or had he? "I wasn't sure you desired company. Some wish to grieve alone." His words and tone sounded formal and stiff, almost priggish, and he sensed that she was amused with him.

"Be assured that I am not one of those."

"Well," he said heartily, "then I know."

Good God, how lame he sounded. His face darkening, Lyttleton glanced across the room to see Montchalmers and Terris headed toward them. Perhaps they would rescue him from this terrible predicament.

"Mrs. Hamilton," Montchalmers said breathlessly once he had joined them, "you are looking absolutely stunning tonight."

"How kind you are, Mr. Montchalmers."

"Not at all." He beamed at her, while Terris simply stared at her.

With growing certainty, Lyttleton realized he was jealous of his two friends and it was the first time he had ever regarded them with such an emotion. He didn't like it, but he couldn't seem to help it. It fact, the jealousy grew as he watched Montchalmers flirt with her and Terris moon over her. Lyttleton curled his lip derisively. Both were fools, and August Hamilton could scarcely be attracted to either one of the vacuous oafs. He glared, but neither man noticed.

The three friends were not alone in their admiration of the widow. The men attending the soirée began drifting over to their small group to flirt with August. Inside Lyttleton the jealousy rose up, twisting his guts until he wanted to shriek at the men and fling himself at them, knocking them aside. His fists clenched at his sides, his teeth gritted, he stood still, refusing to give in to the unworthy feeling.

As he watched her he realized she did nothing to encourage them. She listened to their stories and laughed at their jokes, and was as she was before. Damningly beautiful and tantalizing, and almost aloof. Perhaps, he thought, that made the men want her all the more.

The hours passed interminably for the tense Lyttleton, and by the end of the evening he was prepared to kill each one of the men present, Montchalmers and Terris included. As he glowered at his rivals, he realized what he was thinking, and its violence horrified him, for he had always been a peaceful sort.

Without explanation, Lyttleton turned on his heel and marched from the room. He returned straightaway to his old Georgian house. He told Edgar to bring him a bottle of brandy in the study. He poured a glassful and drank until he could think no more of the shameful feelings he had had toward the woman and toward his friends. And when he finally passed out, Edgar tiptoed in and put him to bed.

Lyttleton slept the sleep of the drunk, and his slumber was disturbed only once toward dawn with warm, liquid dreams.

Wyndham Terris lay wide awake, the darkness of his bedroom enveloping him, and waited. Waited for the dream that came every night, the dream of the woman, the woman who was—

Shhh, one part of him insisted. That was right. He couldn't say her name aloud. Couldn't think it.

Impatiently he waited. He knew she would come, for hadn't she told him the previous night that she would? She had never broken a promise to him yet. She would come . . . and when she did . . .

His sigh rasped loudly in the silence of the room, and he shivered in anticipation. He would lift his arms to welcome her, and they would kiss, long and deeply, and she would surrender to him, surrender as she had before, and he would give himself to her. As he had before.

She would bite and scratch him, and he would call her his little hellion, and she would laugh, and then, and then she would give him what she had promised for so long and had as yet withheld.

Terris groaned aloud as he anticipated what was to come, and in the darkness a husky laugh answered him.

The next two nights after the soirée Lyttleton's sleep was disturbed by an increasing number of unusual dreams, dreams in which Tommy's widow figured.

All of the dreams possessed an erotic nature. In them August appeared in various poses, both dressed and disrobed; sometimes he was stripping off her clothes himself, his hands clumsy in his haste, and sometimes she was removing them herself, slowly, teasingly.

Each time it was as though Lyttleton had never seen her before, and on each occasion he caught his breath when the last article of clothing fluttered to the floor and August stood before him, revealed completely in her nakedness, with her head thrown back, her eyes half closed, her hands resting lightly upon her hips. He would stare hungrily at the long white throat, at the swelling of the full bosom, the dark rose nipples tautening under his gaze. His eyes would travel down her flat stomach, past the rounded hips, to linger at the dark tangle of hair between her thighs.

His body would ache and throb, and he could feel

himself stiffening in response. He would go to her then, and he would find his clothes had been stripped from him without his remembering. He would embrace her, savoring the feel of the velvety hair pressing against his groin, the tips of her breasts brushing against his chest. He would press his fingertips into the small of her back, grinding himself against her small body, his rigid manhood seeking entrance, and she would lean back, beckon, spread her legs, and he would—

Wake up.

Every time he woke up. Sitting bolt up, out of breath, damp from sweat, Lyttleton would wake abruptly and stare wildly about the room, not sure where he was, and then the memory of the dream would return, and he would fall back limply, his eyes closed. Several times he was embarrassed to discover emission. Agitated, he would rise to pace around his bedroom. He would think about what happened. None of it made sense.

He couldn't offer an explanation for the dreams; he wasn't sure that he wanted to.

The next day, at the club, Lyttleton hailed Montchalmers and Terris, who had just entered. They came to sit with him, and he studied them, thinking that in their own ways they appeared as haunted as he felt. His friends seemed nervous and snapped at each other several times. Lyttleton frowned and wondered if he should say anything. It was best, he felt, to share confidences. He told them he was having strange dreams at night.

"Dreams?" Terris set his glass down sharply. "What kind?"

Lyttleton glanced away, knowing he was blushing but not being able to prevent it. Damnit, he thought furiously, he was a grown man acting like a schoolboy. "Dreams of a highly . . . personal nature, Wyndy."

"About the widow?"

Montchalmers and Lyttleton stared at him.

"Why, yes. How did you know?"

"I've had them, too," Terris said shortly.

"I, too," Montchalmers echoed, a little bewildered. He knocked down a glass of wine. "What does it mean?" He looked around at his friends.

"Mean, Henry?" Lyttleton's tone was brusque. "I'm sure it doesn't mean anything at all." He didn't want to discuss the topic any longer and regretted bringing it up in the first place.

"Somehow it must be related to our grief for our late friend," Terris suggested quietly. He was staring down into his glass as if he could divine something from those ruby depths.

"That must be it," Montchalmers agreed eagerly, looking vastly relieved to have his erotic dreams explained away so easily.

Lyttleton wasn't so sure, though, even though that seemed as good an excuse as any, and momentarily he felt relieved. Still, some shame lingered at the memory of the intense dreams, and as he glanced at his friends he wondered how intense their dreams were, then decided he didn't want to know.

"Have you lost weight, Wyndy?" he asked. Terris looked gaunter than usual and hadn't spoken very much. Terris was usually more reticent than the other two men, but tonight he seemed even more withdrawn.

"No; well, yes," said Terris, not looking up. "Some, I suppose. Why?"

"Oh, no reason, old boy." Lyttleton knew he was still upset by the death of their friend, so he dismissed the worry that was forming inside him.

Again that night Lyttleton experienced the strange dreams.

Again he woke, sitting bolt up in bed. When he finally rose at half past ten that morning, he did not feel rested at all.

Better, he told himself, to have sat up all evening than endure that sleeplessness. Tonight, though, at dinner with his friends he intended to do more drinking than usual and perhaps that would put him soundly to sleep. He hadn't given much thought to Terris' odd behavior, although once while he was dressing, he thought that the look in Terris' eyes reminded him of someone else's. But whose he didn't know. Shrugging, he dismissed the thought and went in to have a light breakfast.

At the club that evening Lyttleton was distressed to discover that Terris looked even worse than he had the night before. His movements were jerky, and he continually dropped things. At times his eyes were unfocused, his voice strident when he answered questions.

"Are you all right, Wyndy?" Lyttleton asked abruptly during the excellent meal of roast beef.

"Of course I am," Terris snarled. He glared at Lyttleton.

Lyttleton glanced across at Montchalmers and saw his own concern mirrored there. "I thought you were ill or—" He never had a chance to finish.

"Mind your own business, won't you! I'm perfectly all right. I haven't been sleeping as much as usual, but otherwise I can't complain."

Lyttleton nodded, aware that other club members were looking in their direction, and prudently dropped the matter.

The remainder of the meal passed comfortably enough, although some constraint remained between the three men and Montchalmers chattered too much. Afterward they had their usual brandies, and Terris was the first to excuse himself, saying he had important business to attend to. He left then, and Montchalmers and Lyttleton spent the rest of the evening conjecturing about Terris, but finally, as they could come up with nothing, they let the matter rest.

Lyttleton did not see Terris again until two days later, and he was shocked at the change undergone by the man in that short time. His skin seemed stretched across the bones of his face, the gaunt hollows filled with shadows. His eyes were red, as though from lack of sleep, and the skin underneath black and puffy. His hands trembled with everything he did.

Terris insisted he wasn't ill. His voice was shrill, rising louder and louder until Montchalmers was compelled to shush him, which only served to make him more frenzied.

Suddenly Lyttleton knew where he had seen the look in Terris' eyes before. He had seen the same expression in the eyes of Tommy Hamilton, just days prior to his sudden death.

"Don't you try to quiet me!" Terris shrieked.

"For God's sake, Wyndy, lower your voice," Montchalmers said, leaning forward.

"I won't! I won't let you silence me! I have things to say! Things, I say!"

"Very well," Lyttleton said reasonably, trying to humor the stricken man, "what sort of things?"

"Things," Terris muttered darkly. A lock of his hair, lank and dirty, swung back and forth over his forehead as he shook his head. He pushed it back, and for the first time Lyttleton noticed the man's fingernails were dirty and broken; some were ragged, as though he'd chewed on them. Lyttleton was repelled, and filled with pity, too. He wished he could help.

"Good things, Wyndy?" Lyttleton asked. If he could draw him out by talking, they might discover what was troubling Terris.

"Of course good things!" Terris toyed with his wineglass,

set it down so violently it startled Montchalmers. Nervously he twisted a cufflink, and Lyttleton noticed the griminess of the cuffs, as though the shirt hadn't been properly laundered or as if he hadn't changed it in some time. Wrinkled as well, the shirt was stained in several places. Terris was slipping in every possible way, and Lyttleton didn't know what to do. Terris muttered under his breath, words neither man could understand.

Montchalmers leaned over him, trying to reassure him, and Terris shrank back with a low moan. Montchalmers tried unsuccessfully to mask the hurt.

"She's mine," Terris said.

"What's that?" Lyttleton said, not believing Terris' words.

"She's mine," he repeated, louder this time. "She's mine, do you hear me? I love her, I truly do, and she loves me!" he declared passionately, almost defiantly. He stared at Lyttleton and Montchalmers, his eyes almost glazed. "I'm her true love!"

There was no doubt in Lyttleton's mind whom Terris meant.

"They all want her. Dogs. Each and every one of 'em dogs. I've seen the way they come around her, sniffing and grunting. Terrible dogs. Terrible men." His eyes rolled, the whites showing. "Dogs, sons-of-bitches!" He smirked. "Dogs." Apparently the word amused him for he kept repeating it to himself.

"Wyndy," Lyttleton said, his tone as calm as he could muster, "we understand what you're enduring, and you needn't be alone. We can help. For God's sake, let us. We're your friends."

Terris' expression turned sly. "You can't understand what it's like. How could you? You're both dogs! Dogs! All of 'em! They come after her, you come after her, sniffing and grunting, sniffing and grunting. Coming day and night. After her. And it hurts to see them, to see all of them. I don't like it. I don't want any of them around. I want them all to go away, but they won't, the dogs. Sniffing and grunting. Jealousy," he muttered, not looking at either man, "it's eating me alive!" he whined. "Alive with jealousy! To see them come around, sniffing and grunting around her, around my love, my love." Tears coursed down his face now as the two men stared, horrified. "I can't stand it any longer! I'm her love, and there's no one else. There'll never be anyone else!"

Suddenly Terris leaped to his feet, knocking back his chair, and pulled something from his pocket. He clutched a pistol in his hands. Grinning foolishly, he aimed the pistol shakily at Montchalmers, then at Lyttleton. Both stood slowly, not wanting to startle him. Terris began to chuckle, a low, hideous sound like the laugh of a madman. Montchalmers glanced out of the tail of his eye at Lyttleton, who nodded almost imperceptibly. As one, they lunged forward. They grappled with Terris, trying to wrest the pistol away from him. Some of the braver club members had started toward them, and Lyttleton shouted at them to stay back.

Terris knocked his two friends away as though they were children. Montchalmers fell to the floor, while Lyttleton staggered backward, nearly slipping and falling. Momentarily his breath was sucked out, and when he breathed deeply, he felt as though a knife were slicing through his lungs.

Before Lyttleton could recover, Terris pushed Montchalmers, who was just getting to his feet, down again, and then he rushed from the room. Lyttleton helped Montchalmers up, and they pursued their friend. At the end of the hall they saw a door slam shut. They found it locked and pounded on the wood with their palms.

"Wyndy, for God's sake, let us in!" Montchalmers called. "Please!"

"Come on, old man," Lyttleton cajoled. "Let us in. We'll all talk about it, have some wine—"

From behind the door came a muffled giggle which sent chills down their spines.

"Wyndy!"

"We understand how you feel. We can—"

There was a sharp retort. The two men looked at each other.

It was the sound of a pistol being fired.

Delhi, India: 1857

The sun had sunk below the mountains almost an hour before, and still the heat remained, for the India summer that lasted from March until October was only a month old.

Baked into the white walls of the house, the heat, so intense and overwhelming in midday that it could literally suck the breath out of a man, sighed as it was slowly released, and the leaves of the mango trees shook in the hot breeze that blew from the west. Across the windows and doorways were *tatties*, four-inch thick screens of sweet smelling *kuskus* grass kept wet constantly to reduce the temperature of the air passing through them. Sometimes they helped.

The one-story stuccoed house was large and rambling, with the verandah around all four sides. Behind stood an enclosed, and long-neglected, garden of oleanders, jasmine, roses, and hibiscus. Palms and cypress grew in the dusty front yard.

The house was the residence of a *sahib*, an Englishman

who'd disembarked in India thirty years earlier to seek his fortune, who'd stayed while his comrades had returned to an England of pleasant memories, and who had amassed more wealth than he'd ever dreamed possible while he was growing up in Yorkshire.

Located in the English suburb of Delhi, the house was filled with the finest of everything: delicate etchings and accomplished paintings; silver and gold bowls and service; china brought many years ago around the Cape from England; tables and boxes, small and large, intricately inlaid with ivory and mother-of-pearl; mahogany and cherrywood furniture; brass and silver, gold and gold-plate; and this luxurious residential empire was tended by an army of native servants.

The servants had now retired to their whitewashed baked-mud huts behind the house to await the return of the owner, and so the house was empty, or nearly so, for cockroaches as large as mice scuttled across the floor of the study, while insects as large as a man's hand buzzed through the rooms. Mosquitoes and gnats sought bare flesh upon which to feed, and a lizard darted up a wall by a framed watercolor. On a Louis XIV lacquered writing desk mold marred the thin sheaves of paper. Opposite, on the shelves stretching the length and height of one wall, the book pages curled and rotted and harbored parasites that ate away at the leaves.

The overly warm air was pungent with the odor of rotting mangoes and too-ripe bananas, the perfume of oleanders and hibiscus, the sourness of wet animal dung, and the mustiness of mildew.

Outside, a horse neighed shrilly, breaking the silence, as a carriage rumbled to a stop. A man's deep voice shouted angry orders in Hindustani, and two servants, both dressed alike in *dhoti*, hastened into the house to light the lamps.

Another squatted by the *punkah* in the study and began working it so that a slight breeze fanned the deadened air of the room.

The front door crashed open, knocking loose the lizard which had just reached the ceiling, and a large man, still in his middle years, strode into the room. He was accompanied by a woman some decades his junior.

He slapped his gloves down on a table, ruffling the pages of an open book. He whirled around and tapped his foot.

"Why'd you have to invite him back here?" he demanded harshly. His eyebrows, shot with grey, beetled together into a fierce expression which did not in the least daunt his younger companion.

"Father, the servants." She glanced at the *punkah-wallah*.

"Servants be damned. They're just niggers," he said, glaring at her.

"They still have ears, Father."

He ignored her. "You haven't answered my question, August. Why tonight, of all nights?" He took a step toward her, his arms half-raised at his side. "*Tonight* was to be—"

Stepping agilely away from him, she tugged off her gloves and let them fall to the floor. A servant would retrieve them within minutes.

"I thought it would be an excellent way to pass the evening. After all, Lieutenant Hamilton is *very* handsome. And young." The man paled noticeably. "Besides, I find him extremely intriguing," she added as she carefully arranged her skirts and sat in one of the cane-back chairs scattered about the room.

"So, he intrigues you. There's bound to be more to it than his handsome face, I'll wager." The man regarded her for some moments, while she ignored him and leafed through a book. "Are you thinking of going to England, my sweet?" he asked finally.

"It has occurred to me."

"Ha! I thought so! He's not very important, August. He's merely a lowly lieutenant, not at all influential. And besides, he's just been stationed here in India. He won't leave for some time."

"I'm well aware of that. Now, come sit, Father. Don't stand and bluster about, for it'll make you exceedingly hot and weary."

Sighing, he eased himself into a nearby chair proportioned to his size, and before he could say another word, a servant entered silently and bowed low over the teakwood tray he held. The man took a crystal glass, as did the woman.

When the servant had left, the man resumed the conversation. "You know I've never interfered before with these diversions"—here he placed his hand upon her arm—"and you know I wouldn't mind, August, except that tonight was promised to—"

"Father," she said, a bored expression in her voice as she shrugged his hand away, "I really don't care to discuss it any longer. It is settled. Our guest will be arriving shortly."

"You never consult me, August," he muttered somewhat petulantly as he glared into his glass of wine. She ignored him; his expression deepened into a glower, and still she did not look at him. Finally he gave up and began drinking his chilled wine.

They did not speak again, and in the silence Parrish and his daughter could hear the howling of jackals as they roamed the banks of the Jumna River flowing past the city. Not long after, they heard the sounds of a horseman arriving. A man dismounted, said something to a servant, and within seconds their guest was ushered into the study by yet another servant.

Lieutenant Thomas Edmund Hamilton of the Queen's Sixth Dragoon Guards towered half a head over six feet, had shoulders broadened by summers of swimming at his uncle's estate, and the narrow hips and the muscular legs and arms of a natural athlete. His hair was guinea-gold, his blue eyes guileless, as well as being framed by long curling lashes that were the envy of most Englishwomen in Delhi, and his strong chin bore a slight cleft. He wore the undress summer uniform of a frock coat and white pants. Smiling, he bowed low.

"Good evening, Mr. Parrish. Miss Parrish." Hamilton's voice was resonant, the voice of a young man confident of himself and his abilities.

Cecil Parrish nodded brusquely. "Hamilton. Good to see you again. Care for some wine, Lieutenant? It's been chilled."

"Why, yes, thank you."

The lieutenant sat and gazed unabashedly and admiringly at August Parrish.

Parrish handed Hamilton a glass, then glared at the young officer from behind his wineglass. Hamilton never noticed.

"I'm so glad you were able to come this evening," August murmured, her lashes lowered becomingly over her large dark eyes.

"I'm glad, too," Hamilton responded eagerly, his eyes never leaving her face. "I have seen you before, Miss Parrish. That is, before tonight at the concert. From afar, though." He grinned at her.

She lifted a dark brow. "An admirer from afar? Is that correct, Lieutenant Hamilton?"

"Oh yes," he breathed.

Parrish made a disgusted sound and drained his glass. He poured more wine.

"It's true, Miss Parrish," Hamilton said, undaunted. "I've admired you for so long—weeks, in fact, ever since I saw you at the Turners' party last month—and I've wanted to meet you from that very moment, but until I saw you tonight, I didn't know how to go about it, and then, when we fell to talking"—he grinned at Parrish, who didn't return the expression—"and when you invited me back, well, you really are most kind, Miss Parrish."

"Not at all," she said, her voice low.

He grinned again; she answered with a smile, and he took a quick gulp of his wine. A bead of sweat trickled unnoticed down the side of his face.

Hamilton cleared his throat, looked at her, then at her father, then back at the young woman. He evidently wanted to speak, but he was too shy. August smiled encouragingly at him.

"I was wondering . . . that is, I had wanted to—would you care to go to the Oswalds' dinner party this week, Miss Parrish?" His words rushed together in his nervousness. "I know that it's probably impossible, as I've given you such short notice, and you probably already have an escort, but if that isn't the case, I would be most happy if you would attend with me." His tone, as well as expression, was eager.

"I would be most delighted, Lieutenant, to attend with you."

"You would? Wonderful!" Hamilton smiled, elated. "Excellent. I'll make further arrangements tomorrow." She nodded, and he finished his wine, then stood. "I think I should go. It's growing late, Miss Parrish, and no doubt your father and you will be retiring soon."

"No doubt," she said.

Hamilton bent over her hand and in a courtly fashion brushed his lips across the top of it. It was customary for men and women to shake hands.

"Would it be permissible for me to call upon you tomorrow morning?"

Social calls in Delhi, as in the rest of English-dominated India, were most often conducted in the mornings, well before the enervating heat of the day had become unbearable, while the two best times to go riding were three a.m. and nine p.m.

"I fear I do not rise early, sir, as is the custom with so many of my women acquaintances. And later in the afternoon I have household matters I must attend, and which I cannot neglect."

"I understand perfectly," Hamilton said. "I have only the greatest of admiration for your ability in running your father's household so capably, Miss Parrish. It is an excellent quality." She murmured her thanks. "May I call upon you in the evening then?"

"That would be fine, Lieutenant Hamilton, for I should be completely rested by then. I look forward to seeing you."

Hamilton smiled again at her, shook hands with a reluctant Cecil Parrish and thanked him for inviting him to his house, then left.

In the abrupt silence Parrish glanced across at his daughter, who had a slightly dreamy expression on her red lips. He pressed his lips together and spoke in a tight voice.

"I don't like you encouraging him."

"You don't like me encouraging anyone," she countered. "Besides, I'm not encouraging him." She trailed her fingertips along the arm of the chair and paused to rub a worn spot.

"Like hell you're not!"

August looked appropriately shocked. "Father! Your language!"

He glowered. Sweat trickled down the sides of his face, matting the grey hair, and a dark stain spread downward on his starched collar. His lips were dry, the skin cracking and flaking.

"He vows he's interested in me." Her voice was coy. "Can I help that?"

"Yes, you bloody well can."

"Come now, Father. Don't be so angry. After all, you must realize that—"

"No, I won't let it happen! I won't let some boy still wet behind the ears sweep you off your feet. I won't have it, do you hear, August!" His chest rose and fell rapidly with his hoarse breathing.

"He's hardly a boy," she demurred. "He's a man, Father, *and* as I understand it, the only son of a wealthy family."

"They're all boys," he muttered, wiping a hand across his darkening face. He glanced at his hand, then took out a lawn handkerchief and rubbed at the sweat dabbing his face. "Inexperienced, young, stupid. I've seen it too often, August. Too often. We haven't been in Delhi that long—don't spoil things for us."

"I won't, believe me. This is different," she said softly. "That I promise you."

"Hmmph."

"It is different," she repeated, then cocked her head slightly to one side. "You won't ruin it this time, Father. I'm giving you fair warning. I have been tolerant in the past."

Parrish said nothing.

In one graceful motion she rose and walked toward him, her skirts swaying seductively. She bent down to give him an affectionate kiss upon the forehead. "There now, Father, don't you feel better?"

"No, but I do know what will make me feel better," he said thickly. He glanced up at her and his harsh expression relaxed a little.

With a faint smile curving her red lips she clasped his hand.

"Tommy's got a girl," said a grinning Malcolm Grant.

The Queen's Sixth Dragoon Guards cantonment, or military station, was located in the town of Meerut, almost forty miles to the northeast of Delhi. Hamilton had arrived late the night before from Delhi, giving his friends ample opportunity to discuss his absence.

"The arrows of Cupid have found the heart of our cherub," Grant continued. Hamilton's brother officers called him a cherub because of his fair hair and guileless eyes. He was also considered an innocent, for he'd been in India for scarcely two months. The regiment had been sent home from Crimea the year before and was about half its usual strength. Grant had been with the Dragoon Guards the longest of the four officers; his family had served in the regiment since the days of Queen Anne.

"A girl, eh?" said Bert Flaxley, winking at Grant and Richard Rutherford. "Wouldn't be one of the native girls now, would it, Tommy?"

"Good God, no! Haven't lost my mind from the beastly heat yet."

"Besides, keeping a mistress takes money, and Tommy wants to keep what his father's left him!" Grant teased. "Don't blame him myself."

"Maybe she just came over on the Fishing Fleet," Flaxley suggested.

For some time large numbers of unattached English girls and women had flocked to India, seeking available men as husbands, and this use of India as a marriage mart was termed by the local British as the Fishing Fleet. By and large, the women were successful, too.

"Those long-faced spinsters!" Rutherford said. "Tommy has better taste than that. Don't you, old man?"

"That's right," Flaxley said. "Come on now, Tommy, who is it? You can tell us! We're your friends!"

Hamilton grinned good-naturedly as he stretched out his legs so that his servant could remove the dusty boots. "Why should I tell you fellows?"

"Why not?" Grant said.

"Well, if you can keep a secret, I'll tell you."

"We can, we can!" the three men exclaimed.

"I doubt it, but I'll tell anyway." He took his time with his rum while his friends grew impatient. Finally he grinned. "I'm going to the Oswalds' dinner party, and I will be escorting Miss August Parrish."

One of the men whistled appreciatively.

"I've heard her father is as rich as Croesus," Rutherford said, a note of envy in his voice.

"To hell with her father," Grant said, "she's a rare beauty, and an unplucked jewel, I've heard, too. My God, Tommy, how'd you do it? Her name hasn't been linked with anyone's; she and her father keep to themselves, and I don't think I've seen her above five times. Her father might as well keep her in *purdah* for all that we see of her."

"You haven't seen much because they've only been here a few months," Hamilton explained. "I believe they came from the north, around Cashmere, I believe."

"Incredible, Tommy, simply incredible." Flaxley's hazel eyes became sly. "As for motive . . ." He made a gesture which caused the others to laugh.

Hamilton just grinned.

The shadow glided across the dirt street. The night was black; no moon hung overhead, and there were no streetlights. Even the open windows of the crude houses were black. A foul odor arose from the gutters where garbage and sewage lay rotting in the heat.

A pack of dogs, their ribs protruding, rummaged through the reeking piles, then bristled and growled as the shadow approached. Suddenly they turned, and with tails tucked between their scrawny legs, ran. A sound like faint laughter followed them, then drifted away in the torpid night air.

The shadow listened.

Down the street drifted an infant's hungry cries. Nearby a man and a woman shouted in Hindi, while across the street several children giggled. Far away a cat yowled. These were the sounds of the city settling for the night, while along the river jackals barked as they prowled for food.

Another sound was added to this: footsteps.

Veiled in darkness, the shadow waited.

The footsteps became bare feet slapping against the dirt. Closer and closer.

Around the corner of a mud house a youth no more than twelve appeared. He was a handsome boy with large eyes and a ready smile. Strong-limbed, clean, healthy. He was running an errand for his ill mother, and he had promised her he would be home soon.

Smiling, the shadow waited; then, when the boy was only a few feet away, the shadow slipped away from the wall.

The boy stopped, thinking he'd seen something in the darkness. "Come here," the shadow whispered in the boy's own language. The boy took a step forward, then stopped. "Come to me." The voice was insistent.

The child melted into the shadows, and cool, soft hands crept around his neck, while icy lips touched his.

The boy laughed.

"Have you seen the bloody *Gazette*?" Flaxley waved the Delhi newspaper in front of him.

Today the April heat, worse than usual, had robbed the four officers of whatever strength they'd had left. In the morning they had paraded briefly, then been dismissed to rest. Even the *tatties* failed to keep the oppressiveness from the room. The *punkah-wallah* sat in one corner, and a slight breeze stirred the room's still air. A huge green fly buzzed around the ceiling.

"What's that?" Grant was busy shuffling a deck of cards, for he and Rutherford were engaged in a friendly wager. Pausing, he took out a handkerchief and wiped it across his gleaming face and neck.

Hamilton, who could barely manage to find enough strength to write a long letter to August, paused and looked up. "Saw it yesterday." He seemed far more affected by the heat than the others, for he had been in India less time. Grant had assured him that he would grow used to it. Sometime.

"They've found a third native child dead, it says here.

Something about the blood. Seems it might be a new disease, although they can't say for sure as some animal—probably the dogs—got to it."

"Bloody wogs," Rutherford muttered. "Damned heathens. I'll be glad when the missionaries convert them all and this sort of thing will stop." He shook his head, a disgusted look on his face. "Murders now, and those rumors about the *sepoys* and their damned unrest. I told you before and I'll tell you now—you can't trust any of 'em. Go ahead, Grant, deal."

Flaxley opened the newspaper to read more. "Children and young men have died. All in the same manner. Terrible, just terrible. It says the bodies were—"

"Please, spare us the gruesome details," Grant said softly.

"Might have something to do with their religion, Bert," Hamilton said. "Like *suttee*. Or the Thugs. That's what it sounds like to me."

"I don't think so," said Grant. "No, this seems different."

"How?" Hamilton asked as he returned to his letter. He wasn't really interested, for he was a man in love and love had no patience for unpleasantries such as death.

"I don't know," Grant said, shrugging slightly. "Just different somehow."

"It's the heat," Flaxley stated firmly. "It's turning everyone into beasts." Sweat trickled down his neck, and his hair lay limply across his forehead. He grimaced and reached for his drink.

"The Indians are accustomed to these summers, though," Grant pointed out.

"Doesn't mean it don't make them go mad," Flaxley asserted.

"Goddamnit, Grant, deal the cards!" Rutherford said, scowling, and downed his rum.

Grant obliged, but continued talking. "The sawbones think it might be a fever that's killing them off. God knows, the place has enough." Like the others, he'd endured his share of tropical diseases and fevers since coming to India. Before, in the Crimea, he had almost died of a battle wound.

"Amazing," Flaxley said. He reached for his glass, found it empty. He clapped his hands. "Chand!"

The summons was answered by a short Indian of middle years; he bowed low. "Yes, Lieutenant-*sahib*?"

"More rum and arrack," Flaxley said.

"Yes, Lieutenant-*sahib*."

"Chand." The man waited.

"These deaths—what do you think caused them?" Flaxley carefully folded the newspaper.

Fearfully the Indian servant glanced over his shoulder as if he expected something to be lurking there. His voice dropped to a whisper. "Demons, Lieutenant-*sahib*. There are demons loose. A *shaitan*."

"Good God!" Rutherford exploded into raucous laughter. "I told you they were a superstitious bunch." He guffawed and winked at the others.

Even Grant was smiling. "What sort of demons are they, Chand?"

"Demons," the servant said, incapable of elaborating further. He gestured wildly. "It is best if the *sahibs* stay inside at night. The demons come from the north, it is said."

"That's enough, Chand. Well, that explains it," Flaxley said, once the Indian had left the room, "there are demons about." He made a grotesque face.

"And witches," said Rutherford.

"And goblins," said Grant.

"And I've had enough of this nonsense," Hamilton said, smiling as he finished his letter. "I've got to get ready now." He pushed away from the writing desk and stretched.

"Where are you going tonight, Lieutenant?" Grant asked. He winked at the others, who tried hard not to grin.

"As if you didn't know."

"Ah yes, to visit the fair August. When do we meet your—should we term her your fiancée as yet?" Grant raised his eyebrows hopefully.

Hamilton blushed. "No, not yet."

Flaxley nudged Rutherford. "Hasn't popped the question yet."

"I'm sure he's popped something else, though," Rutherford said slyly.

Angrily Hamilton wheeled on him. "Take back those words, Rutherford! Miss Parrish is a fine, genteel young lady, and I won't have you implying she's some sort of common—"

"Easy now," Grant said, resting a hand on his friend's arm. "I don't think Dick was serious."

"Apologize, Rutherford."

Rutherford scowled. "Oh, very well. I'm sorry, Hamilton, for I'm sure she's a fine lady."

Hamilton started for the door. "Tommy," Grant called. "When will we get to meet Miss Parrish?"

"Soon; very soon, I think," he said.

"We'll be looking forward to it. Have a good time."

"Thanks, Malcolm." Hamilton flashed an easy smile at him and left.

The three men glanced at one another. Flaxley spoke first. "I've never seen him like that before."

"I know," Grant said, while Rutherford nodded.

"It's as if he were . . ."

"Possessed," Grant supplied.

"Yes." Flaxley stared thoughtfully through the open door and watched as Hamilton's tall form receded across the compound. "Yes, it is."

"Maybe it's the demons from the north," Grant said, and they all laughed.

He hadn't meant to react violently, for he knew Rutherford had just been gibing him. Or had he? Rutherford always rode him hard. No, he assured himself, it was just in jest.

Hamilton reached the far side of the compound and entered his quarters, glad to be out of the hot sun. He rubbed a hand across his forehead, feeling the grime on his fingertips, and wiped his hand on his pants leg. He would get shaved, dress, then start the long ride to Delhi. He poured himself a glass of arrack, downed it quickly, but it was warm and tasted bitter.

He dropped onto the bed and closed his eyes. Delhi. And August.

His August. He saw her so clearly, so intensely. The smell of her perfume seemed to waft through the air, and the musky scent brought back many memories.

He wanted her so badly it hurt. At night he ached for her, wanted to hold her tightly in his arms, longed to kiss and stroke her. He wanted her under him, wanted to be one with her. Yet he would remain the gentleman and would wait until he'd proposed marriage to her and they were lawfully wedded. After all, he loved her with all his heart, and he would not dishonor her. She was a lady, a woman of refinement. He couldn't touch her in the way he had the native girls.

As difficult as it was, he would wait. Wait for the night

when he came to her bed, when they would embrace, kiss, and he would taste the sweetness of her full lips. He would slip off her negligee, revealing her lovely body. She would blush becomingly as he stroked her breasts, the nipples hardening under his careful fingers, and she would lie back, moaning that she wanted him. His hand would rub the silkiness of her skin, and at the juncture of her legs she would be wet and inviting. He would kiss the soft hair there, flicking the pink bud of her passion with his tongue, and then he would roll on top of her and thrust inside her virginal tightness and—

The world exploded behind his closed eyes as his body bucked. Bewildered, Hamilton sat up and stared around the room, then down at his pants. A great wet smear spread across them. Mingled with it was blood.

Alarmed, he stripped off his sticky clothes and searched, but could find no wound. He examined his pants again. The blood was gone.

Hamilton shivered, suddenly chilled in the terrible heat of the afternoon.

On the first of May, Tommy Hamilton was invited to dine with the Parrishes. He regarded this as an important step in his courtship of August, for he'd never dined there before and he hoped he'd have a better chance of impressing her father. Too, he had important news to give them.

For Tommy wanted desperately to marry August, and in deciding that, he had set about to campaign for her by bringing her bouquets of the most exotic blossoms, boxes of delicacies imported from France and Italy, and once a volume of poetry bound in fine Morocco leather. And he spent his time with her whenever possible. He was very much in love, so much that he thought of nothing but her day and night. Even what little sleep he found during the nights of stifling heat was disturbed by intense dreams, dreams of them together, dreams that left him exhausted and drenched with sweat.

Once at the Parrish house Hamilton formally greeted Cecil Parrish, who was curt as usual. Hamilton knew the man didn't like him, and he was determined not to let it deter him. August soon joined them, and Hamilton smiled at her, his eyes never leaving her face. Shortly after that they went into dinner. She toyed with her food, excusing herself by saying she'd been ill that day from the extreme heat. Hamilton nodded with sympathy, for the day had been particularly bad.

As they chatted of approaching parties and a cricket match scheduled next month, Hamilton became aware of the glances Parrish directed toward her. Glances not of fatherly love, but of something else. Lust? But surely they were nothing as sinister as that. At times she seemed to return them. Hamilton shook his head, dismissing this notion as a product of jealousy and the heat.

Turning toward him, August smiled, and it took his breath away; he felt as though a hand were squeezing his chest, and he was aware of his body's response to her. God, how he wanted her right now. In this very room. On the table. Her lips shone wetly, so red and lush, and he wanted to kiss them, wanted to touch her tongue with his, to feel her.

"Lieutenant Hamilton," came the waspish voice.

He blinked. "I'm sorry, sir, what were you saying?"

Parrish glared at him. "I was talking about the chances for the cricket match."

"Their team doesn't stand a ghost of a chance, sir."

Parrish looked like he was going to argue the point, when August said, "Come, gentlemen, before you grow too involved in this discussion, let us retire."

They nodded, following her into the study, where they found chairs that caught the errant breeze blowing through the opened windows. As always, the *punkah* fanned them.

The native butler brought a silver tray laden with a cut-crystal decanter and matching goblets. He poured the port, then disappeared just as quietly.

When they were alone, except for the *punkah-wallah*, Hamilton leaned forward. "I must speak with you both about an important matter."

"Umm?" Parrish was more concerned with pouring himself another glass.

"It's confidential. Does the *wallah* understand English?"

Parrish shook his head. "Now, what is this confidential matter?"

"I believe, sir, that there might be trouble."

"Trouble? What do you mean by that, Hamilton?"

"The *sepoys* seem restive, sir, and I sense trouble."

"The native soldiers? What've they to do with this?"

August, her dark eyes fixed on Hamilton's face, listened as he spoke. "There've been isolated incidents recently—incidents that give me increasing concern."

"I haven't heard about them," Parrish said bluntly.

"Of course not, sir, for they aren't publicized, but they do exist. This past January there was just such an incident at Dum-Dum. Too, it's rumored among them that we're trying to force them to break their caste with the new cartridges for the Enfield rifle."

Parrish sat back, an astonished expression on his face. "That's absolute nonsense."

"Of course, sir; you and I know that, as does any European, but these Indians are an ignorant lot. Too, several English ladies have encountered unpleasantness while traveling. Most unusual, for generally the Indians are courteous. And recently an Indian soldier in the Thirty-fourth Regiment went on the rampage with a loaded musket. He's been dealt with, but I worry."

"I think you're imagining things," Parrish said.

Hamilton shook his head. "No, sir, I'm not. I believe the Indians are growing tired of the British yoke."

"British yoke! Fine words from one of the Queen's Dragoons!" Parrish grunted.

"Sir, please," Hamilton said quietly. "I fear the Indians misunderstand what we are doing here, and due to this fear and distrust, an uprising could occur. It is, after all, not without precedent, sir. As distasteful for personal reasons as I find this, I would suggest that you and your daughter put your affairs in order at once and leave the country. For your own safety."

August's red lips curved slightly, and his pulse quickened. "No one will force us to leave India. India is, after all, my home."

"India is home to many, but that may not be sufficient to save them," Hamilton responded gloomily.

"I think," she said as she reached out to brush his hand with her fingertips, "that you worry far too much, Lieutenant Hamilton."

He was completely unaware of anything except her touch. His mouth had gone dry, and with effort he concentrated on his words. "If I hear further tales, then I recommend strongly that you leave." She simply smiled. "I'm concerned about your safety, but I don't wish to alarm you."

"Well, you're certainly doing that!" Parrish exclaimed, his words slurred. He pressed his lips into a thin line and belched.

A clock in another room chimed the late hour, and Hamilton pushed back his chair and rose with reluctance.

"I fear I must leave now, Miss Parrish. I know you're tired and hot, and you must get your rest." He bowed over her hand. "Good evening, Mr. Parrish, and thank you for the dinner."

Hamilton was shown from the house by the butler,

while the father and daughter remained seated in the study. Parrish sipped his port, slopping a little on his hand.

"He's head over heels in love with you," he said roughly.

"Is that such a terrible thing?" she asked lightly.

"Yes, damnit!"

She laughed, a chilling sound. "We shall see, Father. There is time yet."

Pretending he did not hear her, he busied himself with pouring more liquor, which he drank in one swallow.

They continued to sit, without speaking, and the only sounds in the room came from the sweeping back and forth of the *punkah* and the buzzing of the insects around the flames of the candles.

The deaths of native children and youths continued, now counting some two or three a week, and within the European community in Delhi the fear grew that they would be next. They cared little that the Indians died, only that death might not always prove so discriminating.

Hamilton found the topic discussed wherever he went in the European suburb, as well as in the Delhi and Meerut cantonments. It even surfaced in the Parrish house a week after he'd first dined there. He and the Parrishes had just finished a sumptuous meal of curried chicken, raisins and almonds with rice, and were lingering in the study over brandy. Candlelight gleamed on several brass urns in the corners and on the dark bindings of the books. The *tatties* had been raised to allow the evening breeze to drift into the room. Far off in the distance an elephant trumpeted. And somehow the subject of the recent deaths was introduced.

"Our serving boy Chand says there are demons loose," Hamilton said. "What do you think, Miss Parrish?"

She smiled languorously, and once more Hamilton felt his pulse quickening. "I fear I must agree with the Indians. There is something loose in the night air."

He saw the humor in her dark eyes and laughed. Parrish glared, downed a glass of brandy, then abruptly stood.

"Excuse me," the older man said curtly. He left the room without a backward glance.

Hamilton was surprised at Parrish's reaction. Had he inadvertently said something to offend her father?

"Forgive my father, please, Lieutenant, for he is not well."

"Of course, Miss Parrish."

She rose and spoke quietly to the *punkah-wallah*. Hamilton couldn't follow what she was saying because he knew few words of the local dialect, but the old servant stilled the cloth fan almost immediately, bowed, and left.

Hamilton and August were completely alone for the first time since he had met her.

An errant breeze wafted into the room, ruffling the pages of an open book, caressing his face. Excitement surged through his body, ebbing and eddying, tantalizing him. He pushed back his chair and took a few steps forward until they were no more than a few inches apart. He raised his arms, and taking her into them, he kissed her.

Her kisses were ice-cold, burning-hot, and flamed the smouldering fires within him, fanned them until he thought he would explode. His body ached and tingled, and he was more aware of it than ever before. He knew where the blood flowed and pulsed, what grew rigid and engorged, what beat rhythmically inside him, demanding release. His hands skimmed along the velvet-soft skin of her arms. His trembling fingers lingered at her full breasts. He rubbed them with his palms and watched as the nipples thrust against the tight material of her gown.

She guided his hand as he unbuttoned her dress. Pushing the material off her shoulders, he kissed her milky skin, so cool against his fevered lips. Her hand slipped into his tunic to tug at the hair on his chest. Quickly he stepped away, and her dress slipped with a whisper to the floor. She wore nothing underneath it. And now—as in his dreams, he thought wildly—she stood nude before him, and she was just as beautiful, just as desirable as he had imagined. He pressed his fingers against the nipples which stiffened at his touch, traced the curving line of her hips, trembled at the soft hair below. His blood was on fire; he was in agony.

She pressed herself against him, grinding her hips against his, and his knees nearly buckled under him. Impatiently she tugged at his pants, and he unfastened them, shrugged out of his shirt as she kissed his chest, shoulders, lips. She studied his nude body.

"You are so handsome," she whispered. It was the first time she had spoken.

"You're so beautiful, August." He was almost sobbing, for her beauty burned him, making his insides twist with pain and desire, and he had never wanted a woman more than he wanted her. He was already aroused, already ready for her, and she clasped his throbbing penis in both hands, raking her nails lightly down the shaft. He gasped in pain, and pleasure, too. No longer able to contain his passion, he grabbed her by both arms, nearly throwing her down upon the floor. She rested upon her elbows, and as she gazed up at him, she laughed.

He knelt before her, between her legs, and rubbed the satiny skin of her inner thigh, and his fingers trembled as he approached her sex. Provocatively she arched her back so that her hips were raised slightly, and he saw a tiny drop of moisture glistening in the dark strands. Lowering his head, he buried his face within the glorious juncture, and the musky perfume overwhelmed him. He lapped at her, tonguing and flicking, savoring her sweetness, and she twisted her hips, moving constantly, so that sometimes she was tantalizingly close, sometimes inches away, and it only served to further inflame him. She lifted her legs easily and clasped him behind the neck, forcing his face into the dark and dewy silkiness, where he breathed deeply of her womanly fragrance and kissed the half-hidden lips.

His hands continued stroking her legs, her stomach, her breasts, and beneath them he felt the pulsing of her blood. Her hands reached out to grab his shoulders, and her long nails sank like talons into his skin, drawing blood. The pain mixed with desire, exciting him even more, and he could wait no longer. He had to have her, now, no matter what he had vowed to himself.

Hamilton flung himself upon her, smothering her face, neck, breasts with frenzied biting kisses. He gazed into her beautiful eyes, so dark, so dizzyingly deep, and found himself diving and losing himself in those depths. He reached down, touched her hand as she guided him into her. He bit back a cry of pleasure as he thrust deeply.

Suddenly something grasped him by both shoulders, ripped him away from her, flung him across the room. He crashed into a table, then looked around, his body shuddering in its denial.

A shadow fell across him: August's father.

"Get out!" Parrish yelled, shaking as though he were suffering from apoplexy. His face was deep red with fury. "Get out of my house! I won't allow you to touch her! Do you hear? I won't! Get out or else!"

Hamilton grabbed his clothing, tried to look back at August, but Parrish had stepped in front of her, blocking his view, and then he was hopping first into one leg, then the other of his pants. By the time he reached the verandah he was fully dressed.

From inside the house he could hear Parrish's voice shouting with anger. "How could you, you slut? In our house? How would that look?"

The words of an outraged father, Hamilton thought as he tucked his shirt in. Almost. Except that something more underlay those words; something he didn't understand. As he hurried down the steps he listened for her reaction. He waited for tears, for entreaty, for something. Instead, silence followed.

Puzzled, he looked back at the house. Had Parrish somehow hurt her? Slapped her? Knocked her senseless? No, even he wasn't that brutal a man. Then Hamilton heard it slowly rising . . . the reaction.

Instead of weeping, he heard laughter. A cold and chilling laughter that made the hair on the back of his neck rise.

Hamilton mounted his horse quickly and kicked the animal into a fast trot so that he could escape from the horrible sound, the wild laughter that followed him through the streets of Delhi.

On Saturday, May 9, in Meerut, under a dark sky that promised a storm, the Third Light Cavalry, the Sixth Dragoon Guards, the first battalion of the Sixtieth Rifles, the Eleventh and Twentieth Native Infantry, a troop of horse artillery, a light field battery, and a company of foot artillery assembled on the infantry parade-ground into three sides of a square. The seventeen hundred European troops, numbering fewer than the native troops present, were armed, their guns and rifles loaded.

Through the fourth side came eighty *sepoys*. In April these men had been ordered to learn the new firing drill for the Enfield rifle, which had been issued in Meerut at the beginning of January. The Indian soldiers had thought they would have to bite the cartridges, as was the case with the old ones. As the new cartridges were rumored to be greased with beef and pork fat, the former anathema to Hindus, the latter to Moslems, the *sepoys* refused to attend the drill, seeing this as one more attempt by the British to destroy the caste system and their religious customs.

Hamilton and his friends watched silently as sentence against the eighty was read and as they were stripped of their uniforms. Shackles were hammered onto their legs, and they were led to the New Gaol.

Hamilton and Grant exchanged glances at this further humiliation of the *sepoys*, but they did not speak. No one was allowed to protest. When they were dismissed, the four officers returned to their quarters to discuss the sentence against the *sepoys*, all of whom had served the British faithfully, some of them for upward of forty years. Grant and Hamilton thought the sentence of imprisonment with hard labor for ten years unreasonable, while Rutherford and Flaxley thought it would simply teach the natives their place.

Sunday, May 10, dawned hot in Meerut. The monsoon season was still some weeks away, and the air remained listless, suffocating. Hamilton and Grant attended church together, greeting H.H. Greathed, the Commissioner of Meerut, and his wife. They returned to find that the evening church-parade, usually held at six-thirty, had been postponed until seven because of the stifling heat, and for that they were relieved.

Hamilton wrote a note to August, explaining he would be otherwise engaged for the next week or so, but as soon as possible he'd call upon her—if still permitted. He tried not to think of what had happened after the dinner Friday night, and most of the time he was successful. At night, though, when he couldn't sleep because of the heat, he remembered, remembered how good she had felt beneath him, how troubled he had been by her laughter afterward.

They were just beginning to dress for the parade when they heard the pounding of a horse's hooves outside. Chand ran into the room.

"Lieutenant-*sahib*! Lieutenant-*sahib*!" he screamed, running to Flaxley.

"What is it, Chand?" Flaxley demanded of his servant.

Grant had gone to the window. "My God, there're fires out there!"

From outside came a rattle of musketry fire as Flaxley tried to calm the Indian so he could speak.

"The Native Infantry lines are on fire, Lieutenant-*sahib*!" Chand managed to say at last. "It is the *sepoys*, Lieutenant-*sahib*. It is mutiny!"

Quickly the four officers pulled on their uniforms, grabbed their weapons, and dashed outside to see beyond the palms and sugar cane clouds of smoke billowing up from the burning bungalows, while Chand followed, explaining what had happened.

The other *sepoys*, resenting the treatment of the eighty, had suspected the European troops were planning to disarm them. They had gathered outside the regimental magazine, and then, when the English Colonel of the Eleventh Native Infantry rode up, his horse was shot out from under him; then he had been shot as well. Within minutes his regiment rose up, ransacking the arms and shooting every European they saw.

By now the four men could distinguish wild shouting and cries over the sound of continued gunfire. Even as they watched, native soldiers ran back and forth through the streets, brandishing torches which they applied to the thatched roofs of the mud huts. Smoke and flames hurled upward into the sky.

"You must leave, *sahibs*," Chand pleaded. "At once, or they will kill you! I have seen what they are doing to the *sahibs* and the *memsahibs*."

"Not bloody likely," Rutherford said. He leveled his rifle, drew a sight, and fired. A running Indian soldier fell.

"My God, Richard!" Grant knocked the other man's rifle down. "He might have been one of ours."

Rutherford's teeth gleamed in the flickering light of the fires. "There aren't any of them on our side now, Malcolm. You'd best realize that before it's too late. I'm going off to kill some of these bloody wogs before they kill me. Are any of you joining me?"

"I'll go," Flaxley said grimly.

"We'll stay together," Grant replied, nodding to Hamilton.

Hamilton nodded as he stared at the nightmarish scene. Rapidly Chand told them what he had seen: A pregnant Englishwoman, wife of the Adjutant of the Eleventh, had been murdered and mutilated by a Muslim butcher; a dead European woman was repeatedly stabbed as she lay propped in a covered wagon; the Surgeon-Major had been shot; many other English had been wounded, killed, were being hunted down. The mutineers, Chand explained hoarsely, planned to free the eighty imprisoned *sepoys*, as well as the hundreds of other prisoners in the old jail, then raze Meerut, killing every English man, woman, and child they could find; then they would march on Delhi to do the same.

Delhi. August was there. Grant looked over to his friend, sensing his thoughts. A chill went through Hamilton, and he handled his rifle with numb fingers. He had to warn her somehow. The telegraph! He could send a telegram to Delhi, warning her to leave.

"The telegraph office, Chand! Is it all right?"

The Indian shook his head sadly. "I am sorry, *sahib*, but they have torn down the lines."

He couldn't leave her to that awful fate. He had to do something. At that moment he saw one of the mutineers creeping along the verandah. He raised his rifle and shot the man through the forehead.

"Tommy! Malcolm!" a man on horseback called. It was Flaxley, who had just left them minutes before. "We're to meet at the parade-ground of the Sixtieth Rifles."

"We haven't horses!" Grant yelled.

"Others behind!" Flaxley shouted, or something very similar, for at that moment a crack sounded. Flaxley screamed and was flung off his horse, landing in a crumpled heap at their feet, a great red stain spreading across the back of his shoulders.

"C'mon, Tommy. We're just sitting targets for those bloody bastards."

Hamilton nodded numbly. Grant grabbed at the reins of Flaxley's horse.

"Take me with you, *sahibs*," Chand pleaded. "They will kill me as well, for I have served you."

"Come on," Hamilton said to the servant, looking around for another horse. He started toward a riderless animal as Grant mounted the first. Chand was right behind him, then staggered and dropped to his knees. He pitched forward onto his face. For a moment Hamilton stared down at the dead Indian, who had doubtless saved their lives by alerting them; then he vaulted onto the back of the second horse, and the officers turned their mounts in the direction of the parade-ground.

A screaming mob of Indians—soldiers, troublemakers from the bazaar, servants, villagers—swung around the corner at that moment, heading in their direction. The mutineers brandished torches, and *tulwars* and *lathies*, and the two men could hear them shouting *"Maro! Maro!"*— "Kill him! Kill him!"

Hamilton and Grant looked quickly around, assessing the situation. They had little choice. They could ride into the line of burning bungalows or they could chance it through the crowd. They might make it, being on horseback; going by foot would be fatal.

"Through the crowd!" Hamilton shouted. Grant nodded.

They spurred their horses forward and lashed left and right with their crops as the Indians tried to pull them off their horses. Grant shot two men wearing only part of the uniform of native officers as they raised rifles to their shoulders, while Hamilton kicked one man in the chest, knocking him back into the others.

"We'll never make it this way," Hamilton shouted. "We've got to find someplace to our advantage. A high place that we can defend, but one where we can't be smoked or burned out, at least until we find the others." Grant nodded that he understood.

By this time they had managed to push through the crowd, which in its frenzy was turning to pursue them. While the moon was not yet up, they could see quite well from the light of the fires. They galloped through the streets until Grant pointed at the stone church.

"Up there."

They crossed the street and rode behind the building, slid off their horses, and led the animals inside the building. They barricaded the double doors with pews they tore loose from the flooring; then the two officers climbed the stairs up to the choir loft to look around. There they found the minister, his throat slit, his belly cut wide open like a hog's.

"My God," Grant said. He wiped his mouth with the back of his hand.

Horrified, Hamilton turned away and looked around. "Over here, Malcolm!"

They set their rifles down by a window, then peered cautiously outside. The mob roamed through the streets, setting fire to buildings, breaking glass, and still shouting *"Maro! Maro!"*

"How many rounds do you have?" Hamilton asked.

Grant checked, shook his head. "Not enough, I'm afraid. Should have picked up more."

"I'm afraid we won't be able to accomplish much. Still, we might take some of them with us." Hamilton stood. "I'll check downstairs and see what I can find." Grant nodded, raised his rifle to his shoulder, and stared out the window as he waited.

Hamilton returned within five minutes, bringing three more rifles and about ten boxes of cartridges. "Found these among the prayer books."

"Good," Grant said. "Take a look."

In the flickering firelight the mob had split into two, one section heading off down the street and the other remaining in front of the church. The latter surged into the building across the street. When the mutineers came outside, they were dragging three English soldiers behind them.

The mob drew back, then reformed to create a circle into which the Englishmen were roughly pushed, and Hamilton was reminded of the humiliation of the eighty *sepoys* the day before. The British soldiers were thrown to the ground, and when they tried to rise, they were kicked brutally in the chest and face. The three men raised their voices, pleading for their lives. Someone laughed, a cruel, harsh sound.

One of the mutineers raised a *tulwar*, the native sword, above his head. It came hurtling down, slamming into the neck of one of the British soldiers. He screamed as the *sepoy* sawed at his neck. The head, finally severed, bounced away, spewing blood across the mob. The smell of this fresh blood enraged them even more, and they seethed forward, attacking the two remaining men, who were screaming for mercy. When the crowd moved back, the two other soldiers were dead, their bodies pierced with dozens of knives.

Drawing a bead on a tall *sepoy* who seemed to be one of the mob's leaders, Grant opened fire. His bullet struck the man squarely in the chest and he dropped, while Hamilton aimed at those mutineers in front, hoping to scatter them. The mob screamed and pounded at the doors of the church, then turned around as about two dozen horsemen rode down upon them, shooting their rifles and hacking with swords.

Hamilton and Grant fired until they had no rounds left; then Grant went down in search of more cartridges. He found a few more and returned in time to see the soldiers outside setting up a cannon. It fired in a burst of orange, and the mob scattered. The two officers gathered their rifles, went downstairs and out into the street to join the others.

As midnight approached, the mutineers began disappearing, and the European troops straggled back to the cantonment. Grant and Hamilton gathered with other members of the Dragoon Guards; Captain Rosser proposed to go after the mutineers on the road to Delhi, but was ignored by the commanding officer. Rutherford, like Flaxley, had died early in the battle, while Grant had been wounded slightly in the arm. Because their barracks were burned, the soldiers had to sleep that night on the barrack square.

In their camps they told the horror stories of what they had seen. European women killed, their children speared and hung on walls. The pregnant wife of an officer, mutilated, her belly cut open, the unborn child squashed upon the floor. Loyal Indians and English alike killed, butchered by the frenzied *sepoys*. Some of the English families had managed to escape, but too many of them had been taken by surprise by servants and soldiers they'd previously trusted.

Hamilton, aching from exhaustion, listened to the stories and thought only of August. The mutineers were sweeping across the dry plains outside Meerut toward Delhi. Toward Delhi and his love. She would die like the others he had seen. Mutilated, hacked, burned, or even worse. He closed his eyes against the nausea and pain, and knew he could not sit there any longer; he had to go to Delhi, had to warn her, rescue her somehow.

When Grant had fallen asleep along with the others around him, Hamilton rose and steathily ran from the square. He found a horse that looked less exhausted than the others, climbed into the saddle, and rode away from the camp. He reminded himself to take care; no doubt he would encounter bands of *sepoys* along the road.

What he was doing wasn't wrong, he told himself, as he rode out of Meerut. He wasn't deserting his station; he was rescuing an English citizen. And after all, one man might ride there faster than a large number. At least he hoped so. As he spurred the horse onward, he prayed he would not arrive too late.

PART II

Delhi, India: 1857

Hamilton reached Delhi by late afternoon the following day, Monday. Most of his time had been spent avoiding the bands of mutineers and robbers who roamed through the countryside, terrorizing and murdering any Europeans they found. He kept away from the road and skirted settlements, fearing the villagers would surrender him to the *sepoys*.

Whenever he'd crossed the road to Delhi, he'd seen the signs of the rebellion. Bodies of Europeans, as well as Indians, lay mortally wounded or murdered, while blood pooled alongside the corpses and overturned carriages.

A mile away from the walled city he turned his horse loose and set out on foot, knowing he could hide more easily in the undergrowth as he approached the city. The shadows lengthened as he approached Delhi, and he knew that the light wouldn't last much longer.

When he was just on the other side of the Jumna River, he paused to check the gates. Delhi had two main entrances, the Lahore and Delhi Gates, as well as six smaller ones.

The one across the Bridge of Boats was closed. Either the Europeans had been alerted to the mutiny in Meerut and had shut all the gates, or else the mutineers had closed them when they arrived in Delhi. Either way, he couldn't get in there. The Red Fort loomed upward some one hundred and ten feet; thus its walls were unscalable.

He tried to remember what he'd learned about the defenses of Delhi when he first came to India. Eight gates, and— Wait. He rubbed the grit from his face as he concentrated. There might be one left open yet—a small water gate at the far end of the palace wall. But first he had to get past the guards on the walls, and he could hardly just stroll across the Bridge of Boats.

He glanced back and in the twilight saw clouds of dust rising from the road. Another band of mutineers, no doubt. He'd better act soon, then. There was a shout from the walls as the guards spotted the horsemen.

Now! he told himself, and keeping to the underbrush, he moved to the river's edge. Then he raised his rifle over his head to keep it dry, waded into the river, and began swimming toward the walls. The guards were too engrossed in the approaching mutineers to notice him.

The gate was still open.

Hamilton swam through the gate and found he was at the end of a drain. Some feet past the gate he found a ledge hewn from rock. He pulled himself out and crawled along it until he could stand. He made his way into the lower levels of the palace, past fountains and sunken baths. Here he moved more cautiously, for he didn't know how the palace occupants would react if they found him.

He slipped through the labyrinth of marble corridors and floors, at one point seeing several of the king's attendants coming around a corner. He ducked into a small room, readied his rifle, and held his breath while the armed men went past. Finally, when he no longer heard their voices, he searched the room for robes to wear. He wouldn't fool anyone for long at a close range, but perhaps he could buy some extra time with the marginal disguise. Then he sought a way outside. When he at last left the Red Fort, it was still dusk. He hadn't spent as much time inside the palace as he'd thought. Now to reach the Parrish house, and he prayed he would not be too late.

Above the city hung a pall of dark smoke, and in the distance he heard shouting and screams. He walked and ran through the maze of filthy streets, past mud and thatch houses, past enclosed courtyards and dark holes and corners, past the many bodies of Europeans, some sprawled across the doorways of their still-burning homes.

Finally he entered the street where the Parrishes lived. Many of the houses were now in ruins, some still burning. He approached their house slowly. It had not been burned, but it looked deserted, and he wondered if he had come too late. His stomach churned at the thought.

He darted across the street and into the unlocked house. The fires outside cast a reddish light through the windows, by which he could see the *punkah-wallah*, his throat slit, lying inside the front door. Beyond him sprawled the bodies of the butler and the cook, as well as several *sepoys*.

The parlor was in a shambles, the furniture smashed, cloth shredded, the paintings torn from the walls, and the glass in shards.

"August?" Hamilton called. His voice was weak, and he realized he hadn't eaten anything in over a day. He cleared his throat. Called again. Heard nothing but the soughing of the wind.

Hamilton licked his dry lips as he stepped into the next room and discovered half a dozen more bodies. Servants, and more Indian soldiers. His voice hoarse, he called out again for August. Again no other voice responded. Panic and despair entwined within him, but he couldn't believe—wouldn't accept—that he had come this far to face only grief.

He found Parrish in the study. He recognized the older man only by the clothes he wore for Parrish's eyes had been gouged from his face which was masked in blood, the blood still damp. Bloated flies, so many that the dead man's head was nearly black, crawled across the wounds.

Nearby were two *sepoys*, their throats ripped out and expressions of terror on their faces. He estimated that none of them had been dead for much longer than an hour. Of August, though, he saw no sign. He continued searching, in each room calling her name. He looked through the garden and the servants' huts, and still he couldn't find her.

She must have escaped somehow, he told himself wildly as he returned to the house. Surely she'd flee. But why hadn't her father gone with her? Perhaps he had been delayed, was to meet her later, and then had been caught unawares by the *sepoys*.

Or what—and this chilled him—what if she had been carried away by the Indians? Who knew what those heathens had done to her. He buried his face in his hands, feeling the exhaustion of the past two days and his grief overtake him. He was too tired to fight, to go on any longer. He would sink down to sit upon the floor and wait for whatever came.

Behind him he heard the whisper of cloth. It must be one of the marauding *sepoys*, he told himself wearily, who had heard his voice and had come to kill him. Hamilton gripped his rifle and whirled around, prepared to defend himself one last time.

It was August.

As she glided slowly toward him he could not believe that he was actually seeing her. It has to be a dream, he told himself. He was feverish, or perhaps out of his head from hunger. He shook his head and rubbed the dirt from his eyes, and she was still there.

As she came closer he saw that droplets of blood had ruined her beautiful gown.

She was injured! That explained why she hadn't responded immediately to his frantic calls.

"August! My darling!" he said, his voice breaking with relief. He rushed toward her, his arms outstretched to take her into them. It would be so good to hold her, to know that she was safe. He would tend to her, and she would heal, and then they would leave this house of death and return to safety.

A foot or so away he stopped as he realized that the blood seemed to come from her mouth. Shocked, he stared at her. What sort of injury was this? Was she bleeding inside? Perhaps even dying? His heart gave a lurch at the thought.

"Tommy," she whispered, and the sound raised the hair on the back of his neck. "Tommy, my love, I'm so glad you came."

The blood around her mouth frightened him, for now that he examined her more carefully, she didn't seem injured. But where did the blood come from? He backed away, stumbling over the body of her father, and she still approached.

"What happened here, August? Tell me what happened today!"

She shook her head and pressed against him, slipping her arms around his neck. The smell of blood mingled with her scent of musk and sickened him. Her eyes, their depths dark and unreadable, gazed up into his. "I am so glad you have come to rescue your dear August. I've missed you so much, my love."

He wanted to respond, but his body wouldn't, and so he stood, his arms hanging loose at his sides. "What are you?" he demanded.

"I don't understand, Tommy. Why are you being so horrible to me?"

"I've sorry, August. I don't know what's the matter with me." Hamilton passed an unsteady hand over his face. "I've gone through so much in the past day, and after the mutiny began in Meerut yesterday, I feared you would be killed. All I could think of was you and your father, and I came here as fast as possible. Thank God, you're safe!" He managed to hug her a little, but even to him the gesture felt remote. "I don't understand who killed the Indians? Was it the servants? Your father?"

"It was terrible," she murmured, her body shivering against his, but not, he thought, with fear. "There was so much shouting from outside, and such awful threats, and then they began hammering on the door. Finally it gave way, and the mutineers ran in, killing all the servants and my father, everyone they could find." She shuddered, and he thought her voice was colored by an unholy excitement, but surely he was wrong? Wasn't he? "Poor Father. They found him hiding in the study, and threw him down upon the floor and blinded him first. He begged, screamed, for a merciful death, but he did not receive it, for then they drew a sword across his stomach, cutting him wide open. He died slowly, agonizingly slowly."

"Shhh," he said reassuringly, "try not to think of what happened." He rocked her in his arms. "How did you escape the carnage, August, my love?" he asked.

"Why weren't you attacked?" The smell of blood, he realized, was on her breath.

"I wasn't here," August explained. "I had been in hiding, for Father had listened to your warnings, and he feared that something terrible would happen. The *sepoys* did not find me until I at last showed myself, and by that time it was too late."

She'd spoken as though she had explained it perfectly. "I-I don't understand," he said. He shook his head. "Did you try to help the survivors? Are you injured, my love? Where did the blood come from?"

August parted her stained lips for him, and too late he saw the long white teeth. Weakened from exhaustion and hunger, from fear and disbelief, he did not resist when she kissed him with her icy lips, and blackness swept down across him, claiming him for its own.

As the long night of Monday, May 10, drew to a close, she roamed the stinking streets of Delhi, skirting the heaped bodies of the dead and the dying.

She hunted for the living.

She ignored the cries, the entreaties, the pitiful begging, the outstretched arms of those injured, those soon to die, for they would not satisfy her.

Vultures and wild dogs had been at the dead since earlier in the day when the mutineers had stormed the city, and the overpowering sun and stifling heat had done their work as well, putrefying the bloated flesh until the noisome stench of death arose everywhere, and already pale maggots crawled and burrowed through the lumps of meat that had once been human. Pools of dark blood, stagnant and with great clouds of black flies hovering above them, had formed in the cracks between the cobblestones, in the holes in the streets, and occasionally animals—dogs, perhaps—could be heard lapping at puddles.

Daintily she raised her long, graceful skirts to avoid the worst of the gore and paused in the hellish glare of the surrounding fires to inspect the lonely street. A dog, its ribs showing through diseased skin, slunk away.

She continued walking, searching, ignoring the bits of flesh on the streets, the arms and legs, fingers and hands that had been lopped from European women and children before they had been raped and butchered. She spared no glance for the men who sprawled on their sides, bellies ripped open, their intestines glistening wetly in the firelight, or for those whose skin had been delicately peeled away to reveal the raw muscles and ligaments and bones.

These meant nothing to her. She had witnessed far worse in her long life, farther back than the time of Agamemnon, and doubtless she would see worse in the years to come. Whatever surprises mankind might hold for her, its capacity for cruelty to its own kind found her unastonished. Too often had she seen it expressed.

Far better to be what she was, she thought as she hunted for her prey, for she did not kill in the name of religion, state, revenge, jealousy, greed, or any of the artificial contrivances man had invented to explain his blood lust.

She killed simply for the blood and the life that it brought her. No more, no less.

At a slight noise some distance away she paused and narrowed her eyes. There was a slight movement by a gate to a walled garden. A young man. And European. As well as uninjured. She breathed deeply, smelling the vigorous blood as it pumped through his healthy body.

Her bloodstained lips pulled back into a smile, and she drew closer to him. The young man—he was, she realized with some satisfaction, hardly more than a boy—had become aware of her now and was trying to hide himself, thinking she was one of the mutineers returned to kill him. Her smile widened, and she held out her pale hand to him as she approached. He was afraid, and his blood coursed faster, his fear exhilarating to her.

He had been crying. His family was dead. His world gone.

She opened her arms to comfort him. "Come to me," she said ever so gently. "Come to me."

Nodding, the boy sniffled and crept into her arms, then nestled his head against her shoulder. She bent her dark head and kissed his soft lips, and he cried out as a fire stirred in his loins.

Together, they sank to the ground, and as she kissed and caressed his silky hair and tender throbbing flesh, she gave him release and death.

When Hamilton woke at last, he was in a bed, and at first he didn't know where he was or what had happened. But as his eyes focused, he saw that it was nighttime and that August Parrish tended him.

"How do you feel, Tommy?" she asked solicitously, her dark eyes concerned. She was cleaned, her gown fresh, and he wondered if the blood covering her had been only a nightmare.

He shook his head and drew his brows together as he tried to remember how he had come to be here. Was he sick? Had his fellow officers called for her? He remembered coming to Delhi, because of the mutiny. He had come to see if August and her father were all right, and in the Parrish house he had found . . . he had found blood and her and—all too swiftly his memory returned, and he closed his eyes at the remembered sights.

"What *are* you?" he whispered. Once more he could see the blood on her face and dress, on her lips.

Apparently she hadn't heard him, for she placed a cool

hand upon his feverish forehead and he shivered at her touch. "You fainted, my love. You mustn't worry now, for I will take care of you."

Hamilton cringed, recalling how he'd ached for her touch and love, how he'd longed to embrace her. He wanted to be repelled, but even now his body was betraying him and desire writhed within him.

Quickly she slipped into the bed beside him. He tried to roll away, but found he couldn't move. What was wrong with him? he wondered. He was so tired, exhausted as though he had gone through an ordeal. The day before he had been a strapping officer of the Dragoon Guards. Now he felt as insubstantial as the fluff from a dandelion. One strong gust of the wind and he would float away, float away into nothing. His eyelids grew heavy, and he didn't think he could keep his eyes open any longer, for it was such an effort. He closed them and drifted into the greyness close to sleep.

Something cold and damp, like the mist from a graveyard, caressed his stomach, slithered down his legs, then between them and up to his groin to cup his testicles. He groaned at the strange touch, tried to raise a hand to brush whatever it was away, but was unable.

Then slivers of ice kissed his face, his neck, his bared chest. Fragrant hair, hair that smelled of musk and blood and jasmine, brushed against him, tickled him, and his lips drew back in a grimace.

August, he thought vaguely, it must be August. Who else—what else—could it be? The kisses, so cold, rose to his chest, then fell down to his stomach, down to his groin, and razorlike teeth nipped at him. Moaning, he arched his weary body, felt a tongue curl around him, and he was throbbing, hardening at the velvet touch, and wanting her so badly. Hundreds of fires seethed in his veins, and panting heavily, he reached out for her, but he couldn't find her. Again her teeth dragged across his loins.

He howled in pain and desire as the pounding in his temples and groin doubled; he rocked his hips as he tried to ram into her, but found only air. He had to have her. Now. She was on top of him, then off to one side, stroking and fondling, rubbing him until he moaned; then she was on top again, teasing him with fingers and nails and teeth and tongue, and he grunted, and stabbed upward, thrusting higher with his engorged shaft, and higher, seeking, thrusting, and he couldn't wait, couldn't wait any longer to find her. He thrust up once more, and it spread through him, burst outward in a final paroxysm of lust, and as he climaxed wildly, teeth sank into the tender flesh of his neck.

He screamed once, then fainted into the well of blackness.

Night after night she visited him, and each time he woke, Hamilton desired her more than before. He spent his days in a half-waking state, and in his dreams he saw the destruction of Delhi and the murder of the English. He saw horrible scenes, and tears squeezed out from under his eyelids. He saw villagers fleeing from an unseen terror that hunted them by night, and as they fell, they cried out, for nothing could save them.

Blood and dust mingled, painting his dreams with a terrible tint. The villages of India stood empty, the living having fled, and yet that which hunted them remained, and always it was behind him, and he didn't want to turn, but he had no choice, and he would turn, and he'd feel the sharpness of its teeth.

Once or twice he managed to stagger to his feet, and unclothed, and not even noticing, he stumbled through the house, blinking in the unaccustomed brightness of daylight.

Large black flies buzzed around the rotting bodies on the floors, and the fetid odor of death clung to him and sickened him.

He heard nothing from outside and wondered what had happened. Were any English soldiers left, or was he the last one? This amused him, and he laughed, but the laughter dissolved into tears that streamed down his dirty cheeks. Sobbing, he slumped to the floor, and when he awoke, he was in bed and August was slipping in beside him.

Once, he tried to escape. He made it as far as the doorway to the outside when faintness overcame him, and he leaned against the door to rest, and when he looked up next, dusk had breathed into night, and she was standing before him. He began weeping, and ever so gently she led him back to bed.

As the long days and nights continued, his strength ebbed away. When she came to him, she would talk, and he listened to her tales of an India long ago, an India before the English had come, before even the Mogul, before Alexander had come to conquer. She had lived here too long to remember, she told him, and before that Greece had been her home, for her and for her sisters. But over the centuries her sisters had been scattered across the world, and she no longer knew if they lived.

Lilith, she said, had been one; others had not been so famous, though. And then she had kissed his lips, chilling him, and her mouth had slid down his chest, past his stomach to his loins, had slid to the tip of his member, which she touched softly with her tongue, and despite his exhaustion, he had felt the stirrings of passion once more. He cried out for her to have mercy, and she had answered him with the cold laughter of something that was not human.

Tommy Hamilton awoke to the drumming of rain on the roof and knew the monsoon season had come while he slept. Cautiously he opened his eyes; seeing grey light, he could not tell if it was morning or dusk. He felt more clearheaded than he had for a long time, less feverish, and he was encouraged.

He listened for any sounds which meant August was close by, but he could hear nothing but the rain. Slowly he swung his legs over the edge of the bed and sat up. His head pounded, and vertigo swept through him, but gradually the dizziness abated, and he was able to stand, albeit somewhat shakily.

He looked around for his clothes, found only white trousers and a shirt too big for him. He tucked its length into the waistband of the pants, and he knew it had belonged to August's father. Or rather the man who had masqueraded as her father. She had told him that she had found Parrish years ago and had lived with—and off— him, and he had lived to serve her. When he was no longer of any use, she had killed him.

He slipped on sandals and left the bedroom. He was aware of an overwhelming hunger, as if he hadn't eaten for days, and as he looked down at himself he saw how pitifully thin he had grown. His skin hung upon him; his wrists had shrunken almost to the bones, and he shuffled along like an old man.

He bit back tears and went into the kitchen, where he inspected a basket of rotting fruit black with flies and insects swarming over it. He stared at it hungrily, but could not bring himself to eat the decaying fruit. In the pantry he found a few pieces of molded bread. He wolfed it down, then vomited immediately. He poured wine down his throat, then realizing he was about to lose that, too, he stopped and sipped it more cautiously. Bottle in one hand, he left the room, and as he walked, he would take a swig of the wine.

Momentarily weak, he sat in a chair in the kitchen and stared around at the bodies as though he'd never been there before. How long had he been under her spell? Days? Weeks? Months? Or worse, years? But if it were years, wouldn't someone have entered the house and found him?

He drank more wine, the tepid liquid soothing his burning throat. He couldn't continue as her slave. She might kill him or do something even worse. What that was he didn't know, nor did he wish to find out. So he must do something. He wasn't strong enough to escape from the house yet. And if he did, she would just hunt him and bring him back to her lair. Therefore, he had only one choice. He must kill her.

Hamilton wiped the wine from his unshaven chin with the back of his hand and frowned. How? For after all, what was August Parrish?

A creature of the night, of dark dreams, and in that moment he realized how stupid he had been. While he courted her he had never seen her in the daytime, and never once had he thought it strange. He'd called upon her after dusk, dined with her at night, kissed her in the light of the moon. He laughed, but his throat muscles were stiff from disuse, and the sound came out a sob.

To kill her he had to find her.

Slowly he explored the house, covering his nose and mouth as he passed the mouldering corpses in the rooms filled with the odor of rotted flesh. He searched through wardrobes, under beds, into every enclosed space he could find. He drank more wine, and again dizziness swept over him. He should return to bed and rest. No, this might be his last chance. If he went to bed, he would fall asleep, and when he woke, *she* would be there, waiting.

She had to be in the house; elsewhere she might be too easily discovered. She was here. Somewhere.

In the kitchen he found a door locked from the other side. He looked around for something to hit the doorknob with. He found a cast-iron pot, hefted it, then swung it against the door. The knob flew off; the door swung open and a cool damp darkness assailed him. He found a candle, lit it, and held it aloft. Steps led down into what had to be a cellar. He started to descend.

The candle's flame flickered when he reached the bottom of the stairs, but the air in the cellar was still—too damned still, he thought. He knew she was here, but as he looked around, he despaired, for dozens of boxes and crates were stacked against the walls. Where would she be? Behind one of these crates? And even as he thought it, he knew the answer.

Wearily he began pulling the tops off the boxes one by one and stared at the contents. Dust rose in great clouds, choking him, and from time to time he paused to take a sip from the wine bottle. It was nearly empty; he should have thought to bring another one, but now he couldn't stop to fetch another bottle. He wanted to find her before it was too late.

Before him sat an ornately carved teakwood box, about six feet in length and four feet high, and when he raised the heavy lid, the sweet odor of cloves and sandalwood rose. She slept inside on a bed of dried spices. Or at least he thought she was asleep, for her eyelids were closed, her black lashes sweeping across her cheekbones. She was so beautiful it brought tears to his eyes. He bent to kiss her, then stopped. He had come here to destroy her. He didn't know where his rifle was, so he would have to use something else. In a pile of tools he found a hammer, and he hefted it. Heavy, it would prove deadly. He returned to the box and gazed down at her. All that loveliness . . . all that evil, and the love and hatred he felt for her warred within him.

Taking a deep breath, he raised the hammer. He would bring it down in one swing and smash her head open like a ripe melon. The horrible image was too clear in his mind and nearly stayed his arm. He had to act now, before he gave in. His arm swung downward, the hammer hurtled, down and down, and midway he stopped, the heavy tool snapping against his wrist. He did not feel the pain.

He stared at the woman he had loved. He could not destroy her. He no longer had the will to do it; he couldn't live without her. He wanted her, needed her. Even as she was. Even as he was.

He dropped the hammer, which clattered to the floor. His weight sagging his knees, he collapsed against the box, huddling on the floor, his head resting against the box. Closing his eyes, he wearily drew in a ragged breath and waited. He was there when dusk came and she awoke. He heard a slight sound, and then she was beside him, stroking his hair. "You shouldn't have left your bed, my sweet," she chided softly, "for you aren't yet well."

He nodded, but he could not speak. She helped him to his feet, and he leaned against her as she guided him up the stairs.

"I think we have been in India overlong," she said as they reached the bedroom and she eased him onto the bed. She pulled the covers over him, then caressed his cheek. His eyes blank, he looked upward; she smiled tenderly at him.

"Perhaps we will travel to England, where the race is younger and much more vigorous." She paused, lifting an elegant eyebrow. "What do you think, Tommy?"

A sob escaped him, and he nodded feebly.

London, England: 1859

In the span of less than two weeks Lyttleton had lost two close friends. He was shocked by the deaths, and he grieved for his friends. For poor bedeviled Terris and poor shrunken Tommy. Such odd, abrupt deaths. And both had had that tortured, hunted look in their eyes toward the very end of their lives.

Lyttleton frowned, something else bothering him about the deaths. What could it be? He concentrated, and then he had it. For some reason, he thought, there was a connection of sorts. But what connection could there be?

Tommy Hamilton had loved August. Wyndham Terris had thought he loved August. Now both men were dead. Surely this tenuous connection was a coincidence at best, Lyttleton told himself. Or was it?

Both had known the woman; both had died. For God's sake, what was he thinking? Others knew her and hadn't died. For that matter, *he* knew her and was very much alive. Henry Montchalmers was an admirer of hers, and he most certainly wasn't dead.

He was imagining it, he told himself. No connection existed. He was tired, distraught at his friends' deaths, and his mind wasn't reliable at the present. Still, he sensed a strangeness about the deaths, a strangeness that he did not understand, and he was not sure he wanted to.

Lyttleton saw August Hamilton the day after Terris' funeral, when he attended a dinner party given by the Ashfords in honor of their son's return from his travels abroad.

Lyttleton, who had been kept busy all day, arrived slightly out of breath and a little late at the Belgrave Square mansion. He relinquished his hat and cane to the butler who greeted him at the door and informed him that the other guests had already gathered in the library. He was shown into the room, where he went straightaway to his host and hostess and proffered his profuse apologies.

"Quite all right, Lyttleton," said Lord Josiah Ashford, a vocal member of the House of Lords and a staunch proponent of the Irish Home Rule Bill. He clapped his guest heartily upon the back and thrust a glass of wine into his hand. "Come in, come in, and meet the others. I'm sure you know most everyone, though."

Lady Blanche Ashford, who had never spoken much to Lyttleton in all the many years of their acquaintance, nodded shyly and murmured that she was happy to see him again.

Lyttleton looked about the room. Two walls held books from floor to ceiling, while in a third wall French doors opened out onto a terrace. Several velvet chairs were located by the French doors, and Lyttleton noticed a clump of men gathered around one of the chairs. An older man walked away momentarily, and in that instant Lyttleton could see who sat in the chair and commanded the undivided attention of the men.

It was August Hamilton, and she was looking at him.

He shouldn't have been surprised, he thought wryly, for somehow he had come to expect to see her wherever he went.

August looked away as one of her admirers asked a question, but Lyttleton saw that she flicked a glance back at him a few minutes later. In the meantime Lord Ashford had strolled off to talk with several newly arrived guests. Lyttleton smiled at Lady Ashford and devoted his full attention to her. Some years younger than her husband, she had been scarcely out of the schoolroom when she married and her son was born. A daughter had followed shortly after that, then three more children, and somehow the attractive brown-haired woman had managed to retain her girlish figure. Lyttleton wished suddenly that he had talked with her more thoroughly through the years.

A burst of laughter sounded from the direction of the French doors, and Lyttleton could hear the low husky tones of the widow.

"I wasn't aware that you were acquainted with Mrs. Hamilton, Lady Ashford," he remarked casually. Certainly the Ashfords had met Tommy, but Lyttleton had never seen them in the same company.

"Who is not these days?" Blanche Ashford asked, her grey eyes fixed on the other woman.

Surprised at the heavily ironic, almost hostile tone, Lyttleton glanced at his hostess. Her lips pressed tightly together, she was frowning.

"Is it correct for me to assume from your words and tone that you do not like the young widow, Lady Ashford?"

She gazed at him, her eyes wide with candor. "In all honesty, Mr. Lyttleton, I must confess that I do not care for Mrs. Hamilton. There is something . . . foreign . . . about her."

"You are accustomed to foreigners and their odd ways from your many journeys abroad, Lady Ashford. I have never heard this particular complaint before," he replied mildly, intrigued by her reaction.

"Yes, I know, Mr. Lyttleton, and that puzzles me all the more, for I really shouldn't be disturbed, and yet somehow I am." Blanche Ashford sipped her sherry. "All the men are fascinated. Both my husband and son have been dancing attendance upon her since she arrived, and I have scarcely had a word with either." She paused as she regarded him. "And how is it that you are not among her group of admirers?"

He smiled. "Let's say that while I'm acquainted with the lady, I'm not yet caught up in her web." He knew she hadn't missed the faint irony in his voice.

"Her web," the woman mused. "Yes, it's an excellent term." She looked truly distressed. "I'm sorry, Mr. Lyttleton, you must think me impossibly ill-mannered for speaking so of a guest, and prejudiced as well."

"No, not at all," Lyttleton replied thoughtfully. "One moment, Lady Ashford, before you leave." She paused. "Could it be that the word you were thinking of was not *foreign*, but rather *exotic*, or *alien*? Possibly even *strange*?"

"Yes," she replied without hesitation. "*Foreign* isn't appropriate. I grant you she is most decidedly exotic— much like a dark-hued jungle orchid among pale English tea roses. And yes, I think she may be described as strange. That is, there is nothing odd about her, but yet . . ." Words seemed to fail her.

Had he found someone who felt as he did? If he wasn't the only one with misgivings about August, then perhaps it wasn't simply his imagination playing him false, as he'd begun to believe. "Yet would you say you sense something about her, something not precisely correct, not in the sense that she is socially unacceptable but rather in the sense that something is distorted?" He looked intently at his hostess.

"Distorted," she said. "Yes, I think there is something not right about her, something I find—" But what she was going to say Lyttleton did not discover, for Lord Ashford chose that moment to beckon to his wife. "I'm sorry, Mr. Lyttleton. I fear I must see what my husband wants. Until later, then." She smiled warmly at Lyttleton, then hurried off.

Lyttleton sipped his wine thoughtfully as he studied the group tightly gathered around Tommy Hamilton's widow. None of the men had moved from her side.

The wives of the men stood apart as they chatted. From time to time, singularly and collectively, the women glanced toward the knot of men with bemused expressions on their faces.

Interesting, he thought, that only he and Lady Ashford had noticed something odd about August Hamilton. Certainly his friends, like these men, had not.

The butler announced that dinner was ready. Lady Ashford stood nearby, and Lyttleton offered his arm, for her husband had abandoned protocol. For a moment they watched while the Ashfords, father and son, vied to escort the widow into the dining room. The son finally won, and after flashing a triumphant smile at his frowning father, he led the woman away from the older man.

During the meal, which was excellent, Lyttleton concentrated on the widow, seated across from him between the two men of the house. She spoke little, for Josiah Ashford and his son Gerald dominated the entire conversation as they vied for her attention. Only occasionally did August raise her head, and then it was to look across at him.

The rivalry could almost be amusing, Lyttleton thought, except that the two men seemed so intent, so serious. This was no lighthearted flirtation; yet he knew Ashford adored his wife and had always been faithful to her, unusual within their society. Too, now that Gerald Ashford had returned from abroad, he planned to wed Lucy Chandler, his childhood sweetheart, in a few months. But these men didn't act like men in love. Indeed, all evening both wife and fiancée had been pointedly ignored, almost as if they did not exist.

Lyttleton saw the anger and hurt in Lady Ashford's eyes, emotions to which her husband was obviously impervious tonight. She was talking too rapidly to her other guests and darting quick glances at her husband. Finally she directed a question to her husband. He neither turned his head nor acknowledged her, and Lady Ashford dropped her gaze as her cheeks turned crimson. Lyttleton felt sorry for her, and as he glanced around the table he realized that the only diners actually conversing were Bethany and Lady Ashford, Mrs. Cleveland, Edith and Lucy Chandler, Honoria Young and himself. Mr. Cleveland stared raptly at August Hamilton, while his son Timothy, a year younger than Gerald Ashford, gawked adolescently. The near-elderly John James Chandler and considerably younger Francis Young wore miserable expressions of unrequited love that could almost have been laughable, too. But somehow they weren't.

With the strained conversation Lyttleton was uncomfortable for the remainder of the dinner, and afterward, when normally the men would have remained at the table to smoke cigars and drink brandy while the women would have gone to a parlor, Lyttleton was surprised to find the diners all headed together toward the library. At least August Hamilton, with her retinue of men, retired to the library, while the wives and daughters followed. Lyttleton trailed after them; stopping just inside the doorway, he narrowed his eyes as he found August once more established in the corner and encircled by the Cleveland and Ashford men as well as Chandler and Young.

"I find it most shocking," Bethany Ashford stated. She, too, was looking at the widow.

"What is that, Miss Ashford?" he inquired politely, although he already knew.

"Mrs. Hamilton is a recently bereaved widow, not yet out of mourning," she replied forcefully, "but you would hardly know it for all the social appointments she keeps."

Lyttleton glanced at the young woman. Bethany Ashford was a pretty girl, not at all beautiful, with intelligent eyes, a slender refined nose, a small mouth, and a pointed chin in a face with rosy cheeks. She also had a sensible nature, and he did not believe that maliciousness inspired her observation. "It is indeed extremely odd, Miss Ashford. I am at a loss to explain this phenomenon, although one of my friends claims that she is far too young to remain secluded in mourning for long."

Miss Ashford turned large brown eyes toward him. "Do you truly believe that, Mr. Lyttleton?"

"No, I do not." His look was sympathetic.

For a few minutes they listened to the rising conversation from across the library. The widow's admirers were trying to outdo each other with various flattering tales of their prowess, most of them greatly exaggerated. The Chandler women, Mrs. Young, and Bethany's mother had retired to the opposite end of the room to glare at the knot of men. The young woman next to him pressed her lips together tightly.

"You don't like her, Miss Ashford?" Lyttleton asked, and her reply surprised him for the depth of its passion.

"Like her? Indeed, I do not. I confess I . . . hate her!" With that Bethany Ashford whirled and left the room.

August smiled across at him, for the first time acknowledging his presence in the library, and he had the most uncanny feeling that she knew what he and the Ashford daughter had been discussing.

Impossible, Lyttleton told himself, but could not divest himself of the unusual notion. Increasingly uneasy, he lingered in the library and talked to the women as long as he could manage, but when another hour passed and he felt he would not be accused of being uncivil, he warmly thanked his host and hostess for their invitation and returned home.

He stayed up until long after midnight reading, or trying to, for as soon as he opened the book, the words blurred and his thoughts returned to the evening's dinner and the woman who had been the focal point of everyone's attention.

Finally, when he realized he couldn't read, he told himself to go to bed. Once there, though, he found no rest, for his dreams were filled with visions of the voluptuous beauty. Her lips were parted in a mockery of a smile, an expression that filled him with dread.

Lyttleton found August Hamilton at all the theater and dinner parties he attended, and in fact, he'd come to expect her presence, not that he would have been disappointed had she been absent. Or would he? he mused. In one respect, she seemed to be dogging his steps, but that was impossible, he countered, for she'd have no way of knowing where he'd be next. And yet he did see her often.

The widow's name appeared more frequently in the social columns of the London newspapers than ever before, a circumstance no one—except Lyttleton—found unusual. Sometimes he found it hard to remember she was in mourning, while everyone else appeared to have forgotten it completely.

To add to this faintly bewildering affair, Henry Montchalmers, apparently casting himself in the role of Boswell, reported faithfully each step the woman took until Lyttleton desired nothing more than to shake his good friend into silence. Good manners, however, would not permit him; instead, he endured Montchalmers' rapturous accolades.

"She's become the absolute toast of the city!" an euphoric Montchalmers declared two nights after the Ashfords' dinner party. He and Lyttleton had met earlier, then had dined together at a restaurant they had often frequented with Wyndy Terris, and now they had gone to the club to talk further.

"Is that so?" Lyttleton asked.

"Yes, it is," Montchalmers replied, oblivious to his friend's irony. "Why, we've gone to the Sunday Populars at St. James' Hall, been for a drive through the park in the evenin', and tomorrow night I'm takin' her to the theater to see some French comedy."

Lyttleton drew his brows together. "I don't know if that's wise, Henry. Perhaps you shouldn't."

"Why the devil not?" Montchalmers rasped. He scowled at his friend.

"Why the devil not? I'll tell you why not, Henry! May I remind you that August Hamilton happens to be the widow of our recently departed friend, and I don't think you honor his memory by escorting his widow about the city so soon after his death."

Montchalmers looked astonished. "Good God, Lyttleton, you needn't look so furious! What's the matter with you, old boy? You were never one for toeing the mark. What's wrong? Jealous, are you?"

Montchalmers had missed his point, and Lyttleton knew it would be futile to further explain why he felt the widow should observe the mourning. Montchalmers would simply get his back up and listen to his friend less than he already did.

"Never mind," Lyttleton said with a slight sigh as he waved a desultory hand. "Go on, and enjoy yourself while you may."

"Well, we certainly intend to."

"And by the way . . ."

"Yes?"

"I am not jealous."

"Oh, very well, if you insist." Montchalmers' normally good-natured face had taken on a faintly petulant look, and Lyttleton was reminded of Terris.

Busying himself with the cigar he'd just drawn from a pocket, he turned to his own thoughts while Montchalmers expounded the many glories of August Hamilton. After their brief exchange Montchalmers appeared even more determined to prove how wonderful a woman the widow was.

The trouble was that Montchalmers wasn't alone in his single-minded adulation. These days everyone of Lyttleton's acquaintance acclaimed the woman. Not only that, but Lyttleton had observed—and heard about—his friends being seen continually in her company, escorting her to various functions, calling upon her, riding with her in the park as well.

By definition, yes, August Hamilton was the toast of the town, probably the most sought-after woman in London. All within the span of about forty days since the death of her husband. It wasn't right, Lyttleton told himself; Tommy had been his friend. She should observe a full year of mourning.

And it wasn't right because of something else. Only he didn't know what that something-else was. Sometimes a glimmer of some elusive thought brushed his mind, and he would try to grab it, but it was gone before he could concentrate fully. And so the something remained, the something that prevented him from enjoying the company of August Hamilton, the something that kept him from being enamored of her.

Too, he remembered certain things, such as the inexplicable half-smile on her face as she talked about the Indian Mutiny and the ice-cold touch of her hand after Tommy's death.

Like the breath of a grave. He shuddered and rubbed a hand across his face, aware that Montchalmers had been talking for some time now and he had absolutely no idea about what. He was tired tonight, and irritable, and no doubt it would be best for him to go home before he picked a fight with Montchalmers. He didn't have too many good friends left.

Lyttleton smiled at Montchalmers, listened as the man finished his story, then drained the last of his glass. He yawned, then stretched.

"I suppose I should be going, Henry. It's been a long day, and I'm tired."

"Well, I'm glad we could have dinner tonight," Montchalmers said cautiously.

"I am too," Lyttleton replied, and he meant it. They stood and shook hands and agreed to meet again for dinner soon.

Once outside the club Lyttleton breathed deeply. Damned strange October, he thought. The sky had remained overcast for several days, and a sultry heat had settled across the city. It was almost like summer again, and Lyttleton wished it would rain and sweep the heat away. He waved a hansom cab along, indicating he wanted to walk. It wasn't far, and he needed to be out in the night air to do some thinking.

Of course, he told himself as he strolled away from the club, he was thinking too much lately. He was brooding about matters and magnifying them far beyond their scope. He was saddened by the deaths of two friends in such a short time, and he was uneasy about the attention being paid to August Hamilton. Or was it jealousy of the other men? No, it wasn't that. He didn't know what it was, but it certainly wasn't jealousy.

Lyttleton reached a corner, crossed the street after a carriage rumbled past, and continued strolling.

Perhaps he should retire to the country for a month or so, maybe spend Christmas there. He could do some writing, or just read and rest and generally rusticate. Or he could visit his family in America. His sister had just married, and he supposed he should meet her new husband now that he was part of their very small family. Yes, that sounded good. He would have to begin making plans. First, he'd write Sophie, though, for she might not want visitors right away.

He passed the mouth of an alleyway, then stopped in the globe of light from a street lamp. He frowned, then turned around, and gripping his walking stick more securely, he walked back to the alley and peered into the darkness. He could just make out the usual jumble of crates and boxes and a broken barrel. And something more, too. A dark shape lay crumpled amidst the heaps of rotting garbage. Lyttleton knelt and lit a match, then stared down at the shape.

It was Gerald Ashford. And he was dead.

When Lyttleton returned home, morning was half gone. He'd reported the death to the police, who had asked Lyttleton to return to the station with them so that he could tell them everything he knew. Which, he realized, wasn't much. Still, he cooperated, telling them how he had been going home and had passed the alleyway and something glimpsed from the corner of his eye had caught his attention. He had walked back and found the body of the young man, whom he knew.

The police had questioned him closely, and for a while he suspected they thought he had killed Gerald Ashford. Obviously, though, they had dismissed that idea, for not long afterward they let him go. He hailed a cab and went home.

Drained by exhaustion, he collapsed fully clothed into bed and dropped shortly thereafter into an uneasy sleep disturbed by visions of a laughing August and the corpse of Gerald Ashford.

When Lyttleton awoke later, he felt just as tired as

when he had gone to bed. He stared into the mirror at his bloodshot eyes and the pouches under them, and he could have sworn he'd spent a night drinking heavily. If only he had, he thought as he splashed cold water on his face, then rubbed it vigorously with a hand towel. His skin tingled, but he didn't feel much better.

He changed into the clothes set out by Edgar, went down to a simple breakfast of tea and toast, all that his queasy stomach could tolerate for the moment, then deemed it best to call upon the Ashfords. He did not look forward to this.

Lyttleton found Lord Ashford's usually stolid demeanor broken; the man's eyes were filled with tears and his voice choked, while Lady Ashford was weeping openly, a delicately embroidered handkerchief crumpled in her hand. The grieving parents greeted him, and Lyttleton offered his condolences on the loss of their son. The house's atmosphere was tense, strained, so very unlike the evening of the dinner party, and for the first time Lyttleton felt uncomfortable in the Ashford house.

Again Lyttleton said how sorry he was, knowing that his words sounded awkward, but neither Ashford noticed. He said nothing about his having discovered Gerald; that, he believed, was best left to the police. He stayed as long as politeness dictated, then took his leave. On his way out he met Bethany Ashford in the hall.

"I'm very sorry about your brother," he said softly, taking her hand.

She nodded, started to speak, then pressed her lips together. Tears had darkened her eyes, and he saw grief there, and something else, too. Something akin to anger.

For a moment they did not speak as Lyttleton gazed at the young woman. She seemed to make some resolution, for she suddenly moved away, then whirled back to face him.

"It's her fault," Bethany stated in a murderous voice. Her hands were clenched at her sides.

"I beg your pardon?"

"Gerald's death is her fault." Her voice was still low.

"Her fault?" he repeated stupidly. For some reason he wasn't following. Whatever was the girl talking about? He frowned as he tried to concentrate on her next words.

"Yes." She leveled her gaze at Lyttleton. "It's August Hamilton's fault. She came here, and now Gerald is dead."

He looked as astonished as he felt. "Surely, Miss Ashford, I know you dislike that woman, but even you cannot blame her for—"

"Oh, but I do, Mr. Lyttleton. Mark my words: She is an evil woman, and she will destroy others."

"Bethany!"

They both turned around. Lady Ashford stood by the stairs.

"Come here, my dear." Her daughter obeyed quickly. Lady Ashford turned eyes reddened from weeping toward him. "I'm sorry, Mr. Lyttleton. Please forgive Bethany's melodramatic accusations. She is very upset by her brother's death."

"Of course," Lyttleton murmured, "I quite understand, Lady Ashford. Please, if there is anything that I may do for you, let me know."

Where now? he asked himself once he was outside. As he walked away, he glanced back at the Ashford house, black crepe draped across the front door. He sighed. He could go home to sit and think about last night, or he could be with friends.

He chose the latter.

As he walked briskly to the club, Lyttleton puzzled over

Bethany Ashford's angry eyes and bitter words, her unusual accusation. He understood the girl's grief over her brother's death, for she had been close to him, but how could her anger be explained? Particularly when it was directed so vehemently at August Hamilton?

As he arrived at the club and handed his hat and cane over, Montchalmers hastened across to greet him.

"Did you hear about Gerald Ashford?" Montchalmers asked excitedly, pumping his friend's proffered hand.

"I found him," Lyttleton said quietly.

"Bloody hell you say." Montchalmers gaped at him. "Come in, come in, and sit down."

Lyttleton allowed himself to be settled into his favorite chair and took a glass of brandy in hand. It was a bit early for liquor, but he'd needed it after the night before. Taking a long swallow, he closed his eyes as the burning liquor trickled down his throat.

A faint noise came from Montchalmers, and Lyttleton smiled at the sound of impatience. He opened his eyes again. Montchalmers was sitting forward in his chair, an eager expression on his face.

"Well?"

"Well what, Henry?" Lyttleton countered.

"Tell me about it."

"It? If you mean the death of Gerald Ashford, I don't know what to say, Henry. The police suspect foul play, but they have no one in custody at the time."

"Come on, old man, that's not precisely what I meant." Montchalmer's tone was goading.

Suddenly Lyttleton realized what his friend wanted to hear. Montchalmers wanted the *particulars* of the death, all the details—gory and otherwise, and preferably the former.

Lyttleton curled his lip, barely able to contain his disgust. "I'm sorry, Henry, but there really isn't much to tell."

"But you say you found him!"

"Yes," Lyttleton heard himself saying somewhat irritably, "yes, damnit, I did find him, but there was nothing to see. The boy was dead. I happened along well after the event."

"How'd he die?"

Lyttleton shook his head. "I don't know, Henry. I'm no expert in those matters. You'll have to wait to hear from the police or read the newspapers."

"Oh." The other's voice softened with disappointment. He leaned back in his chair and looked grumpy.

This previously unseen side of his friend disturbed Lyttleton. He hadn't known Montchalmers had a penchant for the ghoulish, nor did he particularly like it. Curiosity was one thing; this was altogether another.

As for what he had told Montchalmers, it was quite true. There *was* little to tell. After he'd lit the match, he had stared in shock at the familiar face. The match had burned to his fingers before he dropped it, and cursing his clumsiness, he lit another. Gerald Ashford had still been handsome in death, although his skin had grown grey, his lips almost waxen in appearance. The hideous grimace on his face had upset Lyttleton even more, for he could not help but remember the horrible expression on Tommy Hamilton's face in death. He shook himself, brought himself back to the present.

"I called on the Ashfords before coming here," he said. "I'll go see them later."

"It was hard, you know, finding him dead like that, and so soon after I'd last seen him alive. His poor fiancée." Lyttleton shook his head sadly, and he remembered his own youth when it had been the young woman who had died, leaving the young man bereft. Yes, he could sympathize with Lucy Chandler.

"Yes, rather."

"Henry?"

"Yes?" Montchalmers stirred, for he had been dozing. He yawned and sat up.

"Don't you think it's odd, all these recent deaths?"

"Recent deaths?" Montchalmers stared at him. "Whatever do you mean?"

"I mean, Tommy and Terris have died, and now Gerald Ashford, and while he wasn't a particular friend of ours, we were acquaintances." He paused. "What I'm saying is: Don't you think it's strange, the number of deaths within our circle?"

"It's only three."

"Yes, but when was the last time such a thing happened?" Montchalmers looked blank. "And the three men who died were young and in good health."

"Tommy wasn't," Montchalmers pointed out.

"No, but he had been two years before."

"Accidents do happen, you know. Why the morbid interest, old boy?" Montchalmers stared at his friend through slitted eyes.

Lyttleton found the expression disconcerting, and oddly unpleasant. Apparently, Montchalmers didn't see anything amiss in the deaths. Why should he, then? Perhaps they were nothing more than phantasms of his imagination. Except . . . Except nothing, he told himself firmly.

"Well," he said in what he hoped was a hearty tone, "I suppose you are correct, Henry. Accidents do happen." He stood. "I should be leaving now, I think." He saluted his friend and prepared to stroll off when Montchalmers called to him.

"Lyttleton."

"Yes?"

"Do be careful."

Lyttleton nodded, collected his hat and his cane, and it wasn't until he was outside that he realized that he had broken out into a cold sweat.

Timothy Cleveland was the next to die. He was found the next night behind the carriage house at his parents' London home. Once more foul play was suspected.

Lyttleton shuddered as he put down the afternoon edition of the *Times*. He glanced around the reading room of the club. Only the older members were here today. He was the youngest man present.

Not as young as those who were dying, one part of him whispered.

He tried to force the voice away, but it wouldn't leave.

You're afraid of dying, it sneered.

No, he whispered half aloud. No, I'm not afraid of that, but he knew it was a lie.

He pressed the heels of his hands against his burning eyes and shuddered again. Then he dropped his hands and rose shakily, the newspaper sliding to the floor. He had to have fresh air.

Outside he stumbled away from the club. He kept his eyes on the pavement as his legs took him farther and farther away. He had no idea where he was going. He walked on, not caring. All he could think of was that his friends were dying, that they were all young, and that something was terribly wrong. He walked. After an hour he felt the strain in his legs. He ignored it and walked on.

Finally, as the light began fading from the sky, he raised his head to look around. At first he didn't recognize the neighborhood; then he realized where he was. He stood in front of the Hamilton house.

The sky had darkened and was streaked with brooding clouds. Occasionally lightning pierced the clouds, and he heard the rumble of faraway thunder above the clatter of the city. The air was damp, and his hair was plastered to his forehead; his clothes clung wetly to him.

Upstairs one window was lit, and as he stared at the yellow light he wondered if August were in that room. He thought he saw the faintest flutter of a curtain, but he couldn't be sure.

He waited. The wind rose, swirling dust through the street, and a crooked branch of a tree whipped back and forth. Abruptly he turned and walked away. What had brought him here? Sheer madness.

Lyttleton consulted his pocket watch. It was well past six, and he had a dinner party to attend at eight. He walked home quickly, changed into his formal attire, then left again, and to his vast relief he arrived only a few minutes late.

Most of the conversation centered on the recent deaths of Gerald Ashford and Timothy Cleveland. There had been two additional deaths last night—Phillip Thomkins and Birkey Davenant, acquaintances, not friends, of his, as had been Gerald Ashford. Murdered, the police thought.

People were uneasy. It was as though someone was out

to murder their sons. Lyttleton listened intently as the conversation whirled around him.

"The police think it's some horrible axe murderer," said a youngish matron whose chest was covered with glittering plaits of diamonds and rubies. She sipped quickly at her wine.

"There's no axe involved, Helena," said her husband with a faint Scots burr in his voice. "I've told you that before. They haven't found any blood by the victims."

"No blood?" asked another man seated close by. "Here now, what d'ye mean, Dr. Napier? No blood? Were they strangled? That wouldn't leave any blood now, would it?" The elderly woman seated next to him looked as though she were about to faint.

Dr. Napier shook his head. "It wasn't a strangulation that killed these men, Mr. Peterson, and it's quite true that no blood has been found at the scene of the deaths or on the victims themselves. That's why the police are beginning to question whether these were murders." He glanced at his wife. "But this is hardly a topic for the dinner table."

"Come now," Helena Napier replied briskly, "I haven't been a physician's wife these past ten years for nothing, David. You've told me far worse. Go on."

"That's true, my dear," he admitted. He took a bite of his chicken and thoughtfully chewed. When he was finished, he sipped his white wine.

"Yes, do," said Peterson. He was clearly impatient to hear more.

"What else would you know, Mr. Peterson?"

"Well, if it's not a murderer that's doing them in, how've they died?"

"Some of my distinguished colleagues are talking of natural causes."

"Not one of the victims was above the age of thirty! And they all enjoyed excellent health!" Peterson said. Lyttleton judged Peterson, who was decidedly nervous, to be close to five-and-twenty.

"Such men have died before."

"No doubt, Dr. Napier, but don't you find it odd that these deaths came so close together?"

"Odd?" Napier beetled his brows threateningly and looked as though he were about to scowl fiercely at the other man. "Why, of course I find them odd, Peterson! It's not natural causes that are killing these men, but I'm damned if I know what is."

"Some of David's other colleagues are suggesting it's some type of new disease," Helena Napier said.

"Disease?" asked Peterson. "What sort of disease?"

"If I knew, I probably wouldn't be here having dinner with you. I'd be doing something about it. It's just a suggestion, after all." Even as he spoke, though, Napier glanced at his wife.

He knows more than he's saying, Lyttleton thought, and he planned to take Napier aside later to find out what it was.

Dinner passed amiably enough, and they were leaving the dining room when another guest arrived. Lyttleton heard the voice before he saw who it was.

"I'm so sorry, Colonel Latimer, that I was unable to join you earlier," said the soft sultry voice.

A shiver ran down Lyttleton's spine, and he clenched his fists at his side.

"That's perfectly fine, my dear," said the jovial host. "I'm just pleased that you could come at all. Have you met all my guests?"

As the introductions were made to the Petersons and

Napiers, Lyttleton stood stock-still. He waited until the others had moved away.

"Have you met Mr. Lyttleton?" Latimer asked.

"Yes, Mr. Lyttleton and I have met before," August Hamilton said with a smile.

"Good, good."

Latimer tucked her arm through his and led her off, much to Lyttleton's relief.

Lyttleton settled down by himself with an after-dinner drink, but found the widow staring thoughtfully at him from time to time. Or at least he thought her expression was thoughtful. That further unsettled him, though, and when he could gracefully leave, he did.

He returned home to find a cold sweat had broken out over his body. The second time in a few days. Was he ill? Or was it something more? He threw off his clothes and crawled into bed.

She had smiled at him, almost as if she had expected to find him there. Of course, that was nonsense. They moved within the same circles, so of course she would come to expect to see him as well.

Nonsense, he told himself, it was all nonsense—his uneasiness about her and the deaths. It was simply nothing more than the fact that he was obsessed with her. Thoughts of her filled his waking hours and that disturbed him, for nothing had taken hold of his mind like this before. Nothing.

Lyttleton slid slowly beneath the covers. Gradually his eyelids drooped as he fell asleep and dreamed strange dreams.

He stood in a dark cavern, and nearby he could hear the lapping of water. A chill in the air sent shivers through him, and he wondered how he had come there when he'd last been in bed. He looked around, seeking a way to leave, when he heard the sound. His breath held, he waited, listening.

A faint footstep. Then a second, and another. Closer and closer. He held his breath, and his heart pounded as he waited.

Off to his left something white glimmered, and he thought he detected the smell of musk. There was a faint laugh, or was it the water?

Then he saw her. Gliding toward him, and as she approached, she shed her clothing. Soon she stood in front of him. She stepped closer.

Her dusky nipples pressed against his chest, branding him. He groaned as she slipped her hands inside his shirt and playfully tugged at the hair on his chest. He fastened his mouth on hers, probing with his tongue and greedily sucking at her breath. As they embraced, he stripped his clothes off. She traced the lines of his arms and shoulders with her fingertips, and his skin tingled. He grabbed her roughly by the arms and threw her down on the uneven floor.

Laughing, she arched her body, inviting him, and with a strangled cry he fell upon her. He bit her arms, kneaded her breasts harshly while her mocking laughter filled his head, echoed through the cavern, and maddened him. He wanted her now, and he would have her.

She bucked, twisting and turning like a wild animal under him as he tried to enter her, and he kept missing, and he cried out in his frustration. That seemed to amuse her, for she laughed even more, then took his member in both hands and cradled it for a moment before digging her nails along the tender skin. He cried out, jerked away, then thrust deeply into her and screamed as the barbs tore cruelly into him.

He woke, screaming, and sat shuddering in his bed, his

head resting on his drawn-up knees. For a long time he did not move. He had never had a dream like that. And never had he treated a woman like that. He closed his eyes, trying to force the images from his mind. Finally, when he was calm, he rose and slipped on his dressing gown and sat down to read. He would sleep no more that night.

The next night he did not sleep, for he feared the dreams that would come. The day after, in the early evening, he went to see Dr. Napier at his office, which was adjacent to his fashionable West End house in Hanover Square.

"I remember you from the Latimers' party," Dr. Napier said once Lyttleton was settled opposite him. "As I recall, you were quite interested in our topic of conversation, although you didn't say anything."

"Several of my friends were among those who have died recently."

"I see." The physician leaned back and thoughtfully studied the other man. "Is that why you've come here, Mr. Lyttleton?"

"Partially," Lyttleton confessed, "but also because I have had problems sleeping."

"What sort of problems?"

"I've been having terrible dreams—nightmares, really—

and I wake up screaming. Afterwards I'm so shaken I can't go back to sleep, knowing it'll just happen again."

"When did the dreams begin?"

"I don't remember. Quite some time ago, I think. They weren't terrible at first, but later they grew worse."

"What are they about?"

Lyttleton blushed. "They're dreams of a highly personal nature."

Dr. Napier's voice held amusement. "That's natural, Mr. Lyttleton, as you're a young and healthy and virile man. But," he said, frowning, "you say you wake up screaming."

"Yes."

"And the nature of the dreams is terrible."

"Yes."

"What is the 'highly personal nature' of these dreams?"

"I can't remember all, although there's a woman in them, and it's always the same woman, but in the dreams I feel as though I'm being consumed alive."

"I see." Dr. Napier steepled his fingers. "Is this woman one whom you visit often?"

"No, it isn't. That is, she is . . . No." He didn't say any more. He might inadvertently reveal her identity. That would not be gentlemanly. Too, he wasn't sure he wanted Dr. Napier to know who it was.

"Do you think of this woman often in your waking hours?"

"Yes, I do."

"Do you love this woman?"

"No."

Dr. Napier peered at him. "You're very sure of yourself, Mr. Lyttleton."

"Yes, and I don't love this woman."

"Yet you think often of her, and she figures in your

dreams." Lyttleton nodded. "As an object of adoration, perhaps?"

"No. I am scarcely worshipping her in my dreams." His mouth quirked into a wry smile.

"I see." Dr. Napier's eyes gleamed with amusement for a moment; then he grew more serious. "You say that several of your friends have died recently." Lyttleton nodded. "Hmm. And I assume that this woman is somehow inaccessible to you?"

"I don't know if that's the proper term. It's not precisely that she's inaccessible, but rather that she's a . . . no, rather she's . . ." He faltered to a stop, unable to go on.

"May I ask you something?"

"Of course."

"Is the woman in your dream August Hamilton?"

Lyttleton stared, unable to believe he had heard correctly. "Why, yes," he admitted after a moment's silence, "but how did you know? I don't understand."

"Mr. Lyttleton, as strange as this may sound, you aren't the first man to come to me about this particular kind of dream, with this woman in it." Dr. Napier gave him a kindly smile.

"I'm not the first?" Why should he find that surprising, Lyttleton wondered, when he remembered how his friends— particularly Montchalmers and poor late Terris—had acted around the woman.

"No. Indeed, in the past month or so, many of my patients have complained to me of these dreams, and not all the men were young, either. There is one difference, though, from what you said."

"What is that, Dr. Napier?"

"To a man my patients claimed to be in love with her. You did not. I find that very interesting."

Lyttleton frowned. "I don't understand how a number of different men come to have similar dreams around the same woman."

Dr. Napier said with a slight smile of modesty, "I've given this matter much thought over the past weeks, Mr. Lyttleton. All of you move within the same social circles as did the dead men. From this I deduce that you—yourself and the others—are upset by these sudden deaths, deaths of men you know and who were your age. I think the dreams might well be part of your own fear that you will die too.

"Another factor is added: that of the sensual in the presence of a beautiful and exotic woman. Not long ago she came to London, and since then her husband, known and liked by you and others, has died and she's been elevated to a center of attraction, in part because of her recent widowhood and in part because alluring women such as August Hamilton, from the time of the Greeks to our own, are rarely ignored. As she is a widow, and set apart and thus unobtainable, she enters the fancies of young and old men alike. She's pursued in dreams because she cannot be otherwise." Dr. Napier paused. "What do you think of this explanation, Mr. Lyttleton? Does this hold merit for you?"

"Yes," Lyttleton allowed slowly. "I think it does. It holds as much merit as anything I have thought of, Doctor. Still, the problem remains. However, I suppose that as long as Mrs. Hamilton is in London, I will have the dreams." Dr. Napier nodded. "Then what am I to do? I can't continue without sleep."

"Ah, that's a simple prescription. I recommend long brisk walks and rides, a trip to the seaside for its air. Avoid rich food, but drink as much wine or champagne as you desire—although not to excess—before retiring at night.

These often prove excellent sleeping aids." Dr. Napier's eyes twinkled with amusement. "I don't doubt that in a few days your sleeping problems will be solved."

"Has this worked for any of your other patients?"

"None has returned with this complaint."

Lyttleton nodded. "Then I'll try it." He paused, not knowing how to broach the next topic, the second reason he had chosen to come to Dr. Napier rather than his own doctor.

"I see we're not yet finished with our consultation."

"No, sir." Lyttleton cleared his throat. "The matter I wish to discuss is a delicate one. Another one," he said, faintly smiling. "You are correct in saying that I was interested in your conversation at dinner the other night, not only because several of my friends have died but also because I have a certain interest in the topic.

"Not out of morbidity, though," he added, in case the doctor thought otherwise. Apparently, Dr. Napier did not, for he continued listening intently. "Excuse me if I falter, but this is hard for me. The other night I thought that you were planning to elaborate upon the topic under discussion but that you stopped before saying any more. Might I ask what it was you were about to say?"

Dr. Napier studied him for a long moment, and Lyttleton began to wonder if he had somehow overstepped some invisible boundary and offended the doctor. Perhaps the physician would tell him it was none of his business.

"You're correct in your observation, Mr. Lyttleton. I had planned to say more, but I changed my mind as I didn't think it wise. I fear I was not completely truthful with Mr. Peterson, either." Lyttleton sat forward, aware that the other man had grown more serious now and the Scots burr had thickened. "I told him we haven't determined the cause of death in these four men. But we have. Or rather, what was the cause of imminent death."

Lyttleton felt a tingling inside as he waited, breath held.

"The bodies of the victims—Ashford, Cleveland, Thomkins, Davenant—were all almost completely drained of blood."

"Drained of blood?" Lyttleton stared at the doctor, unable to comprehend what the man had just told him. "But how can that be? Weren't there wounds?"

"Slight ones on the throats and groins that looked more like a rash or insect bites. Hardly the sort of wound that would bleed profusely. Too, none of the areas around the victims was drenched with blood."

In Gerald Ashford or Timothy Cleveland or Phillip Thomkins or Birkey Davenant, Lyttleton thought numbly, barely a single drop of blood was left in their veins.

"I still don't understand how it's done," Lyttleton said, horrified by the revelation. He had never heard of anything more fiendish in his life.

"A number of suggestions have been made ranging from attack by an animal to disease. There were also other suggestions, far less probable, made."

"Do you credit any of these?"

"I don't know what I do believe. I've seen bodies mangled by maddened animals, but these corpses were not mangled. They looked as though they'd fallen asleep; there were none of the usual signs of violent struggle—unless, of course, the victims had died elsewhere and had been brought to the places where they were discovered—" He stopped.

"Yes?" Lyttleton prompted.

"There was something violent, as I recall. Their faces. Their eyes were wide open, and their faces were twisted into expressions of—"

"Terror," Lyttleton said.

"Yes." For a moment the doctor looked puzzled; then he nodded. "Ah, yes, you discovered Gerald Ashford."

Lyttleton nodded, and once more he saw the expression on Tommy Hamilton's face. "That's one of the reasons I'm interested in these murders."

"One? There are others?"

"Yes," he said slowly, "I had another friend who died with just such a look of terror on his face, and I thought perhaps the cause of death might be the same." He was reluctant to elaborate at present, and perhaps Dr. Napier sensed that, for he did not pursue it.

"I've never seen more hideous expressions in all my career, and I have seen men dead from many things."

"If an animal killed those men, surely it would have savaged its prey and surely the area would be drenched in blood. If it's disease, I cannot fathom what sort. I've never seen a disease that evaporates blood."

"What about the wounds?"

"What if they're something else entirely? Perhaps a rash that breaks out in only two areas? Or begins over the entire body, then retreats, collecting at the throat and groin just before the time of death. Perhaps they're blisters that burst."

"If the deaths resulted from disease, why haven't more

people in London died? And why would the disease have attacked only young men in perfect health?"

"I don't know."

"Their expressions . . ." Lyttleton said slowly.

"A physical condition caused by disease or perhaps a seizure might account for that. Might, although I doubt it. Someone also suggested that the deaths were the work of a human."

"My God! It would have to be a fiend or a madman!" Lyttleton exclaimed.

"Just so," Dr. Napier said, nodding. "I'm afraid we'll never know, though, unless someone else dies."

Lyttleton thought of the streets he had walked through to the doctor's house. Now that it was evening he would be returning home in the dark, and what, he wondered, danger might he find there? Along the street, in an alley, around a corner. Danger from beast, human, disease, or something else? He recalled that night he thought he had been followed. No, it wasn't the same, he told himself. It couldn't be.

"I must go," he said, standing. "I'm sorry to have taken so much of your time."

"Not at all," Dr. Napier replied graciously. "I'm glad I could be of some help to you. Do as I suggested, Mr. Lyttleton, and please let me know if you do not begin sleeping easily once more."

"Thank you, I shall."

They shook hands, and Lyttleton left. Napier sat down at his desk again and thoughtfully drummed his fingertips against the polished wood.

Lyttleton knew more than he was telling. Napier had sensed that several times during the conversation. Once or twice the other man's eyes had refused to meet his—a most telling sign, in the doctor's mind. He wondered what

Lyttleton was concealing. Very interesting, Napier thought, and he wondered what Helena would say about it. He glanced at the silver pocket watch she had given him five years ago. Nearly time for dinner, and no doubt his dear wife was waiting patiently. He stood up, and imagined her face when he introduced this subject as their dinner conversation.

Lyttleton hailed a cab after he left Dr. Napier's office. Tonight he would not walk. Tonight he could not. Not after what Napier had told him. He glanced out the window and stared at the dark mouths of alleyways. Did another Ashford lie out there, waiting for discovery? He fervently hoped not, but he would not be surprised to hear of another murder.

Closing his eyes, he thought about their conversation. The doctor's suggestions for easing his sleeplessness had been quite practical, but Lyttleton suspected none of them would work. At least he would try them. Perhaps one might help.

Had he said too much about August Hamilton? Perhaps he should have kept quiet. Too late now, he thought. Still, he merely acknowledged that she appeared in his dreams, as she did with other men. Lyttleton frowned. There was something wrong . . . but he didn't know what. Even as he thought, sleep came to him and claimed him long before the cab had turned into Eaton Square.

"You are so handsome, my love," she whispered in the darkness.

Arthur Ives stroked her long hair and breathed deeply of its musky scent. "And you are so beautiful, so very beautiful." He bent to kiss her, and her strong teeth playfully nipped his lower lip and drew blood. She gently licked the blood away, and he shivered at the touch of her tongue.

He stroked her soft body, and she laughed, then rolled over on top of him.

"Now," she said in the husky voice that sent thrills through him, "I will show you how to make love, Arthur."

"But, haven't we—" he began, bewildered.

"Hush," she said, laying a finger against his lips. The cut still seeped a little blood, and she rubbed her finger back and forth across the damp surface of his lips, spreading the blood across his mouth. "Now, I shall instruct you."

"Very well," he murmured. What could she mean? She was the most magnificent of any of his many bed partners, Ives thought. He had never slept with a woman more knowledgeable, a woman able to bring his body to greater feelings.

She kissed him, then reached down to caress his thighs, his flat abdomen. Her fingers twisted through his curly hair, and he groaned aloud. He could feel himself stiffening already. They had made love five times already tonight. How could he have anything left? And yet he did. He grinned in the darkness.

Her hands slid down his length, flicked the tip of the shaft, and she eased back onto him. He thrust deeply into her as she bent to kiss him, and for Ives the world exploded into glints of shimmering white and crimson, as searing pain tore through his neck and his groin. For a moment, he didn't know what was happening, and then, when he opened his eyes, he screamed in terror.

"Good afternoon, Dr. Napier."

"Good day, Mr. Lyttleton. What brings you again to my office so soon?"

Lyttleton laid the newspaper down on the doctor's desk and said quietly, "Another man has died."

Napier's eyes flicked to the story, then back to the man in front of him. "Yes, I know."

Lyttleton sat. "I knew him, too. Arthur Ives and I went to school together. He was an athlete, one of the fittest men I have ever known, excelling in all sports he tried. And now he is dead." Napier remained silent. "I don't understand. Arthur was never ill, was always strong." He paused. "His blood . . . ?"

"Gone."

"Where does it go? Why is it drained? Why are they killed this way? So many *why's*." He leaned back and rubbed a hand across his face. "Could this be the work of some unscrupulous doctor?"

"For what purpose?"

"I don't know. None of it makes sense."

"No, it doesn't," the doctor agreed. "I pray that the deaths will end, that the cause will be found and stopped. But for now, unhappily, we have another death." He tapped the newspaper. "And the ignorant grow fearful. The reports of sightings of odd creatures have begun, just as I thought they would. Huge cats and dogs prowling the streets. Immense birds wheeling through the skies of London. Someone even claimed to have spotted a wild ape in the East End. Incredible nonsense."

"But no reports of human predators?"

"None so far."

"There's something else I wish to discuss, Dr. Napier. Are there victims from other classes, or are only wealthy men dying from this?"

"Hmm." Napier leaned forward and tapped his fingers on the desktop. "An interesting question, Mr. Lyttleton, and one I cannot answer. Frankly, I doubt anyone has investigated it, but I can promise you that I'll look into the matter for you. I have contacts throughout the city hospitals."

"I should go," Lyttleton said. "I intended to stay only a few minutes." He stood.

"One moment, Mr. Lyttleton. How have you been sleeping?"

"Rather well of late. The dreams come and go, but they seem less terrifying. Perhaps I am growing accustomed to them, or perhaps they are milder now. I'm just grateful to be able to sleep the night through."

"Good, good. I'm glad to hear you're getting some rest." The two men shook hands. "I'll look into this matter for you."

Relief surged through him as he stepped outside. Dr. Napier would find out for him. Even if the deaths were caused by a man and even if the killer preyed only on the wealthy, what did that prove? He didn't know. Perhaps he would understand then. He felt as if he had stepped around a corner this evening. Somehow he was closer to—

To what? To whatever lay beyond.

It was close to sundown, and he should be getting home. He didn't want to be out on the streets after dark. He began whistling under his breath and quickened his pace. The sultry air closed around him, thickening and tightening as night dropped through the streets. He looked around for a hansom cab, didn't see one. He couldn't wait; he would have to walk.

Once or twice he thought he heard soft footsteps behind him, but he didn't see anyone. He was relieved to reach Eaton Square and quickly went up the steps to the door. Once inside he breathed more easily.

Lyttleton lingered over his dinner, and later he read for a while, then retired to bed with a wine decanter and glass.

He drank one glassful, glanced out the window at the darkness, shuddered, and poured himself another one. Finally, when he could drink no more, he turned off the gaslight and settled down to sleep and prayed that he would have no dreams.

She draped her arms around his neck, but this time she spoke, calling him by name. And the sound of her voice was agony. The soft huskiness burned into his veins, his brain, and he twisted away as he sought escape, but he could find none. And then she was upon him, and the pain before was as nothing. He shrieked as his life drained from him, and in that moment he climaxed, and she leaned back, baring her white throat as she laughed at his torment.

Lyttleton woke, screaming and panting heavily. He sat up abruptly, and momentarily the room swirled around him as dizziness assaulted him. The bed sheets clung wetly to him, and he peeled them away in disgust, then stood, his legs trembling beneath him. He had to hang onto the bedpost for support. He looked about the room, fearing the blackness he saw, and finally, when his legs steadied, he turned on the lamp by the bed. Napier's advice had worked—for a while. The glasses of wine he'd consumed in bed hadn't kept the dream away. Nothing would now, he suspected, and he shuddered at the thought.

He belted his dressing gown around him, then went to a table across the room. He sat, and head in hands, he stared at the floor. Had Wyndy Terris dreamed of her? he wondered. Of all the men of Lyttleton's acquaintances who had died recently, Terris had been the only one to die by his own hand.

Which didn't mean he wasn't murdered. Now, Lyttleton thought with a frown, what did that mean? But Terris had fancied himself in love with Tommy's widow—precisely what Dr. Napier's other patients thought.

The deaths had begun with Tommy's. His wasn't the same as the later ones, though. Or was it? He didn't know. If he could talk to Tommy's doctor—but August said she hadn't called one. Again he thought that odd. Still, there had been a gap of time between Tommy's death and Terris', and Gerald Ashford's, and the others'.

But what if other deaths similar in nature had been occurring in those gaps? Deaths of which he had no knowledge? The deaths hadn't begun until the Hamiltons had arrived in London, but there might have been other deaths before that. The police would have records.

What then? he asked himself.

If this sort of death had occurred before the Hamiltons returned to London, all right. And if the deaths had only begun afterward, then . . . then what? Then somehow, he thought grimly, somehow August Hamilton was implicated in them. No. Not implicated. That was too strong a word. But then there existed a connection of sorts between the deaths and the widow. If, if, if.

But what sort of connection could this be? Was she an accomplice to some madman or criminal mind? What madman? What criminal? She scarcely knew anyone in London—or hadn't. Perhaps she had lied when she said she had no family left; perhaps there was a brother, father, uncle, cousin, some relative who lived in England, and for a long time they had conspired together to—

Lyttleton smiled briefly. August and her unknown relative conspired to kill men of quality. A truly absurd notion. Besides, hadn't August Hamilton said she'd lived in India all her life?

Or so she claimed.

What if, Lyttleton proposed, she were the murderer? Good God, he must be losing his mind. No gently nurtured woman could be capable of such horror. How could anyone, much less a woman as frail as August Hamilton, accomplish such a dreadful act in the first place? Impossible.

Still, if someone wanted to murder a man, wouldn't it be easier to simply knife or shoot him, or even club him with a heavy instrument? Why go to the trouble of removing his blood?

He could not forget that Bethany Ashford had accused the widow of killing Gerald. Still, the girl had been mourning her brother and was doubtless out of her mind with grief.

But no woman he'd met seemed to like August Hamilton.

Certainly, though, that didn't mean she was a murderer. Through the years he had observed any number of women who were greatly disliked by the members of their sex for one reason or another, particularly when that woman proved very attractive to every male she met.

But had any of those women been like August Hamilton?

No, none. He'd never before met a woman to whom men were universally attracted, for whom her admirers would forget and forgive anything at all. Never. It was downright uncanny. Almost unnatural.

And that led back to the dreams which were, in his opinion, unnatural. Nothing could convince him otherwise. Perhaps, as Dr. Napier had suggested, the dreams were representations of his grief for his friend or of desire for his friend's widow. Nonetheless, the dreams remained unnatural.

Certainly Lyttleton had had sensual dreams numerous times before in his life. He was, after all, a healthy male with healthy tastes, but never had his dreams been so explicit, so detailed, so real as these. And never in any previous dream had he made love to a woman only to have her use him and for him to experience pain. Before, his sensual dreams had been pleasant for both participants. In his recent dreams only August achieved satisfaction. And he woke up screaming and drenched in sweat.

No, he thought wryly, not natural at all.

What, then, did these reflections leave him with? Did he, in fact, suspect that Mrs. Hamilton had killed four—no, five and possibly more—young men? Had she grappled to the ground tall and strong men from whom she'd somehow drained their blood? Well, yes, he did suspect her, one part of him admitted, and sheepishly he laughed aloud. Again, absurd. Doubtless she had known the men. He knew she had met Gerald and Timothy at the Ashfords' dinner party. Even so, what did that prove? Nothing. Simply that she had known the murder victims, just as he had, just as did any number of men and women.

Perhaps the widow was a madwoman whose insanity gave her inhuman strength and who was able to conceal her madness. Others had before this. He stroked his moustache thoughtfully. No, that made no sense. He had looked into her eyes and known she was not mad, at least no more mad than he.

He stood and crossed over to his desk to get writing paper and pen and ink. He would write all of his reflections of the past hour down, then draft a copy of it and send it around to Dr. Napier in the morning. Much later in the morning, he thought as he yawned. And perhaps Dr. Napier could make something of it; perhaps not. Lyttleton began writing, the only sound in the room the rapid scratching of the pen nib across the paper. Midway through the first page Lyttleton lifted his pen and paused as he stared down at one sentence.

"Besides," he had written to the doctor, "August Hamilton told Terris, Montchalmers, and me, upon the occasion of our meeting her, that she had lived in India all her life. How do we know this is accurate?"

Indeed, how did they? They had only her word for it. And that, Lyttleton realized, he was not prepared to fully accept now.

She and Tommy had recently left India; no doubt his regiment was still stationed there, and if not, he could find where it was located presently. Tommy's brother officers and friends in the regiment might reveal information about this strange woman and her origins, information that would shed some light on the mystery. When he finished Napier's letter, he would begin writing others. It would be, he thought, a far busier night than he had previously thought.

Lyttleton heard nothing from Dr. Napier, and he began to wonder if Napier thought he was crazy. Then, a few days after he'd sent the note, he received a dinner invitation from Mrs. Napier for the next night.

At the bottom of the note a brief postscript had been penned in another hand. Dr. Napier indicated he had business to discuss with Lyttleton. He sensed that the doctor had made some discovery.

The next evening as Lyttleton dressed, his hands trembled with the inner excitement he felt at the impending appointment.

He wished he had more to report to Napier. He'd been about to post the letters to India when it occurred to him that the regiment might have moved. He checked and found it had returned to England. After readdressing his letters, he sent them out. Only God knew if the letters would reach their destinations.

Still, the letters weren't his last resort. He'd resolved to ask around the city—particularly at the clubs. Perhaps he could find someone who was with Tommy in India—God knows, the regiment had been large enough—and who was now in London or nearby.

Dr. Napier greeted Lyttleton warmly, and the two men settled in the doctor's study before dinner. Lyttleton, the only guest, sat in a chair flanking the fireplace, while Napier paced, his hands locked behind his back. For a few minutes the doctor continued pacing, his agitation clearly evident, then finally he whirled and threw up his hands.

"You were right, damn you! Too terribly right, Mr. Lyttleton." The doctor's burr had grown thick from his excitement.

Lyttleton waited, his breath held, to hear what the doctor said he was too terribly right about.

Napier took another turn around the study, sighing deeply as he did so, then eased himself into a chair opposite Lyttleton.

"In your note you suggested I investigate other deaths that match the ones with which we're familiar. Well, there have been others." Dr. Napier held up a hand before Lyttleton could speak. Scowling fiercely, he leaned forward. "*The very same*, my friend, the very same as the deaths of Ashford and the others. That is, the victims were drained completely of their blood, and in death their faces held that terrible expression we have seen on the others. The police report that over twenty of these deaths have occurred."

"The victims?" Lyttleton said, his voice nearly a croak. "What of them?"

"All were men ranging in age from seventeen to thirty-three or so. All had previously enjoyed good health, and unlike Mr. Ashford and Mr. Cleveland and the others, many of these victims were quite poor. The police found them in the East End, not far from their homes."

Lyttleton stared, unable to believe that any of his suppositions of that strange night could possibly be true. And now not one, but two. Were there others? He was almost afraid to ask.

"Twenty," Napier muttered, shaking his head.

"My God," Lyttleton whispered. "I didn't know. I-I didn't really think that . . ." He couldn't go on as he realized the enormous horror of it.

"Yes." Napier toyed with his wineglass and momentarily closed his eyes, then opened them to look at the other man. "It was far worse than I had thought, too. Terrible, terrible. There has very nearly been panic in the East End, and the police have maintained order only by asking the newspapers not to print each case. *That* is why we had not heard of these."

"The timing," Lyttleton said, "what of that? Did the deaths begin before the Hamiltons arrived, or afterward?" Napier did not speak, and from the look on the doctor's face Lyttleton knew. "My God! Afterward? The deaths began after they came to London?"

"Yes, if the date you gave me for their arrival is correct."

"It is."

"I've listed the date of each death and the name of the victim, as well as where he lived at the time of his death. I think you will find it interesting."

Lyttleton glanced through the columns. Close to thirty names were written there. Thirty. And could there be more that the police had never discovered? Bodies dumped into the Thames? Bodies outside the city? He shuddered at the thought.

"What do we do now?"

"If it's a disease, then there's little we can do but let it run its course and try to find an antidote. If it's not . . ." Napier stopped.

"If it's not disease, then it's a deliberate killing. Either by beast or man."

"Yes, and no factual reportings of animals have been seen, plus the fact that the evidence of the bodies does not support that theory."

"Thus . . ."

"Yes. The deaths must be by human hand." Napier's thick eyebrows beetled as he frowned. "Mr. Lyttleton, I suggested to the police that the two sets of deaths might be linked. Do you know what they said?" Lyttleton shook his head, almost fearing what he would hear. "They told me that the very night Arthur Ives died, another death had occurred, one that we hadn't heard about—one virtually identical with Ives'. The authorities have concluded that the deaths occurred no more than thirty minutes apart as both bodies were still warm when found."

Lyttleton's voice betrayed his excitement as he sat up. "Then that means the crimes have all been committed by a single murderer!"

"Yes, yes, that's what I thought, too, for it is a logical inference, after all." Dr. Napier's voice was very calm, and suddenly Lyttleton's elation began to dim. "As you can well imagine, I told the police my observation that the murderer must be the same. They denied it."

"What?" Lyttleton said slowly.

"Yes. The police said it couldn't be the same killer, for the murders were at opposite ends of the city—Ives' in Kensington, the other in the East End. How, the police asked me, could the killer have gone from one end of the city to the other in thirty minutes or so—flown? The man didn't laugh at me; he didn't have to."

Lyttleton sagged back against the chair.

Napier continued. "The wounds in the throat and groin area are identical. In width, length, depth—all identical.

How could one villain duplicate exactly what his accomplice was doing?"

"I don't understand then," Lyttleton said truthfully. "If it's impossible for one man to have killed Ives and the other fellow, and if it is impossible for two men, separately, to have killed Ives and the other man, then how in God's name did they die?"

"I don't know. Perhaps it's truly some exotic disease of which we're just learning."

The doctor paused to pour himself another glass of wine and held up the decanter to Lyttleton, who shook his head. He suspected he'd best keep a clear head.

Napier continued. "It's true that the police haven't been able to discover a similar crime—let us now call it a death, for argument's sake only, Mr. Lyttleton—before the Hamiltons arrived in London. They traveled from India, a country known for its unusual diseases. I have treated many men and women alike who have returned from India near death from one disease or another, for the doctors there could not cure them."

August Hamilton had said that her husband's fever had reoccurred, Lyttleton remembered, and she had gone from one doctor to another in India, and none of them had been able to cure her husband. And so she had returned to England to save Tommy's life. And yet he had died shortly afterward.

"If either August or Tommy Hamilton had brought this disease back to London, then it could have begun spreading and killing others."

"I suppose it's possible."

"Mrs. Hamilton is quite active socially, from what I've gathered. She could have innocently spread the disease through her contacts at dinners and parties. That's not unknown."

"But wouldn't she suffer from the disease and ultimately die as the others have?"

Napier shook his head. "Some men and women are immune to diseases naturally. They're few, but they do exist. So Mrs. Hamilton might well carry the illness but not be affected by it. This is given substance by the fact that she's lived in India all her life."

"Which leaves us where, Doctor?"

Dr. Napier spread his hands. "I don't know, Mr. Lyttleton. Murder, perhaps."

At that moment someone knocked on the study door.

"Ah, that will be our dinner summons. Shall we go, Mr. Lyttleton?"

As they left the study, Lyttleton paused.

"Tommy Hamilton wasted away before his death," he said slowly, his eyes meeting the doctor's.

Dr. Napier's eyes grew grim. "I think that I should do some more investigation. What do you say, Mr. Lyttleton?"

"An excellent idea, sir."

From the shadows she watched the child play with his spaniel pup behind the house. The full moon cast a silvery light on them as they raced across the grass, the dog barking while the child laughed. Such a pretty sight, she thought, and obviously the child's parents did not know he had slipped outside for a midnight romp with his new pet. Such a handsome, sturdy fellow. And so very innocent.

Suddenly bounding into the air, the dog knocked the surprised boy down, and together they rolled over and over, the boy giggling even more while his pet licked his face. Finally tired, the boy lay on his back, the panting puppy resting his head on the child's stomach.

She stepped out of the shadows into the light of the

moon. The dog lifted its head, drew back its lips in what someday might be a ferocious look, and growled.

"Hello."

The child sat up, suddenly conscious of an adult. The puppy, stiff-legged, advanced toward her.

"Come back, Trifle," the boy called in his childish tones. "Come back."

The puppy kept approaching.

She glanced down at the growling creature, then glided toward the child. He was looking nervously from his upset puppy to the beautiful woman, and slowly he backed up as she drew closer.

"Come here, little one," she coaxed. "I won't harm you. Come here."

The boy shook his head.

Suddenly the dog lunged toward her, his small jaw open to display puppy teeth.

Impatient, she swept her hands in front of her, and the dog stopped as though it had run into an invisible barricade. It whimpered pitifully as it was lifted several feet in the air and flung across the grass to land with a thud against a tree. The boy's eyes widened, and he opened his mouth to shriek.

Close to him now, she reached out to grasp the boy's shaking shoulders with her long fingers. One hand stroked his plump cheek.

"Be quiet, child. Your puppy is not dead. Come to me, my little sweetling." She knelt, and obediently the boy went into her waiting arms. She hugged him close and kissed his soft lips, and he shivered under the icy touch of hers.

Lyttleton blanched and shakily set his teacup down as he read the story in the newspaper. Another victim.

This time, though, a child had died. A boy who'd turned seven that day had been found behind his parents' home. The article said murder was suspected. Curiously, the body of his spaniel had also been found at the base of a tree not far from the boy's body. It appeared the dog had been flung with considerable strength to its death.

He rang for Edgar. "Bring me my writing materials at once," he instructed. The servant nodded and left, and returned within minutes. Lyttleton began writing. When he was finished, he rang for Edgar again and handed him the sealed note. "Have John deliver this to Dr. Napier at once."

"Yes, sir." The servant bowed and left.

Lyttleton wondered what answer Napier would send. He set the newspaper down; he made a half-hearted attempt to finish his breakfast of eggs and sausage but found he'd lost his appetite. He went upstairs and dressed with care.

It might take some time for Dr. Napier to reply, particularly if the doctor was busy, and so Lyttleton thought he'd go to the club. He hadn't seen Montchalmers for a while, and if he did get an answer from the doctor, Edgar would send word to him there.

"I haven't seen you in a long time, old boy," Lyttleton said as he greeted his friend.

Henry Montchalmers smiled wanly. "It's been a while. Well, what with one thing or another, I've been busy."

"Yes, I don't doubt." Lyttleton frowned momentarily. Montchalmers looked terrible; in fact, the flesh on his friend's face seemed to sag and no longer looked as youthful as it had just days before. Swollen pouches lay under his eyes, as though he had missed a great amount of sleep. "Are you still having those dreams, old man?" Lyttleton asked casually.

"Dreams?" Montchalmers asked blankly.

"Yes, you know, Henry. The dreams about August Hamilton. The ones that you and I and poor Wyndy were all having about the same time. Remember them?" Lyttleton shook his head. "Amazing, isn't it?"

"Oh, those." Montchalmers blinked. "No, not at all, old boy. They've gone."

He was lying, Lyttleton thought, and that hurt him. Or perhaps he couldn't tell the truth, even though he might want to. Why did he lie about not having the dreams? Was Henry ashamed? He hadn't been before.

"Glad to hear that," Lyttleton said. As he lit his cigar he glanced at the newspaper that lay spread at his friend's feet. The top headlines caught his attention. "It's ghastly about those murders, isn't it?"

Montchalmers nodded. "Yes, yes, terrible."

"And now an innocent child." Lyttleton's stomach turned

whenever he thought of the boy. His note to Dr. Napier had inquired about the expression on the dead child's face. He was convinced that Dr. Napier would be able to determine that, and if it were one of terror, then—no, he refused to think about it yet. "What a terrible shame. You know, Henry, whoever's doing this is an animal." Lyttleton exhaled and a perfect smoke ring sailed over Montchalmers' head.

"The bloody culprit ought to be shot," said a club member who was passing by.

Lyttleton nodded amiably to Christopher Smyth-Fellowes, a portly gentleman of some forty-six years with a large brood: Of ten children, six were sons, five of them under the age of seven. He also had a petite wife, twenty years his junior, who rarely left her rooms, being exhausted from frequent childbirth, and while the Smyth-Fellowes family was, by and large, rather boisterous, Lyttleton knew that both Smyth-Fellowes and his wife were loving parents. "Better yet," Smyth-Fellowes suggested as he draped his arms across the back of Montchalmers' chair, "he ought to be bloody well taken out and dragged behind a coach, then hanged!"

"Hear, hear," another member murmured as he passed the three men.

"Isn't that a bit harsh—" Montchalmers began timidly.

"Harsh?" bellowed Smyth-Fellowes. Montchalmers winced at the blast of sound next to his ear. "I'll give you harsh! I know the family involved, sir, indeed I do, and let me tell you that I've never met a more Christian family in my life, and that boy, an angel compared to my own ruffians, was their only child—the other children having died in early childhood—and his poor grieving parents are in their fifties and not likely to have another chick in their nest! Harsh, sir, what I recommend? Harsh? Not at all!" He harrumphed and glared at the top of Montchalmers' head, as if daring the man to disagree with him again.

Montchalmers had no reply to this.

"I had hoped—as I'm sure we all do—that the deaths might end soon," Lyttleton said. "How long can they go on?"

"It's this damnable hot weather we've been having," Smyth-Fellowes said, making a growling sound in his throat. He had moved around Montchalmers to sit in a chair between the two men. He sighed as he stretched his legs out. "Strangest October weather I've ever seen. The heat brings out the beast, makes men damned crazy. Mark my words, Lyttleton, these terrible deaths will stop once the heat breaks and autumn begins in earnest. Mark my words!"

"I certainly hope you're right, Chris, old fellow, I certainly do."

"It's all the talk wherever one goes," said another member. The gentleman was Felix Andrews, whose youthful daughter Felicia was becoming well-known in social circles for the colorful travelogue on Egypt which she just had published. "One can't escape it. It's in all the clubs, the parties, dinners." Andrews shook his head. "No one talks of anything else. The papers shout it from the front page."

"With good reason," Smyth-Fellowes said, Lyttleton and Andrews nodded agreement. "Makes me damned uncomfortable, goin' about the city now, what with this beast or madman or whatever running amuck—though," he said, lifting a bushy grey eyebrow and eyeing Lyttleton, "I don't know that we old fellers, Felix, have to worry as much as these whelps do."

Amused, Lyttleton stroked his moustache. "Come now, Henry and I didn't get out of short pants yesterday."

Andrews chuckled. "No, you didn't, but then you're near half our age, and that's what seems to get these chaps killed, doesn't it?"

Lyttleton nodded. "I'm afraid so. Men of a certain age—but now a little boy."

"A sad business." Smyth-Fellowes shook his head. "A sad business, indeed."

"I've forbidden my Felicia to go out at all while this is going on," Andrews said. "I won't have her going out and being hurt."

"I don't believe any women have died," Lyttleton said and glanced toward Montchalmers, noting that he looked distinctly uncomfortable with this topic of conversation.

"Damned, if that ain't right," said Smyth-Fellowes, an awed tone to his voice. "Still, I wouldn't put it past this madman—if it is—to try to fool us all into believing he only kills men and boys and then turning around and slaughtering our women like lambs. No, I'll keep mine under lock and key, see if I don't!"

"Excuse me," Montchalmers said suddenly, "but I must be going now. I-I have another appointment."

"Henry, when can we dine together again?" Lyttleton asked as his friend hurried across the room. "It's been a while, after all!"

"I don't know. Maybe soon. Don't ask! I've got to go now," Montchalmers called, and then he was gone.

"In a damned bit of a hurry, what," Smyth-Fellowes rumbled. He glared at the vacant chair. "That's one of the problems with youth nowadays. Always rushing hither and yon for no reason." He subsided into a surly silence.

Andrews and Lyttleton exchanged smiles, but inwardly Lyttleton wasn't amused. Something was definitely wrong with his friend, something connected somehow to the recent deaths. Could Henry have— No, his friend was incapable of that. Or was he? Surely, though, Henry had been with others when those deaths had happened. Certainly that would be easy enough to check.

Or, Lyttleton thought, what if Henry simply knew something about them? That seemed more probable. Particularly if August Hamilton were somehow involved with the deaths. He thought of his suggestion to Napier of an accomplice. Montchalmers and Mrs. Hamilton? Perhaps, and he did not like the idea one bit.

Later, as Lyttleton was leaving the club, his footman John caught up with him.

"Sir, Mr. Edgar sent me with a note for you, sir," the boy managed to gasp. His face was flushed; he'd obviously run most of the way.

Lyttleton took the sealed note, broke it open, and scanned the contents. Dr. Napier reported that the boy who had died the night before did indeed have a look of terror on his face when he died. Death by the same means, whatever that was. First young men, now boys. Why? Numbly he thrust the note into his pocket.

"Sir?" John asked, his round face concerned. "Is there anything more you wish?"

"No," Lyttleton said absently. He started to walk off, then paused. "It's all right, John. Go on home; I won't be needing you now. First, though," he said, reaching into a pocket, "stop by a confectioner's shop." He dropped a coin into John's hand.

Wide-eyed, the young footman stared at the shilling.

"Thank you, sir." Not delaying a moment longer, he rushed off, turning the corner.

His mind blank, Lyttleton began walking in the direction of Eaton Square. Around him the unseasonable heat pulsed and wavered, shimmering off the streets and the buildings. His skin prickled as a long tentacle of sweat ran down his back, and his starched collar scratched his neck; he was most decidedly uncomfortable. When he reached home, he would read and rest for a while, have Edgar prepare a light meal, and perhaps later, after the sun had gone down, he would feel revived.

He began whistling soundlessly and stopped off at a bookseller's to purchase a volume of poems and to browse a little through the dusty shelves. By the time he reached Eaton Square, the shadows stretched long across the street. He trotted up the steps; the door swung open to admit him, and Edgar stepped forward to take his hat and cane.

"A gentleman and a lady inside waiting for you, sir," Edgar said. His expression was of disapproval: Edgar did not like guests; no doubt, Lyttleton thought wryly, his butler would heartily approve of him becoming a hermit. "I sent the boy after you, but you were nowhere to be found." Again disapproval. Edgar always liked to know where his employer could be found.

"I stopped off at Ramsey's for this," Lyttleton said as he handed the book to the servant. Edgar did not spare a glance for the volume. "A gentleman and a lady, you say?" Lyttleton began sorting through the mail waiting for him on the tray in the hallway.

"Yes, sir. They have been waiting for some time. I told them that I did not expect you soon, but the gentleman said it didn't matter. Their names are Captain and Mrs. Grant." Lyttleton looked puzzled, and Edgar elaborated.

"They said they have come in reference to your recent inquiries regarding Lieutenant Hamilton's stay in India."

Lyttleton dropped the letters he had been holding. "Send them into the library at once, Edgar. I'll be there as soon as possible."

"Very well, sir," the butler replied with a slightly disdainful sniff.

Lyttleton went upstairs to wash his face and hands, brushed his hair, glanced at himself in the mirror, then patted his moustache, and went down to the library. He realized he was trembling. He entered, and his visitors stood and turned around to him. They introduced themselves as Malcolm Grant and his wife Emily. Grant declined Lyttleton's offer of a cigar, then came right to the point of his visit.

"I understand, Mr. Lyttleton, that you are desirous of talking to some of Tommy Hamilton's friends."

"I was particularly interested in those who had known him while he served in India."

"Well," said Grant without seeming to boast, "I'm your man. I met Tommy right after he arrived in India, and I probably knew him better than most."

Lyttleton studied the pair. Malcolm Grant, dark-haired and handsome, was in his late twenties, elegantly attired with carefully tended hands. A three-inch-long scar under his left eye lent him a raffish look. His wife, blonde, with brown eyes tinged with green, was most stylishly dressed in a dress of grey linen, the high-necked bodice trimmed in silver braid. She wore white gloves and a fetching straw bonnet, and was in her early twenties.

"How did you hear about my inquiries?"

"Do you know Charles Beck?" Grant asked. Lyttleton nodded. "You'd talked to some lads at the club, and one of them with a long name and a huge family talked to

Beck, who's a friend of mine, and in turn he relayed this to me."

"Good, good," Lyttleton murmured as he stroked his moustache thoughtfully. Grant seemed friendly; perhaps he'd be candid. For some reason the wife acted a trifle nervous. Her eyes shifted about the room, and only once had she met Lyttleton's gaze directly. "You do know that Tommy died some time ago, do you not?" He didn't recall seeing Grant at the funeral, but as the ceremony had been heavily attended and as Lyttleton had been paying little attention to those around him, he could easily have missed him.

"Yes, I heard. I wasn't in London at the time. It was a terrible tragedy. Just terrible."

"Had you seen Tommy since he left India, Captain Grant, or just prior to his departure?" Lyttleton asked, carefully watching the man.

"No. In fact, I hadn't seen him since the uprising two years before. The last time I saw Tommy Hamilton was when we were both in Meerut the day the Mutiny began. We fought together, and then were separated, and after that I didn't see him again. I made inquiries, but couldn't locate him. From time to time after that I would hear rumors that he was in Delhi, but I could never find him when I was there. I suppose he must have been injured or sick at the time. A lot of us were." Unconsciously his fingers touched the scar.

"Did anyone of your acquaintance see Tommy in the two years following the Mutiny?"

"No, Mr. Lyttleton. At least none of the fellows we served with did, or else they would have said something to me."

"Captain Grant, tell me, please, if you can—do you know anything about his widow?"

A surprised look crossed Grant's face. "Tommy married? My God, to whom?"

"He married a woman named August Parrish. Do you know her?"

The surprise changed to recognition and pleasure, a look Lyttleton had seen on other men's faces when August Hamilton's name was mentioned.

"Why, of course, I know the lady. Tommy was courting her before the mutiny. We used to rag him a lot about it, teasing him about being in love and all that, and he took it well, as Tommy did with everything. Miss Parrish—Mrs. Hamilton, I suppose I should call her—lived in Delhi, less than a day's journey from Meerut."

"Where was she when the Mutiny began?" Lyttleton asked. Emily Grant, he noticed, had clasped her hands in her lap and was keeping her eyes down. Her lips were pressed together, and it was obvious she didn't like the topic of conversation.

"Miss Par—Mrs. Hamilton—was in the capital that day, and when we were under seige that terrible day, Tommy was terribly concerned about her and her father. He kept muttering about going to Delhi to make sure they were all right. I lost track of him after that, and didn't know if he'd been injured or captured or simply separated from the rest of us. But, by Jove, he managed to reach her, then." A smile now curved his lips, and he chuckled at a memory. "By gad, he was in love with her! Some days that's all we heard from him. Miss Parrish this and Miss Parrish that, and at first we thought the old boy was exaggerating because no one could be a paragon the way he described her, but then we all finally met her, and we could see that Tommy had been right on the mark. Isn't that smashing, Em?"

Malcolm Grant might think it was an excellent idea that

Tommy Hamilton had married August Parrish, but by Emily's expression she evidently disapproved as highly of the notion as she did her husband's enthusiasm about the person of August Hamilton.

"Did you know the couple, Mrs. Grant?" Lyttleton asked. Grant was obviously too enamored of the memory of August Parrish to be of any real help. He might find out more from the wife.

"I knew Lieutenant Hamilton only in the vaguest sense," Emily Grant replied, "having seen him at several dances and dinners while I was in India. English families tended to stay together there, and so I knew August Parrish somewhat better."

"And?" Lyttleton pressed.

"I did not like the woman." Her mouth was tightly set, and her fingers curled on her lap.

He thought the feeling was stronger than dislike. Hatred, perhaps. Why? What had August Hamilton done to provoke this woman? Had Emily Grant wanted Lieutenant Hamilton for her own, then lost him to a rival? Or could it be something more?

"I see. Is there anything else you can tell me about her? Perhaps where she and her father came from? Their personal background?"

"May I ask why, Mr. Lyttleton?" She stared unflinchingly at him.

"My interest in Mrs. Hamilton may help us trace the illness that finally felled Tommy," Lyttleton replied smoothly. He had already given much thought to his replies if they questioned him. "I and the doctor I am working with have good reason to believe that either he or his wife may have inadvertently brought some unknown disease to this country."

"Are people dying?" Emily Grant asked sharply, glancing sidelong at her husband.

"Yes," Lyttleton said.

"I see."

Lyttleton didn't know quite how to interpret this answer. "Please, Mrs. Grant, if there is anything that you know . . ."

"When I said I knew her better than Lieutenant Hamilton, I did not mean to imply I was an intimate of hers. I think no one was. I never saw her in the daytime, for she always claimed the harsh India sun burned her, and thus she was only social at night. As for her family, I believe her father once mentioned that they had come from the north of India, and before that he had come from England. Supposedly, she was born in India; of her mother I never heard a word. She and her father"—she shook her head—"they were very close, those two, but I'll wager he took more than a fatherly interest in her." Both her husband and Lyttleton looked shocked at this disclosure. There was no irony, though, in Emily Grant's expression or voice. "August Parrish was like a brightly burning light, the men like moths, Mr. Lyttleton. I never saw men behave more foolishly than they did around her. No, Malcolm, please allow me to finish." Her husband had started to protest, but Emily shook her head and continued.

"I left just prior to the Mutiny, Mr. Lyttleton, for my father was wise and heeded the signs of growing unrest, but while I lived there, a number of young men and boys in Delhi—both European and native—died from some mysterious 'ailment' that the doctors were unable to identify. But then the Mutiny broke out, and attention was drawn away from the deaths."

She paused, then resumed, her tone even more curt than before. "Let me just say, Mr. Lyttleton, that where August Parrish is, men die. I have witnessed it before, and now I find she is here in London and men and boys are dying once again."

"Emily," said her husband in a pleading tone. The officer's cheeks were flushed, as though he were acutely embarrassed, but of what, Lyttleton was not sure. Was it because Malcolm Grant knew he had acted foolishly over August Parrish and was now being censured by his previously demure wife?

"Please, Malcolm." She looked at Lyttleton and spoke slowly. "August Hamilton is an evil woman, Mr. Lyttleton. Totally evil and beyond redemption. I suggest that you leave her alone, that you stay far away from her unless you wish to fall under her spell and die, too. My husband was most fortunate, for he had just met her when the Mutiny began and she disappeared from sight. Otherwise, I suspect he would have been fatally mesmerized too." She stood. "Now, if you will excuse me."

Both men stood and watched as she left the room. Lyttleton glanced at Grant, whose face had now turned a dull red.

"I'm sorry, Mr. Lyttleton. Extremely sorry. My wife is—she's highly strung, that is, delicate . . ." He hastened to his feet, nearly knocking a chair over, and backed toward the door. "I'm sorry that we haven't been much help. Good luck in your effort, though." He flashed a smile, then was out the door.

Thoughtfully Lyttleton sat and stared at the painting over the fireplace. Grant thought he and his wife had not been of much use, but they had. Young men and boys, Emily Grant had said, had died previously where August Parrish Hamilton was. Died in India; then died in London. She might be the carrier or the transmitter of some disease. Perhaps, then, she should be informed, or possibly Dr.

Napier and other doctors could study her to see what could be done to prevent further outbreak of the disease.

If it were a disease that was causing the deaths in London.

How curious had been Emily Grant's reaction toward Tommy's widow. Vehemently she had warned him against having anything to do with August. Mrs. Grant had called August evil and beyond redemption. An interesting choice of words. Could Emily Grant be the daughter of a missionary? Was it simply that she thought August was a woman of loose morals? No, he thought it went beyond that. Lady Ashford, as well as her daughter Bethany, had not liked August Hamilton, either. Did no woman like her? Why, when every man was fascinated by her?

Every man except himself.

He had no chance to think further on this, for at that moment a sharp knock sounded on the door, and before he could answer, the door was flung open and Dr. Napier rushed into the room. Behind him stood an irritated-looking Edgar. Lyttleton waved the butler away. Dr. Napier, his face flushed, was slightly out of breath.

"Lyttleton, cancel whatever appointments you have for the next few hours!" he said briskly.

Lyttleton started to rise from behind the desk. "Why? What's the matter, Dr. Napier? Has something happened?" The doctor seemed greatly agitated.

"I've just come from talking with the doctor," Napier said. "The Hamiltons' doctor, that is." He sat heavily in the chair vacated by Grant and drew out a handkerchief to mop his damp face. He shook his head as Lyttleton pointed to a wine decanter. "Dr. Fillowby did *not* examine the body of Tommy Hamilton after his death, Lyttleton. At the request of the widow, the doctor simply signed the death certificate."

A chill touched Lyttleton. "Then that means—"

Napier nodded adamantly. "She lied, damnit, she lied. And thus, we have an appointment this afternoon."

Somewhat overwhelmed, Lyttleton said, "We do?"

"Yes, damnit, I've made all the arrangements necessary, and I'll just need you along as a witness."

"Where are we going?"

"To the cemetery. We're digging up the remains of Lieutenant Hamilton."

Lyttleton watched solemnly as the two burly men hired by Dr. Napier plied their shovels, swinging the loads of dirt up to the sides of the hole that was deepening with each minute.

The light had all but fled the afternoon sky as the workers, Dr. Napier, and Lyttleton arrived at the cemetery where Tommy Hamilton had been buried such a short time before. Evening was approaching, and now, in the grey twilight, a slight wind had sprung up, dispelling the heat of the day and bringing with it the chill and smell of autumn-to-come and the tangy, slightly sour odor of newly overturned dirt.

The workers traded pleasantries between themselves, joking and occasionally laughing, and never missed a stroke of the shovel, while Dr. Napier, and Lyttleton stood to one side. Both men looked glum now that they were at the cemetery. The doctor's excitement had dimmed as the shovels tore up the grass over Tommy's grave, and as the metal ate through the earth the moods of the onlookers became decidedly more subdued. Lyttleton little liked exhuming his friend's body, but no other alternative had offered itself. Even when Dr. Napier examined the body and even if he found the blood gone, what did that prove?

Sighing heavily, Lyttleton glanced at Napier, who was studying the gravediggers. Poor Tommy. He can't even find rest after death, Lyttleton thought, and now here we are about to dig him up and poke through his remains. He shivered, as much from the wind as from what they were doing. He wasn't superstitious, though, and knew they had to do this, but he still didn't like it.

Napier had said nothing to August Hamilton, for he knew she would try to stop him.

In the past few minutes the remaining light had died, and blackness fell across the cemetery. Thick clouds hid the early moon's light, while occasionally streaks of jagged lightning pierced the cloud cover. Off in the distance came a faint rumble of thunder; the air was oppressive, heavy, and Lyttleton wondered if it would rain. Surely, if it did, Napier would call this madness off; they couldn't continue in the rain. Or could they?

One of the workers lit a lantern so that they could continue digging; Dr. Napier lit a second one and placed it atop a flat tombstone. The yellow light cast strange elongated shadows across the ground, shadows that seemed to stretch toward Lyttleton, and he felt his flesh creep. He'd never been in a cemetery at night, and he wished they could have postponed this until daylight, but Napier had insisted that they couldn't delay, even for a few hours. Nearby the low branches of a tree scraped against a tombstone, and Lyttleton's fingers curled at his side.

Dr. Napier caught his eye. "An uncanny place, is it not? It will be our home once we're dead, but we fear and despise it while we're yet alive."

Lyttleton nodded, little cheered by the doctor's words. Shivering, he thought he heard voices in the moaning wind and wished the workmen would hurry. Then Dr. Napier could do what he had to, and after that they could leave this place of the dead.

"How much deeper?" Dr. Napier asked.

" 'Bout a foot, sir, or so," the man said as he swung his shovel over his shoulder. Dr. Napier stepped back just in time to avoid dirt and pebbles raining on his trousers and shoes.

"Here now, Bert, it's less 'n that," the other said.

For a few minutes longer the men dug in silence, then Lyttleton heard metal scraping across wood. "We're down to the coffin, sir," Bert called. Dr. Napier went to the edge of the hole, while Lyttleton stood still. He was reluctant to go closer.

"That's good. Now pry the lid off."

One of the men worked the blade of the shovel under the lip of the coffin and pushed down. The nails in the lid pulled up slightly. When he was tired, the other worker took over.

"Stop it!"

The low voice was angry, and both Napier and Lyttleton whirled around to see August Hamilton standing some feet away from them. A black shawl was draped around her shoulders and her long hair blew wildly in the wind. Her dark eyes seemed to smoulder.

"You must stop this, for it is wrong. It's my husband whom you are disturbing."

"Mrs. Hamilton, please," Dr. Napier said.

She looked at Lyttleton. "How could you allow this? You were his friend."

"I do it precisely because Tommy *was* a friend, Mrs.

Hamilton. We need to know if Tommy died from the same thing that killed the others."

She laughed, a strident sound that rasped Lyttleton's nerves. The two workers gaped at her.

"I hadn't thought you would profane a grave."

"We're not," Dr. Napier said. "We're not profaning your husband's grave, Mrs. Hamilton. It's important that we stop others from dying, and I think your husband would have wanted us to exhume his body."

"My husband wanted many things before he died," she said, looking once again at Lyttleton. For no reason he thought of the note that Tommy had sent hours before his death. "Man dies from the moment of his birth," she said as she came closer and drew her shawl about her shoulders. The yellow light from the lantern cast waxy shadows along the planes of her face. "You cannot do anything about that, Doctor."

"No, but we can stop some from dying."

Lyttleton said nothing, for he was remembering the dreams in which she had appeared. Almost as if she had sensed his thoughts, she curved her moist lips into a smile, and he felt the warmth stirring in his loins. He cursed mildly under his breath.

"You won't stop?" she asked.

"No, Mrs. Hamilton," Dr. Napier said firmly.

"Very well, then," she said, her voice so low they could scarcely hear it. "I warn you now. You will suffer the consequences, gentlemen. Particularly when the deaths do not end."

With those cryptic remarks she turned and left as silently as she had come. Lyttleton thought it odd he hadn't heard the sound of a carriage or horses, but perhaps he'd been too engrossed to mark any unusual noises. Perhaps.

Dr. Napier cleared his throat. "Continue your work."

The scraping continued until finally a worker called that the lid was loose.

"Bring it up," Napier directed. He and Lyttleton backed away as the coffin was lifted up to ground level by the two sweating workmen. With a deep groan each they set their burden down, then looked to Dr. Napier.

He picked up the bag he'd set down earlier and went to the coffin while Bert pushed back the lid and backed away. Lyttleton drew out a handkerchief and pressed it to his face, then looked at what lay in the coffin. He swallowed quickly and closed his eyes, wishing he hadn't looked.

Undisturbed by the effluvium and the unpleasant sight, Dr. Napier knelt and took a surgical knife from the bag. He slit the corpse's collar and directed Lyttleton to hold the lantern above the coffin; then he cut the material around the corpse's groin, then finally pressed the blade into the arm. He pulled back the skin and muscle.

"Take a look, Mr. Lyttleton."

Lyttleton forced himself to open his eyes and stare. The veins were empty. Where blood would normally have cogulated after this length of time, none was there.

"Only residue left, as with the other bodies," Dr. Napier said. He stood, dusted his hands off with a clean linen handkerchief, and put his surgical knife away in his bag. He directed the men to reinter the coffin and to fill in the hole. Once they were finished, the doctor spoke to them in an undertone, then passed an envelope to them which Lyttleton suspected contained money. He and the doctor walked away from the freshly opened grave and paused by the massive gates of the cemetery.

"It all comes back to Mrs. Hamilton, doesn't it?" Lyttleton asked. He wanted away from these eerie grounds.

"I'm afraid so."

"We could go to the authorities," Lyttleton said.

"Yes."

"But she would have to have an accomplice. I know someone who's been acting oddly and who is in her thrall." Dr. Napier did not speak. "My friend Henry Montchalmers. He's been rather strange lately and seems uncomfortable whenever someone mentions the deaths." Lyttleton could well remember how Montchalmers had been that morning at the club.

"Have you seen him within the last day or so?"

"Yes, and he didn't look . . . right."

"Then I think we should pay a call upon him early tomorrow morning. Perhaps, because of friendship, he'll confess to you—if he has anything to confess."

"Perhaps you're right. We can try. I'll come by for you at eight. Is that early enough?" Dr. Napier nodded.

The moon broke through the clouds just as the doctor climbed into the coach. He paused to stare up at the swollen orb. "A new month begins tomorrow."

"November 1," Lyttleton said, having forgotten the date in the midst of everything else.

"All Saint's Day," the doctor said with a faint smile. "All Soul's Eve. The night when the demons and witches mingle with the living. Where I grew up, they believed the dead came back from the grave on this day."

Nervously Lyttleton looked back at the dark cemetery behind them. He climbed into the carriage and closed the door and wished they were back in the city.

"Nonsense, though, eh, Lyttleton?" the doctor said, laughing. "Well, we have a lot to do tomorrow. I don't know about you, but I don't imagine I'll be able to sleep much tonight."

Lyttleton, remembering the look on August Hamilton's face, whispered, "Nor do I." And wondered then how the woman had known to come to the cemetery to find them.

Lyttleton woke to darkness. Had he heard something? A sibilant whisper? Was it his imagination? A dream? He listened intently, and when he heard nothing, he closed his eyes and burrowed deep into sleep, and did not wake when the hand touched his shoulder and drew back the coverlet. Cool lips brushed his mouth, and his eyes opened.

"August."

"Yes." Her hands trailed across his chest, slipped down his arms, caressed his stomach with a fluttering gesture that made him suck in his breath. Her hands hesitated just above his groin.

"I-I didn't think I would see you so soon," he stammered from nervousness and from the sudden arousal of his body.

"Why? Because I was angry with you at the cemetery?" He knew she had tilted her head to one side. "All things pass, my dear, all things of the human body." She kissed his lips again, and he moaned.

"No, please, I don't think that we should." He stopped, tried again. "Mrs. Hamilton."

"August," she murmured, nuzzling against his neck, her tongue tickling the warm skin there.

"August." Heat roiled in his loins and veins, inflaming his long-denied passions, and he wanted her now, without waiting. Horrified at his thoughts, he tried to push her away, but she had the advantage of position as well as having more strength than he would have thought possible, and he was pinned.

Together they rolled across the bed, fighting for domination, and at last he lay back, spent, while she straddled him. He felt her wetness slide across his loins, and he ached as he had never before for any woman. He clutched at her bared breasts, and she leaned forward to brush the crimson tips against his clawing fingers. He cried out as she nipped his chest with her sharp teeth, then dragged her nails down his sides.

He reached up to bring her face down to his so that he could kiss her. Her long hair swept across his face and neck and chest, tickling him, and he wanted her lips on his, and then she lifted her hips just once, then twisted down upon him, and the exploding heat surged through him, rising and rising, destroying his veins, his body, and he screamed out to her. Pain assaulted his neck, his chest, his groin, and he was dying. He cried out and fought against her, trying to push her off his body.

He wanted her away, wanted to live, but she wouldn't move; she kept sucking his life out of him, out and out, and then he was screaming once more as his body shook with tremor after tremor of release, and he was shaking and shaking and someone was calling his name. Through the haze of white heat the pain and the pleasure, he began to breathe deeply, and the heat dimmed, and the passions cooled, and he opened his eyes to see his manservant standing by his bed.

"I'm sorry, sir," Edgar said stolidly, "but you did leave implicit instructions last night for me to awaken you at six, and it is now five past the hour."

Lyttleton blinked as he stared around the darkened chamber. Edgar had not yet opened the drapes. He brushed the damp hair back from his forehead and sat up somewhat unsteadily. The memory of the dream—if it was that—remained. It had seemed so real. He touched his neck and checked his chest. Nothing came away on his fingers. Edgar coughed discreetly and Lyttleton looked up.

"Would you care for breakfast in bed or the other room?"

"The other room, Edgar. Two eggs and a beefsteak, please. I'll be along shortly. I won't take long this morning."

"Very good sir." Edgar nodded and left to make his employer's breakfast.

For a few minutes longer Lyttleton sat in bed, his back propped against his pillow. What must Edgar have thought as he'd entered his employer's bedroom to see a twitching, moaning heap? With little effort Lyttleton relived the dream. She had come to him; she had actually been there. He threw back the covers to look for an imprint of her body, but he found nothing. It was too vivid to have been a dream; he had felt her presence more than ever before. Had felt her physically more, too, and that thought brought a sudden darkening to his cheeks.

There had been such agonizing pain, too, and he did not like pain with his pleasure. He shook his head and eased out of bed, realizing he felt stiff. He washed, dressed, then went to eat his breakfast. He wasn't accustomed to rising at this ungodly early hour, and yawning, he reached for the volume of poetry he'd purchased at the bookseller's.

The book fell open, and he glanced down at the book as he brought a forkful of eggs to his mouth.

" 'O what can ail thee, knight-at-arms,/ So haggard and so woe-begone? . . . I see a lily on thy brow/ With anguish moist and fever dew/ And on thy cheeks a fading rose/ Fast withereth too/ I met a lady in the meads,/ Full beautiful—a faery's child;/ Her hair was long, her foot was light,/ And her eyes were wild.' "

He blindly reached for his tea as he continued to read the poem.

" 'And there she lulléd me asleep,/ And there I dreamed—ah! Woe betide!/ The latest dream I ever dreamed/ On the cold hill side./ I saw pale kings, and princes too,/ Pale warriors, death-pale were they all;/ They cried—"*La Belle Dame sans Merci/* Hath thee in thrall!" ' "

Lyttleton dropped the cup with a clatter. "*La Belle Dame sans Merci,*" he murmured aloud. "The beautiful woman without mercy." His face burned, and momentarily his eyes dimmed, and when they cleared, he read Keats' poem again from beginning to end.

The beautiful woman without mercy. The beautiful woman. Without mercy. Her hair was long; her eyes were wild. August. A faery-woman. A faery-woman of the poem. Or worse. A demon-woman. A woman who came to men, who held them in thrall—he could have laughed, although he knew it would have been a wild, mad sound, but hadn't he used that word before to describe the hold she had over men? Hadn't he? Well, hadn't he? He nodded to himself and found his cheeks were damp. He rubbed at them, then ground the heel of his hands into his eyes.

A demon-woman. A woman who came to men without a sound, as she had come to him. Come to him in his dream, he'd thought so innocently, but it hadn't been a dream. It *had* been real. No dream, but rather a nightmare, a nightmare that could kill.

Yes, he thought, yes, she was the one who killed, who murdered. She had murdered Tommy, and Gerald Ashford, and Timmy Cleveland, and the little seven-year-old boy, and all the others. He didn't know why. Perhaps there was no reason except that she enjoyed it. There were no accomplices; there was just one woman, the demon-woman, who killed, who killed only men. Young men. Healthy men. Strong men. Like the knight of the poem.

And he was in danger, and Dr. Napier was in danger, and Henry Montchalmers was in danger. All men were in danger; he had to warn them.

He stood up abruptly, knocking his chair over. Edgar stepped into the room and looked at him questioningly. Lyttleton rushed past the butler without a word. If he caught a cab now, he would reach Dr. Napier's shortly before eight.

Luck was with him, and within minutes he found a hansom. Once he was at the doctor's house, he knocked on the massive door.

"Mr. Lyttleton to see Dr. Napier," he said, his voice slightly breathless, to the servant who answered. "He's expecting me, and I must see him at once."

"Sir." The servant looked a little flustered. "Sir, please wait."

Lyttleton heard a woman's voice. "Please allow me, Foster."

"Yes, madam." The butler bowed and permitted Lyttleton to enter, then quietly left Helena Napier and Lyttleton alone in the entry hall. The woman had been crying.

Something was wrong, dreadfully wrong, he knew, and his insides seemed to twist. "Mrs. Napier, what's wrong? Where is your husband?"

She put a crumpled handkerchief up to her eyes. "My husband," she said in a choked voice, "died last night, Mr. Lyttleton."

He couldn't believe it. "Dr. Napier died? That's impossible, Mrs. Napier. He was healthy and . . ." His voice faltered.

"I know," she said mournfully.

That was why the man had died, Lyttleton told himself with certainty. The doctor had died because he, like Lyttleton, knew too much about August Hamilton. Had known about her and had intended to do something about her. And so she killed Dr. Napier. Which meant that she had feared Napier, and perhaps feared him.

He guided the woman into a parlor, and once they were seated on a sofa and she had dabbed at her eyes with the handkerchief, he asked, "When did it happen?"

"Shortly before dawn." Her voice was thick with emotion. "He hadn't come to bed all night—I thought he was working, for he often did that—but this morning, before breakfast, Foster found him in his study. He was slumped over his desk. He had been trying to write something, a note, I suppose, w-when he collapsed."

"I'm truly sorry," he murmured, feeling a constriction inside at the loss of the doctor, whom he regarded as a friend.

"We've sent for our own physician, but he hasn't arrived. I fear it must have been his heart, for David had been working so hard lately, working through the night, and running here and there. I don't know what he was working on, for he wouldn't say. He kept telling me, 'All in good time.'" Helena Napier broke down and started sobbing then, and Lyttleton clumsily patted her hand.

"May I see him, Mrs. Napier?" he asked. "To pay my

last respects?" He had to check the doctor's body, had to know for a certainty.

"Yes, of course. Please follow me."

Outside an upstairs bedroom door she paused to look at Lyttleton. "My poor David. I think he must have been in terrible pain before he died."

Lyttleton swallowed heavily and entered behind her. He found Napier's body laid out on a full-sized bed. The servants had washed and dressed him, and all that was needed was the doctor to check the body.

On Napier's grey face was an awful grimace, much like that on Tommy's face when he died.

"Would you mind if I were alone with him for a moment or two, Mrs. Napier?"

Seeing nothing unusual in the request, she nodded and left the room. Lyttleton stared down at the man's contorted face. He wished he didn't feel responsible, but if he hadn't told Dr. Napier about his dreams, the man would doubtless still be alive. He sighed and slipped out a small knife and pushed back the cuff on one of the arms. Then he pressed the knife into the flesh.

Nothing.

He cut deeper. Not even a slight trace of blood. No blood from the cut, he told himself, because there was scarcely any left, and what remained would have settled at the lowest point of the corpse.

The corpse.

Yesterday this had been a living man.

As today he was a living man.

Ashen-faced, his fingers numb, he backed away from the corpse. He closed the bedroom door behind him just as Mrs. Napier reached the landing.

"I'm sorry," he said hurriedly, "but I must leave. I am truly sorry again, Mrs. Napier, for your loss. Please let me know when the funeral will be held." They shook hands and he rushed from the house.

Outside in the hot morning air, Lyttleton took great gulping breaths to help still his fevered thoughts. David Napier had died last night; earlier in the evening he'd joked about All Soul's Eve, the night of the demons and witches, and a demon had claimed the doctor's soul. Lyttleton shuddered. He had to warn others, but who first? Henry? Yes, for he was enamored of her and thus in danger. He had to warn Henry before he died like Tommy, like Gerald, like Napier.

He walked away from the Napier home and did not look back. Why had August killed Tommy? After all, she'd married him . . . or had she? There'd never been any proof of that; they'd had only her word. Obviously, though, she'd needed Tommy to leave India. Perhaps he gave her a name or papers or respectability, but whatever it was, once she was in England, she had no further use for Tommy, and thus he died shortly afterward.

The first of so many to die. Perhaps, he thought grimly, Dr. Napier would be the last. He must do something; he must destroy her. But how did one destroy a demon-woman? Through exorcism? Through the Church? He knew of no other way. But first he had to warn Henry, and he prayed that he would not be too late.

"Mr. Montchalmers is not at home at present," said Xavier, Henry's butler.

Lyttleton paused, momentarily nonplussed. He had confidently expected to find Montchalmers at home, for his friend rarely rose early and even more rarely left his house before eleven, although he did see visitors then. For Henry Montchalmers to be out before ten in the morning was completely unheard-of. Provided, Lyttleton thought, that Montchalmers really wasn't home. What if Henry were actually inside and had instructed his servant to say he was out if Lyttleton called on him?

Impossible, Lyttleton told himself. Impossible, unless August Hamilton held his friend in complete thrall.

"Do you know when he will return?" Lyttleton asked anxiously. It was nearly half past ten, and he needed to talk with Montchalmers as quickly as possible. They had little time left.

"This evening, sir."

"Damn!"

"I beg your pardon, sir?"

"Please tell your employer that I called, Xavier."

"Very good, sir."

Lyttleton turned around and walked away. He would have to wait until evening to return, but in the meantime what was he to do? He could scarcely go home and sit and do nothing and wait complacently as August hunted him down as she had David Napier. He must look for Montchalmers—check at the club, at other favorite spots; perhaps someone might have seen him.

Lyttleton's first stop was the club, where he encountered Christopher Smyth-Fellowes, who greeted him warmly.

"Have you seen Henry Montchalmers today?" Lyttleton asked, somewhat breathlessly.

"That rabbity fellow?" Lyttleton only nodded. "Can't say I have," Smyth-Fellowes replied expansively, "but if I do, I'll tell him that you're—"

"Yes, yes," Lyttleton broke in impatiently. Smyth-Fellowes glared at him. "Thank you, Chris. I apologize for my brusqueness, but it's very important that I find Henry. You might say it's a matter of life and death." He paused, then plunged ahead. "You see, it's about that Hamilton woman."

"August Hamilton?" Smyth-Fellowes lifted an eyebrow.

"Yes, and I think she's the one's been killing our friends off. She has somehow bewitched them—bewitched every man of our acquaintance—until they have no mind of their own; then she seduces them and uses them for God knows what—" Lyttleton stopped. Smyth-Fellowes was looking at him oddly, as were two or three other club members within hearing. "She did in poor Tommy, and Gerald Ashford, and-and . . ."

"You mean to say you're accusing that beautiful and so

charming woman of coldbloodedly murdering half a dozen men?" Smyth-Fellowes demanded.

"Well . . ."

"I think he's gone over completely," Smyth-Fellowes said to the others.

"Yes. Here, now, Lyttleton, you can't go around accusin'—"

The men had started toward him slowly. He backed away.

What a fool he was, Lyttleton told himself. He should have kept his mouth shut, but he'd thought he could warn them before it was too late for them, as it had been for Napier and the others. He should have known that they wouldn't believe him; he should have known.

He turned and bolted for the door. Someone shouted to stop him, but he plowed through the two men who grabbed at him and ran out and down the steps. He didn't look back, even though he heard sounds of pursuit. He kept running and running, dodging through crowds, racing around corners, and finally, when he felt a pain in his side, he slowed to a walk. He glanced back, saw no one chasing him. He was safe for the moment, but he knew they would go to his house, so he couldn't return there. At least not for a while.

Lyttleton continued walking, avoiding anyone he remotely recognized, and finally, late in the afternoon, he arrived at the Hamilton house. For a long time he did nothing more than stand and watch. He saw no signs of activity within. He knocked on the front door and waited, and when no one answered, he knocked again. Finally he went around to the back, where he found a window unlocked. He crawled through it and stood in the kitchen and listened. Absolute silence. The hair along his arms and the back of his neck prickled as he stepped forward. He heard no sounds of servants moving around, and he wondered what she had done to them.

There was no one to be found on the first floor, and after starting up the stairs to the second floor, Lyttleton hesitated. He shouldn't be here. He should be someplace else, trying to hide from her, because he knew she was going to kill him, just as she had killed his friend, just as she had killed Dr. Napier. She would kill him, but she would wait and allow him to anticipate and fear when she would come to him. The beautiful lady without mercy.

Leave, one part of him insisted, and he ignored it, knowing he couldn't leave now. He had to see her. Step by step he ascended, and when he reached the second floor, he turned left toward the master suite. The brass doorknob squeaked briefly as he turned it, and then he pushed open the door. Inside the room the drapes had been pulled shut against the sunlight, and the dimness forced his eyes to adjust; again the air was redolent of that strange scent he had smelled before.

Opposite the door stood a large bed. And it was occupied. Lyttleton moved quietly across the carpeted floor, then paused to look down.

Henry Montchalmers' eyes opened, and for a moment he stared at his friend without recognition; then it came, and he blinked, obviously puzzled.

"W-What are you doing here?" Montchalmers asked, his voice hoarse. His friend had never looked worse, and Lyttleton was reminded strongly of Terris' appearance shortly before his suicide. Shadows that looked puffy and sore to the touch swelled under Henry's eyes, while his skin had paled from lack of sunlight. His hair lay untrimmed and lank, and he was sweating excessively, even though the room was cool.

"I've come to get you, Henry," Lyttleton said as calmly

as he could, but he wondered if it might not be too late for the man. No, it wouldn't be too late until he was dead, and he was determined not to let Henry die.

"Come for me?" Montchalmers was still blinking, as though he couldn't comprehend what his friend was saying. Had he lost his mind? Lyttleton thought.

"What he is saying, Henry dear, is that he wishes to save you from me."

Lyttleton whirled around, and August Hamilton stood inside the doorway. He thought she had never looked more beautiful, more vibrant, more terrifying with her deep red lips and bright eyes than she did now. She seemed to glow, to radiate life, while Henry was fading, his life ebbing.

"Henry, I must speak with you. Alone and at once," Lyttleton said.

"I hide nothing from Mrs. Hamilton," Montchalmers replied, his voice a harsh whisper. "If you must speak to me, speak to me before her." He licked his lips. "Is it true what she says? That you want to save me from my dear one?"

"Yes."

"I want to stay here."

"She'll kill you. The way she killed Tommy, and Terris—though it was by his hand, she forced him to it—and Gerald Ashford, Timmy Cleveland, that seven-year-old boy, and now Dr. Napier. There were many others, too, Henry, men and boys we didn't know. For God's sake, she doesn't love you; she wants to murder you!"

For a moment Lyttleton saw a faint look of desperation in the other's eyes; then it vanished and Montchalmers was shaking his head. "You're wrong, old man. She loves me. She told me. You'll see that everything turns out all right."

"Yes," August said as she glided toward Lyttleton. "Everything always turns out all right, Mr. Lyttleton. You mustn't worry. Soon everything will be fine." She laughed throatily, and the sound chilled him.

"No! You won't take me like the others!" Lyttleton shouted, and jumping forward, he thrust her away from him. She stumbled backward momentarily, and that gave him the time he needed. He ran down the hall, took the stairs three at a time, raced to the front door, unlocked it, and stumbled outside into the lengthening shadows of evening.

Blindly he ran until he had no breath left, and he bent over from the pain in his chest and side, and only then did he pause. He had done nothing to stop her, had done nothing to save his friend, and he could have wept at his ineffectualness.

He didn't know where to go; he didn't have any place to go; no friends were left; the club members were looking for him and would have him committed.

There was only home.

He looked around to get his bearing and began walking. When he reached the house in Eaton Square, Edgar greeted him with surprise.

"A number of gentlemen have been asking for you all day, sir—"

Lyttleton, ignoring him, went straight upstairs and pulled down a valise from the wardrobe and began tossing clothes and personal items in it. He would go to the house in the country. No, she would find him there. Instead, he would go elsewhere; he would go to . . . to . . . to Brighton. He would hide among the crowds, for surely no one would look there.

"I've heard that Brighton is lovely at this time of the year."

He pivoted slowly. August stood a few feet behind him, and he had not heard the door open.

"Come, my dear, why do you resist me so? Am I not beautiful? Would you not wish our friendship to become more intimate?"

"Get away from me." He took a step backward.

"I won't hurt you."

"Is that what you told Tommy and the others?"

She shook her head. "They were weak men, each one of them. So very unlike you, my dear."

Frantically he looked around for a weapon. All he saw was his grandmother's cross on the wall above the bed. He leaped onto the bed, snatched the cross down, and climbing down, he held the crucifix in front of him with trembling hands as she came nearer.

She laughed, and when she was close enough for him to feel her cold breath upon his face, she stopped.

"These feeble objects," she said as she took the cross from his numb fingers, "hold no power, especially if you do not believe." Her tongue darted out to lick her lips, and he stared at the moist redness. "You're very special to me."

"How?" He could retreat no farther, for the bed was behind him.

"Because you know what I am. You may not know the name, but you know in here." A long finger tapped his chest. "There is a bond between us, one that exists with no one else, and that is why I have saved you for the last." She smiled, and he thought how hideous were her white teeth and red lips. How could he ever have believed she was beautiful? She was a hideous mockery of woman. A demon-woman without mercy.

"An interesting poem," she said, although he hadn't spoken aloud. "Keats. A silly romantic, as are all poets, I fear. Always wishing to die from love and then screaming their regrets when their wishes are fulfilled."

She draped her arms around his neck, and they seemed to burn into his skin. "I won't take you now, my dear," she murmured. "Not yet. No, for you will find that I am patient. Sooner or later I will have you, whether you want it or not. But only after you know." She bent forward, and she kissed him on the lips, and her breath smelled of the grave.

He cried out at the icy kiss and tried to rub the fetid touch of her from him. She laughed cruelly, and as he watched, a dark fog smelling of musk and sandalwood swirled around his feet. He leaped onto the bed to avoid it, fearing what it might do, and again he heard her laugh. Then the mist billowed upward, enveloping him, and he screamed silently, lost to the world.

When Lyttleton awoke much later, he was alone and it was daylight. For a moment he lay there, then rose and dressed mechanically, and without a word to Edgar, left. At Montchalmers' house Xavier answered the door again.

"I am sorry, sir, but Mr. Montchalmers passed away yesterday evening."

Lyttleton could find nothing to say.

He lurched away from Henry's house, grief numbing him, and he walked slowly home. He should not have been surprised; yet he had hoped that somehow Henry could have escaped her. But there was no escape. Yet there had to be. Somehow. Somewhere. When he reached his house, he went to his study and sat. He did not move, did not answer when Edgar came in, and when the light was fading from the sky, he shuddered.

There was only one way to protect himself. He would find a sanctuary.

He picked up his packed valise and left, walked through

the streets of London until he found the street he wanted. At the end stood a massive brick building. For many minutes he stared up at its spires; then he went inside the church.

He would believe. And she would not be able to reach him.

The priest turned to him as he approached and smiled. "Yes, my son?"

"Father, help me, for I wish to enter the priesthood."

PART III

Savannah, Georgia: 1889

He fled.
Father Danicl admitted it freely, for there was no other way to describe his abrupt leave-taking just hours ago when August Justinian had approached him, when his memory had returned, when he'd remembered what she had said to him thirty years before. *There is a bond between us, . . . and that is why I have saved you for the last. You'll find that I am a patient woman. Sooner or later I will have you, whether you want it or not.* Those were the words of August Hamilton, as she had been called then, that night, November 1, 1859, the day before he learned of Henry's death, the night after Dr. Napier's death. He had fled then to save his life, and tonight he had fled again.

But he didn't know if fleeing this time would save his life. He had run away before, but hadn't she found him after all this time?

Surely, it was coincidence, he told himself. Surely. But he knew it wasn't.

Nothing that had happened to him was coincidence.

Certainly not his having forgotten August Hamilton—Justinian, he corrected. Perhaps he had forced himself to forget, or perhaps, and this seemed far more likely, she had had a hand in it.

Daniel felt chilled to the bone. One moment his life had been secure; the next his entire existence became precarious and uncertain. He wanted nothing more than to turn tail and run away from Savannah, away from her. But he couldn't, not this time. This time he had responsibilities, and besides, hadn't she proved that fleeing was futile?

Thus he would have to stay; he would have to face her as he had not done thirty years before. This time he was fortified, though, with the strength of his faith. His faith would protect him.

He almost laughed aloud. Whom had he been fooling?

And so what would he do now? he asked himself as he paced around his small, sparsely furnished room. Would he wait to act until August appeared to him in a dream later tonight—when he finally had the courage to go to bed? Would he simply sit idle until she came to claim him?

Perhaps, he thought somewhat wildly as he glanced into the oval mirror that hung over the washstand, she wouldn't come after him. He was no longer a young man. Thirty years ago he might have proved attractive to her, but not now. While he was still healthy and lean, he was nearly sixty. There were lines in his face that hadn't been there, creases around his eyes that had appeared in the last few years, and grey tinged his temples. Surely she wouldn't want him.

He remembered how she had looked at him earlier, and was no longer sure of that.

There was a knock on the door. He hesitated, then went

to answer it. August would not have used the door, he knew.

It was his nephew.

In appearance Guy reminded him of himself when he was that age, for the young man had the same dark hair and eyes as Daniel and Sophie, his only sister, as well as the same lean face and finely boned hands, but there the resemblance ended, being simply physical. Guy had a single-minded purpose to his life. As long as Daniel could recall, his nephew had wanted to be a doctor. Doctor . . . he suddenly remembered Dr. Napier. After all the years he couldn't recall the details of his voice and face, only his manner.

Guy had never cared for poetry or music, as had Daniel. He wanted to learn medicine, and only that, and its pursuit consumed his entire life. He'd earned his medical degree at twenty-two and had gone on to his first appointment in New York City, where Sophie lived. Later he'd gone to Philadelphia, then south to Savannah. It had been coincidence that once Daniel left England for America, he had been sent to Savannah.

"Ah, Father Flirtation," Guy said, chuckling as he settled in one of the two chairs in the room, "I was quite amazed tonight. You made a remarkable conquest and are the envy of all the men in Savannah." He arched an eyebrow and waited for Daniel's usual flippant reply.

None was forthcoming. All traces of the older man's good humor had fled at the recognition of August Hamilton. Justinian, Daniel reminded himself, and he wondered with ill ease how *that* husband had died.

Guy's face took on a look of surprise as the other man kept his silence. "You're sombre tonight. Is anything wrong?" He frowned slightly. "Did you leave early? I don't remember seeing you after ten."

Daniel nodded. "Yes . . . I wasn't feeling well, so I left." A small white lie, and he reminded himself to attend confession. On the other hand, he hadn't felt well when he recognized her, so it wasn't strictly a lie.

"Perhaps it's the heat," Guy suggested. "A number of my patients have been affected by it."

"Perhaps."

"Is there something troubling you, Daniel? You seem so quiet tonight."

Daniel shook his head. "No, Guy. I'll just go to bed soon, and I'm sure I'll be fine in the morning. There's something I'd like to tell you, but not until I'm sure."

"Sure?"

"Yes." He was unwilling to elaborate. "I trust you had a good time tonight. I've never seen you more social before."

"Sometimes you have to get away from your work."

"Yes." Daniel folded his hands in his lap. "Dr. O'Shaunessey left rather early tonight."

"I believe she has a lot of work in the morning," Guy replied neutrally.

Daniel frowned, for that response wasn't like Guy. Normally, he would have been concerned about Rose leaving by herself. But then, at the party his behavior had not been usual.

"She's beautiful, isn't she?"

"What?" He hadn't been paying attention and didn't know what Guy was talking about. But, of course, he really did.

"Mrs. Justinian. She's beautiful, isn't she?"

"Yes, quite."

"You sound as if you don't like her."

"I do?"

"Have you met her before? I thought you said something about knowing her a long time ago or about her reminding you of someone from the past."

"Er, I don't recall, Guy. I'd have to give it more thought, I think." He knew his nephew didn't believe him, but he could say no more at the present. He remembered how Christopher Smyth-Fellowes had acted when he tried to tell him how evil August was.

"All the rage of Savannah in a matter of weeks," Guy said. "It's a shame she's been widowed so young."

Daniel did not smile, even though he knew that the woman was not young; hadn't been young even when he had known her thirty years before. He didn't like Guy's preoccupation with her, for he feared it would have disastrous consequences, and having lost friends to August, he didn't want to lose his only nephew.

"Why don't you go visit your mother?" Daniel suggested suddenly.

"What? Why? Is she ill?" Guy asked.

"Ill? No, I don't believe so, but it has been some time since you were in New York. I have a letter here from her someplace." He was searching through the papers and bundles that cluttered the pigeonholes and top of his desk. "I know she wrote to say that she missed you. I know it's here," he said, half to himself.

Guy laughed, not unkindly. "You know Mother. She would miss me if I lived on the next street and hadn't seen her for two days."

"Well, you're all that she has left."

"I know. I'll go back sometime soon."

That wasn't good enough for Daniel. He wanted Guy to leave as soon as possible and to stay as long as August was going to be in Savannah. He wanted his nephew well away from her.

Because you want her for yourself? One part of him asked snidely.

Daniel was horrified. Good God, no. The thought hadn't crossed his mind. Or had it? He realized Guy was watching him with a slightly puzzled look.

"You could take Rose with you," Daniel said.

Guy laughed again. "You're determined that we're going to marry, aren't you?"

Daniel smiled. "Yes. You know my opinion on that matter, Guy. I like Rose a lot and think you two would do well together."

"Perhaps." Guy roused himself. "The real purpose of my visit tonight, though, Daniel, is to invite you to dine with me tomorrow night."

"Will Rose be there?" Guy nodded. "Then I would be delighted."

They chatted for a while about current gossip and the unseasonably hot weather; then Guy said he must leave, and as his nephew prepared to do so, Daniel realized he wanted him to stay. As long as Guy was here with him, he wouldn't sleep and the night phantoms would be banished. Foolish, he said to himself. He had to face them sometime.

Finally, Guy would delay no longer, and after arranging a time for dinner, he left. Alone, Daniel looked at his old clock, a castoff from one of the wealthier parishioners. Nearly one. He had to go to bed, had to get some rest.

Reluctantly he did so, and crawled in, although he did not pull the covers up because of the heat. He lay there, rigid, his eyes open, and waited. Nothing happened, except that after a while his eyelids grew heavy, then closed, and he slowly drifted to sleep. He slept the night through without any dreams.

Dr. Rose O'Shaunessey unbuttoned the cuffs on the long sleeves of her bodice and carefully rolled them up to above her elbows. One of her coworkers raised an outraged eyebrow and looked away. Convention and propriety be damned, she thought sourly. She was hot and sweaty, and the material held the heat, as well as getting into the way. Men had coats that they could remove, collars to loosen, sleeves to roll up. Women did not. She reached for a simple handkerchief and blotted it against her face, feeling the moisture soak into the material.

She was not yet accustomed to southern hot weather, although all the natives of Savannah she'd talked with were quick to point out that this type of weather this late in the year was unusual. Nonetheless, she was accustomed to a different sort of heat, being born and bred in Boston. The heat in Boston's summers had never left her feeling as languid as she felt here. She sighed, pushed away a damp strand of hair and picked up her pen, forcing herself to concentrate on what she was writing.

The daughter and youngest child of a husky, good-natured Irish merchantman, Rose had been reared by a fiercely religious mother who had strictly raised—mostly alone, because her husband was out roaming the seas for a good part of each year—her seven surviving sons and single daughter to follow the Ten Commandments and to love their country, God, and the Pope, although not necessarily in that order. Above all, she hoped to instill in them a reverence for the Mother Church. Molly O'Shaunessey had pledged her one daughter Rose and one son to the Church, and it had been the most sorrowful day in her life, so she informed each member of her family who would listen, when Rose showed no inclination toward the life of a religious. Had she been less strong-willed, Rose might have allowed herself to be pushed in that direction by the pitiful pleadings of her heartbroken mother and the adamant prayers of the family priest.

But she didn't. Instead, at an early age she'd shown a most unladylike tendency to want to know the "why" of things, as well as a passion for ministering to birds with broken wings and cats and dogs with injured paws and tails. Perversely, while Mrs. O'Shaunessey frowned on her daughter's fascination with facts, Mr. O'Shaunessey was delighted by his daughter's yearning for knowledge and had further kindled it by bringing her numerous books as presents from his sea journeys.

Mrs. O'Shaunessey, disapproving of the practice, tried to take the books away—just once, when Rose was sixteen. Rose held onto the disputed volume and calmly informed her parent that she wasn't about to give up her books, and if her mother forced her to, then she would leave the house that instant and become a Protestant. After that her mother left her alone. At least Mrs. O'Shaunessey didn't try physically to force her daughter to do her will; instead, she worked on another approach—the spiritual. Molly O'Shaunessey's prayers were filled constantly with biddings unto the Lord to bring "a fine husband" for her daughter so that she would forget these unnatural ways.

A husband hadn't come, for Rose had shunned all social functions in order to study. She wanted to continue her schooling past high school. Her brothers were flabbergasted by this seriousness in a girl; her father was pleased, for no one else in his family had been so bookish; her mother crept off to her room to cry and say the Rosary.

When just nineteen, she applied to the Boston University School of Medicine, was accepted and began working on her medical degree. After graduation she worked for a while in the Boston slums, the only position available to a woman doctor, then heard of a job down south in Savannah. Wishing to travel, she decided she would apply for the position of physician at the hospital. At the age of twenty-four, she was accepted.

She had few women doctors of her acquaintance, as only one other had been in the Boston medical school, and while she hadn't been readily accepted in the North, there'd been little active resistance toward her. The South was altogether different. Here, of course, the concept of the lady continued, even a generation after the Civil War, or as the southerners termed it, the War Between the States. In Savannah she was regarded with general bemusement. Why, after all, would a lady wish to dirty her hands as well as tend sick people who were not her relatives? Rose kept insisting she wasn't a lady. That brought icily lifted eyebrows in response.

There was also the question of her being a Yankee. She frankly didn't know which was more damning in the eyes of the southerners: her being a woman doctor or a northerner, but she rather suspected it was the latter.

She wanted to stay, too, for she enjoyed her work. Working there provided her with a day-to-day challenge, and she liked Savannah, finding it a beautiful city, fortunately preserved from Sherman's burning of Georgia, and she was interested in the unusual scenery, the marshes and pine forests. Too, there was a different mixture of people here than in Boston.

And, of course, there was Guy Maxwell.

Rose closed her eyes briefly at the thought of her fellow doctor. Never had she met a male colleague so supportive of her, and perhaps she had let his friendly manner and his ready acceptance of her go to her head. Within days of meeting him she began daydreaming about him; then he started making nightly appearances in her dreams, the nature of which would have shocked her mother greatly.

But soon it was apparent that she wasn't the only one suffering from this malaise of the heart. The two doctors talked while they worked, once they met for dinner, and then late one pleasant summer's night they'd gone for a walk in Forsyth Park. They had stopped by an immense live oak, embraced, and not long after that became lovers. Discreet lovers as well, for they roomed at separate boarding houses, and doubtless the medical board would have fired both of them—or at least her, she recognized wryly—if word of their affair reached anyone else.

She suspected that Guy's uncle, Father Daniel, knew about their affair, but instead of being censorious, he seemed to approve. She liked him a lot, finding him extraordinarily different from the priests she'd known in Boston.

And since she and Guy had become lovers, his free time had been only for her. Until now. Until that other woman had appeared in Savannah. Rose narrowed her eyes as she recalled how Guy had acted at the party the night before.

He had neglected her, acted almost as though they didn't know one another. On the other hand, Father Daniel had been kind, no doubt feeling sorry for her, but she didn't want that. She wanted no one's sympathy.

Well, perhaps this August Justinian was simply a passing fancy. She fervently hoped so.

Rose sighed again. She'd best push these thoughts from her head or she wouldn't be able to finish her report in time. She completed the sentence and glanced over what she had written earlier. She was preparing the report for Dr. Fredericks to take a look at. While she usually did not lack for work, she did notice that she tended to receive fewer assignments than the male doctors or else she was given those that appealed to no one; consequently, she had more free time to study the latest medical developments and to investigate other areas in the field. Something that had come to her attention this past week was a sharp increase in deaths.

Most of the dead had been black youths, and she thought their deaths could be traced to the high temperatures the city had had the past ten days. Exhaustion, heat stroke, there could be any number of reasons. The boys' employers had reported some lassitude preceding their deaths, but she tended to be faintly skeptical about that, for the white bosses always complained of the laziness of their black workers, whether it was summer or winter.

She'd been allowed to examine only one dead man, for the rest had been buried already with no doctor's examination. The one she had seen had had two small areas of rash on his body, around the throat and the groin, and—astonishingly—only slight traces of blood. She'd looked for wounds that could have bled profusely, but had found nothing beyond the rash. There had also been the expression on the young man's face—one of horror, as though he had suffered greatly prior to death.

At that moment Guy entered the common room of the hospital where she sat and approached her.

"Hello."

She smiled confidently, although she felt a little uncertain. He *seemed* friendly enough. "Good morning, Dr. Maxwell."

They were so formal toward one another in public, as the dictates of society demanded. She deplored it as much as he did, but for a while they had no choice. But for a while . . . how long was that? When would it change? She had no idea.

"Working on your report, Dr. O'Shaunessey?" he asked, indicating the papers strewn across the desk. She was always methodical, if not precisely neat.

She nodded. "Finished it just before you came in. Would you care to look it over?"

"Certainly." He sat on the edge of the desk, picked it up in the fine hands she admired so much, and read through it slowly.

She sat back and watched him. Even at this early hour tiny beads of sweat trickled down the sides of his face into his dark sideburns, and a slight frown of concentration was fixed on his face. He wasn't precisely handsome, not in the traditional sense, she thought, but his face was strong with its aquiline nose, high cheekbones, and pointed chin. Almost a devilish sort of a face, she thought with amusement, and realized her mother would have crossed herself and uttered a prayer under the same circumstances. Under the same circumstances? Her mother wouldn't be here, she told herself wryly.

"Excellent, Rose."

"Thank you, Guy, I was about to take it in to Dr.

Fredericks. I certainly hope he likes it. Would you like to come with me?"

"Sure."

She gathered the papers, and they walked down the hall. They could hear the cries of the sick in the wards. There were others, too, waiting outside to be treated—most of them suffering from the heat. There was little the doctors could do except tell them to stay out of the sun and to rest as often as possible.

Dr. Fredericks was in his office, as Rose knew he would be, and was not too busy to see two of his staff doctors. When Rose handed him her report, he raised his eyebrows.

"What's this, Doctor?"

Dr. Fredericks had not been the man who hired her. His predecessor had been. Shortly after she had arrived in Savannah, the other doctor had died, and Dr. Fredericks, his assistant, had been promoted to the position by the medical board. She and the older man had an uneasy truce, and she thought it would take very little for him to fire her. So far she had treaded fairly carefully. She would like to be in the position for at least a year before being fired.

"Certain of my observations of the past week," she said. "I thought you'd like to see them."

"I see, Doctor." He was a native of the city and had a Geechee flavor to his faint southern drawl, not at all unpleasant. He tapped his fingers on the papers. "Well, I'll try to find time to read it this afternoon or possibly this evening."

"I think you should read it now," Guy said quietly. "It's very important, Dr. Fredericks, that you not delay reading it. There are several points that need to be brought to your attention."

"I see." The administrator glanced at them, then pressed his lips together as he pushed his glasses back on his nose.

Rose thought it was obvious what he was thinking. They were both Yankees, interfering with what they didn't know and didn't understand, and she was a woman, to boot. She almost smiled, but managed to hide it with a hand to her mouth as she pretended to cough. Fredericks began reading the report. At the end of the first page, he looked up. "This is concerning a Negro boy, Doctor."

"Yes, sir." She met his gaze and did not waver. He dropped his and continued to read.

After that it did not take him long to finish it. He leaned back in his chair. "I will take this under consideration, Dr. O'Shaunessey."

"Dr. Fredericks," she said, "as you know, I am not given as many cases as the other doctors—"

"Doctor, we have gone over this time after time," Fredericks said.

"Yes, sir, and this time I'm not complaining."

"You're not?" He sounded surprised.

"No, sir. Because this time, if I can pursue this matter, then my fewer cases won't matter."

"I see. Hmmm. Might this not be a matter for the colored hospital?"

"Yes, sir, I've thought about that. But I am interested in it."

He glanced at her. Disgusting Yankee ways, he thought, no doubt. A white woman . . . "Well, I will think about it."

"But—"

"Dr. Maxwell, Dr. O'Shaunessey," Dr. Fredericks said with a heavy sigh. "It is scarcely ten o'clock in the morning and already it's well over ninety degrees. I have patients waiting, as do you. I will consider this matter, but I am not promising anything." He heaved himself to his feet. "I will see you later."

They stood up and left his office.

"Old fool," she muttered angrily under her breath and glared at the closed door.

"Here, here," Guy said, putting his arm around her lightly. It was too hot for much contact.

"I should have let you present the report to him, Guy. He would have listened to you. No, that wouldn't have been right. It was mine, after all."

He grinned down at her. "Feeling discouraged?"

"Yes, and no."

"Good, that's healthy. Now I think we ought to be getting to work. You know I'll help you however I can."

She smiled slyly. "I do like you, Doctor. You have an evil mind."

Guy bent down to lightly kiss her on the lips. "I try." He straightened. "And speaking of trying, I'm having dinner with my uncle tonight and said you would be coming. Will you?"

"I'd love it."

"Good, it's settled then."

They kissed again, and as they left the office, Rose breathed a sigh of relief that Guy was restored to his old self.

Factor's Row.

Not really a street, but more a cobblestoned walk a level above River Street, built on the bluff overlooking the Savannah River, and a level below Bay Street. The cotton warehouses, five stories high, fronted River Street, but could also be entered from Bay Street on wrought-iron walks as well as from the narrow, dark Factor's Row.

Before the Civil War, River Street and Factor's Row had bustled day and night with the activity that made Savannah the leader in cotton exports; now, many of the warehouses stood empty, neglected, with broken and boarded-over windows, while Factor's Row, with its recessed doorways and the old bridges spanning it, lay completely in shadow. The cobblestones had been the ballast stones of European ships. Once thrown into the river, the stones had formed shoals along the river, though, and so that practice had been discontinued. Ramps laid with the ballast stones led from Bay Street down to Factor's Row, then curved down to River Street.

It was not a well-lit area, and respectable people disdained it, for it was the haunt of derelicts and sailors and those who had no other place to go.

On this hot night in September Factor's Row was even darker than usual, and more silent, the only sounds coming from two strolling sailors who sang in their inebriated state, and in the distance sounded the resonance of a ship's horn. A thick mist rose from the river, blanketing the dockside street, muffling the footsteps of anyone out. The light of the few gas lamps glowed yellow and faint through the fog. After the sailors left, heading toward the heart of the city, the silence deepened.

The silence continued until it was broken by hesitant footsteps.

A shadow slipped away from a doorway. Ahead, a young man who had wandered into Factor's Row was lost. He had left his ship, had a few drinks, and now was trying to find his way back to the dock. He knew this wasn't it, but he wasn't sure where to look.

Behind him he heard the whisper of cloth. He turned and peered back into the white gloom, but could see nothing. Probably a cat or dog, he told himself and shrugged.

He walked on, stumbled over a loose stone, and heard faint laughter. Again, he looked back over his shoulder; again, he saw no one.

"Who's there?" he called.

Silence met his words.

"I hear you," he said. "I hear your breathing." What he heard was his own rapid, fear-induced breath, harsh in his ears. "Stop it!"

Again, silence.

His pace quickened; he stumbled once more, fell, flinging

his arms out so that he landed on his palms. He scrambled to his feet, nursed his scraped hands.

The whisper of cloth.

His eyes were wide and fearful, and a low whimper had started in his throat. He ran now, ran blindly in the fog. Something dark loomed out of the mist, and he cried out as he slammed into it. It was a wall. He slid down to the cobblestones, feeling the blood trickle from the lacerations on his face.

"Poor dear," said a soft voice out of the darkness.

The sailor looked up. "Who's there?" He could hardly move and had just managed to get into a sitting position with his back to the wall. He was stiff everywhere, and his head throbbed from where he had knocked it against the wall.

"I am," said the woman as she knelt before him. She took his bruised hands in her own cool ones and turned them palm up. She bent down as if to kiss them, and he could feel the velvet touch of her tongue against the torn skin as she licked the blood away. He cried out once in pain, but realized after a while that the pain was subsiding and his hands were feeling better. His head lolled back as the waves of pleasure swept up from his hands to his chest, then down to his groin.

Her hands were inside his shirt now, kneading the flesh there, pressing it with her nails, and he groaned, but not from pain this time. He tried to discern the details of her face, but all he saw was the black hair and the white face, and in it the dark eyes that drew him to her.

She was loosening his pants now, and he sucked in a breath as her fingers caressed his genitals. He tried to lift his arms to put them around her, but they weighed so much that he couldn't. He opened his mouth, and she kissed him, jabbing her tongue against his. Then she was crouching above him, and he could smell the muskiness, feel the soft downy hair tickle him, the wetness that told him she was ready for him, and she was pushing down on him, and down and down—

And he screamed silently in agony as red-hot pain, worse than any he had ever felt, exploded in his throat and groin. He could feel his blood being drained, could feel the life fading, could feel all of it leaving his veins, draining, until there was nothing left but a husk, a dried-out husk, nothing but—

She laughed as his cooling body toppled to one side. It would be so easy to dispose of this one. He would roll easily down to the river; with one final push he would be gone. They would not find this one.

And then she would bide her time.

Father Daniel dined with his nephew and with Rose, and enjoyed himself thoroughly, and when they were finished, he returned home.

He paced restlessly in his room, again fearing to sleep. He had to, but . . . what if she came? He walked and walked and prayed, and finally, in the early hours of morning, he slept.

When he woke, stiff and tired, he knew that he had one thing to accomplish today.

Once he was finished making sure the boys in the home were all right, he went about paying visits to various parishioners who had recently promised to pledge money to the boys' home. He had a second reason for going. He was seeking information about August Justinian, and he knew that, Savannah society being as tightly knit as it was, he would soon learn all he wanted about her.

He was correct.

She lived not far from the city on a small island in the

Savannah river and was the recent widow of a wealthy Georgia planter, Hugh Justinian. The man had been relatively young when he married the woman, whom he met while traveling, and he had returned home sick, then had died a week later.

Dismayed, Father Daniel realized the terrible pattern was repeating itself. Always a recent widow, he thought with a shudder. He also discovered that his woman parishioners disliked her as intensely as most men liked her. That, too, was familiar. She had been content to stay in mourning, but had been urged by her acquaintances and her husband's friends not to shut herself away and to come to a few limited social functions. No one knew what she planned to do after this.

This information did not cheer him, and he returned to the boys' home somewhat absentminded. When he could, he returned home and sank down on his knees and stared up at the crucifix on the wall.

The waiting was unbearable. He knew she was waiting, and he knew that she knew he would be aware of it and would be tortured by it.

Let it be done! he cried out silently, but knew he didn't want her to come to him.

The next night the dreams began, and each time he sank into sleep and the dream began, he woke up screaming. He wrapped his rosary around his hand, kissed the cross, and went back to sleep; he was not further disturbed that night.

But he knew the dreams would return, and she would be stronger the next time.

The confessional was dark and smelled of dust and sweat and old sin.

Daniel waited for the other priest to enter the confessional, then bowed his head. He had been too ashamed to go to his own church, St. Patrick's, and too intimidated to go to the Cathedral of St. John the Baptist, so he had walked to the southeastern section of town to the parish of the Church of the Sacred Heart. He knew none of the priests here.

The small door slid back to expose the grille.

"Bless me, Father, for I have sinned," Daniel said, his voice scarcely louder than a whisper. "It has been one week since my last confession. I have committed the following sins. I have had impure thoughts. This I have done three times." He knew it was more frequent, but could not bring himself to admit that. He was so ashamed; he had never confessed to impure thoughts before. "For these and all the sins of my past life, especially these sins against purity, I am heartily sorry." His confessor would never know how sorry he was for his present sins and his past—all of them, he realized bleakly, which could be traced to August.

"Are these impure thoughts directed in general to all women or to a specific woman?"

"To a specific woman, Father."

"Then do not see her again, and if you cannot avoid seeing her, then see her in the presence of someone else."

That, Daniel knew, would be of little help.

"You must say the Act of Contrition now."

"O my God, I am heartily sorry for offending thee, and detest all my sins because of thy just punishments, but most of all because they offend thee, my God, who art all-good and all-deserving of my love. I firmly resolve with the help of thy grace to sin no more and to avoid the near occasions of sin."

Daniel listened as the priest gave him absolution and assigned his penance: He must go on a fast, say six Hail Marys, and say a novena to St. Joseph. Daniel nodded, even though he knew the priest couldn't see.

"Go in peace," the priest murmured.

When Father Daniel left the Church of the Sacred Heart, he did not feel satisfied. His sin had not been purged as he had hoped, as he had needed. His sin would remain as long as August Justinian remained in Savannah.

Perhaps if he fasted as the priest had suggested . . . perhaps if he denied his body enough, the dreams would stop. He almost smiled at that.

That first night of his fast he didn't dream, and when he woke in the morning, he was relieved. But as afternoon came, he began to dread the night, dread it because he knew with a certainty that he would dream again. The fast hadn't kept him from dreaming.

August was toying with him, and he could have sobbed with frustration. Instead, he went in to check on the boys at St. Mary's. The dormitory contained about twenty beds, and the older boys and younger ones slept there. At the end of his bed each boy kept a trunk with his belongings, for the most part donated by members of the parish, and next to each bed was a desk so that the boy could do his schoolwork.

The windows were high—the better to keep the boys from climbing out on one of their escapades—and they were open. A slight breeze wafted in to stir the stifling air.

One of his favorite boys, William, a twelve-year-old with big brown eyes and dark blond hair, was busy with his schoolwork.

"And how are you today, William?"

"Oh, Father." The boy scrambled to his feet. "Very well, sir. I'm doing my mathematics." He made a face. "Sister Agatha's favorite subject."

"Yes, I know," Father Daniel said. He was well acquainted with the stern Sister Agatha, who cared more for numbers than her God, or so he secretly believed. Oh dear, he thought suddenly, and knew he would have to add this to his already-lengthening list of sins for his next confession.

"Are you ill, Father?" William asked, staring up at the older man.

"I'm fine, lad, just fine. It's the heat, as I'm sure you know." The boy nodded. "Well, continue." The boy smiled shyly at him and sat down once more.

Father Daniel moved away and chatted with each of the boys: Peter, the two Michaels, the three Johns, and all the other boys.

At the end of the dormitory he glanced back. William was still working, and some of the little boys were pretending to do the same, although he knew very well they weren't. He smiled, feeling very good for the first time in a long time, and left.

All he needed was some rest, he told himself, and for the heat to break. That was all.

By week's end the unseasonable heat wave still held Savannah in its grip.

Guy, coming to visit his uncle early one morning before the heat became too unbearable, was appalled when his uncle opened the door to admit him.

"My God," he said after he was seated, "what's happened to you?"

Daniel frowned. "What do you mean? And good day to you, too, Guy."

Guy stared at him. "You look as though you've aged ten years! Are you ill?" He peered in what his uncle called his medical way.

"No, it's just the heat," Daniel said.

"God, the heat, I know. Are you sleeping well, Daniel?"

Father Daniel shook his head. He had been shocked to see his haggard appearance just that morning in the mirror. Surely he didn't feel as bad as he looked.

"What about eating?" He was no longer the priest's nephew, but rather the physician, and Daniel was touched by his concern.

"I've been fasting a little lately," he admitted reluctantly, uncomfortable with Guy's line of questioning, and wished that he could divert the conversation to some other topic.

"Drinking?" Guy asked.

"No. I've given that up."

"Curious." Guy drummed his fingertips on the arm of the chair and studied his relative.

Daniel feared his nephew would press him for details of the malady, and he knew he'd be forced to tell the young doctor that it was a private matter. He couldn't tell Guy the truth, at least not yet. Truth of what? That his dreams, all of them centered upon August Justinian, were becoming increasingly sensual? He blushed a little.

"Come now," he said, "there's no mystery. The heat has simply taken its toll upon me as it has others. Surely you have other elderly people similarly affected by the rising temperatures?" He knew Guy did, but he wanted to draw attention away from himself.

"Yes, Daniel. There've been a number of deaths from the terrible heat. This damned weather. Maybe it'll break in a day or so, and we'll have some rain to cool it off. I don't know what we're to do if the temperature gets any higher. Every bed in the hospital is already occupied. And there are ten on pallets in the halls." He shook his head. "I pray that the rains will come."

"How is Rose?" Daniel asked innocently.

"She's fine," Guy said, smiling, recognizing the other man's ploy. "When she's not helping with the heat victims, she's busy working on a project of her own."

"Don't let her work too hard," Daniel cautioned.

"I won't." He rose slowly to his feet, "I'd best be heading to the hospital. I was there all night and just went home a few hours ago for rest."

"Take care of yourself, Guy. I don't want you to fall ill."

Guy grinned. "I won't. I'm strong as a horse, and so is Rose."

They chatted at the door for a few minutes more; then Daniel went to St. Mary's. Every morning he made it a habit to greet the boys before they went in to breakfast. He thought they enjoyed the time, for he was less formal then with them, and they could ask him whatever they wished. Within reason, of course.

Outside, the heat glimmered off the buildings, and the leaves of the magnolias, mimosa, and azaleas drooped. Few people were out on the streets, even at this early hour, he noted as he stopped at the corner to fan himself with his hand. Luckily, he didn't have far to go. Daniel reached St. Mary's and opened the door to the dormitory. The usual rain of childish voices greeted him. It was still dark in the room, the inside shutters closed to keep the heat out, and he went down past each bed, saying hello and talking with the occupant for a few minutes.

He stopped at William's cot. The boy did not sit up at his approach.

"What's this? Still asleep?" He chuckled. "What a sleepyhead!"

The boy didn't respond, and Father Daniel shook the child's shoulder to wake him. He was cool to the touch. No, it couldn't be, Daniel told himself. He shook the boy again, harder. The boy's eyes remained closed. He checked for breath, for his heart, then stood up slowly, painfully.

The boy was dead.

"Do you agree?" Guy asked. Rose straightened from her examination of the dead boy and pulled the sheet up over his pale face.

She nodded. "Yes, I'm afraid so." She glanced over at Father Daniel, whose face was almost as white as the dead child's.

"Agree about what?" the priest asked anxiously. After he'd recovered from the shock of finding William dead, he'd sent one of the other boys straight to the hospital with a note begging his nephew to come at once. Guy and Rose had arrived within an hour. Since that time Daniel had refused to think about anything, particularly about the nature of the boy's death. There could be any number of reasons, he told himself, any number, except . . . No, he wouldn't allow himself to think about it.

"Cause of death," Guy replied as he wiped his hands on a cloth and closed his medical bag.

"Which is?"

"Death from loss of blood," Rose said. She had cleaned

up and was jotting notes in a small black book she kept with her.

"Loss of blood," the priest whispered. He sat abruptly on another cot. He shook his head, almost dazed. "No, no, not again. Not again." A shudder passed through him, and unblinking, he stared straight ahead as though he had fallen into a trance.

"Father? Are you all right?" Rose asked. She glanced at Guy, who went at once to his uncle.

"Daniel?" Guy knelt and shook him lightly by the arms. "Daniel, what's wrong?"

Awareness seemed to fill the priest's eyes and he looked down at his nephew. He passed a hand over his face and shook himself a little.

"I'm sorry, I didn't mean to—it's just that with the boy's death . . ."

"I understand. If you'd like, we'll check the other boys while we're here."

"Yes."

As the doctors moved down the aisle, examining the boys, Daniel did not move. He was almost paralyzed by what had happened. He felt responsible, too. He could have prevented William's death. Or could he? What could he have done?

Nothing. No similar deaths had occurred before, as far as he knew, and if he had said anything about August causing the deaths, then he might have been put in an asylum. There was no way he could have protected the child. Just no way.

It took well over an hour for them to complete the examinations, and once they finished, Rose and Guy returned to him.

"Well?" he asked eagerly, and yet dreading what they would say.

"There are signs of illness evident among some of the other boys," Guy said.

"Oh, my God." Daniel swallowed, then asked, "What are the symptoms?"

"Right now, I would say paleness and listlessness," Guy replied. "A general weakening. I can't say any more because we haven't studied them completely enough."

"We'd like to take the afflicted boys back to the hospital," Rose said.

"It won't help," Father Daniel said flatly.

"What do you mean?"

He shook his head. "They won't be safe in the hospital or here, or anywhere." He groaned and clasped his head in his hands. "I think it's too late."

"Too late?" Guy said. "What do you mean?"

Daniel shook his head.

"You know something about this, Daniel?"

"I saw something . . . similar . . . once, a long time ago."

"Where?" Rose demanded.

"England. Thirty years ago. Strong men and boys fell to this, too."

"Tell us, Daniel," Guy said quietly.

"I can't," the priest said mournfully. "Not yet, not now. I don't know that it's the same. I'm just guessing. I can't say."

"Damnit, Daniel, if you know something that will help us—" Guy began. Rose touched him on the arm, and he quieted his tone. "I'm sorry, but I don't want any more little boys to die."

The priest turned anguished eyes to him. "Nor do I, but there is so little we can do. So very little. There is no hope for anyone."

"I don't believe that, Daniel," the doctor said. "I'm

sorry. We'll take the boys who are ill and tend to them; then we'll see you later."

Daniel nodded mutely and watched the two doctors go back to collect the three boys who were ill. Overpowered by what he feared was coming, the priest could only watch and dread what was to come.

"I don't understand what's wrong with Daniel," Guy said, pacing back and forth through the room. Occasionally he would run into a chair in his haste, but it didn't slow him down. "There's something wrong, Rose. He's changed. I think you can understand that."

"He's scared."

"Scared? Of what?"

"I don't know, but I could see it in his eyes this morning. He's afraid of something, something he's not willing to discuss."

"He'd better talk about it, damnit! It might help us save other lives."

"But you can't force him to tell us," Rose pointed out reasonably. "I do think he'll confide in us, and fairly soon, but I suggest in the meantime we work on seeing why these boys are ill." Guy nodded. "This is the first time this illness, or whatever it is, has affected a white child."

"I know. I think it's time to go above Fredericks' head," Guy suggested as he swung around to face her.

"Yes, I agree, although I suspect the Board of Health won't listen. They're just like Dr. Fredericks. Hidebound."

"Pompous."

"Old-fashioned."

Guy grinned and leaned across the table to kiss her on the lips. "To work then, Doctor."

"Very good, Doctor."

"I'm sorry," the head of the Board of Health stated, "but I don't see that an epidemic exists."

Exasperated, Guy stared at him, while Rose pressed her lips tightly together. If she did, she couldn't speak, and if she couldn't speak, then she couldn't yell at this dense man for his stupidity.

"Dr. O'Shaunessey has documented a number of cases, and now we have the death of this boy, as well as the illness of the three others," Guy said.

Rose wondered how her colleague managed to sound so even-tempered when she knew that underneath he was just as angry as she at the resistance they'd met so far to their theory that Savannah faced an epidemic of some unknown disease. Dr. Fredericks and the board of the hospital had been willing to meet with them the day before, but less willing to listen to what they said, and had tried to discourage them from taking this any further. It hadn't worked.

Now, on this hot afternoon in an airless chamber, they stood and listened to these old gasbags, Rose thought crossly. A large blue-green fly buzzed around the room, and occasionally one of the board members took a swipe at it with rolled-up papers. He seemed more concerned about the fly than the two doctors facing the board.

"I don't see enough facts here," the head of the board said, tapping Rose's report. His accent had been deepening in the past half hour, a good indication, Rose thought, that they were irritating him.

"But—" Rose began.

"I'm sorry, Dr. Maxwell, Dr. O'Shaunessey, but I wish to hear nothing further on this matter. Good day to you both."

They were dismissed. Guy started to speak again, but Rose tugged his sleeve.

"Come on," she whispered. "Let's leave. We can't do anything now."

Outside the building the two doctors paused in the shade of a live oak and fanned themselves and caught their breaths. The heat outside seemed so much less than that inside the airless room.

"Well?" Guy asked as he squinted in the brightness of the afternoon sunlight. "What do we do now? The entire hospital board and health board think we're a pair of damned fools, no doubt."

"No doubt," she replied dryly, "but we know we're not fools."

"Small comfort."

Automatically they turned in the direction of the hospital and began walking.

"I know we're right, Guy. If we can just prove it to those old fools."

He didn't reply, and she knew he was angry, not at her, but at the authorities for not believing them.

They did not speak again until they reached the hospital,

and there they went their separate ways. Guy was called to attend several victims of the vicious heat, while Rose decided to check on one of the boys from the orphanage again.

True to Father Daniel's dire prediction, the boy, a handsome boy of some eleven or twelve years named John, had not recovered during his stay in the hospital, and in fact seemed worse than when he had been admitted. His breathing had grown shallow, and his heartbeat had slowed; Rose stared with frustration at the flushed face. The boy was slowly burning up, dying, and she could do nothing to keep the disease from ravaging the youth.

Disease. If it were a disease, she told herself. Yet what other alternatives existed?

She bent over the sleeping child to check him again. She had checked him and the other boys time after time, but she might have missed something. Carefully she examined the boy from head to foot. The boy's skin was dry to the touch, and on his chest was a slight rash that Rose hadn't noticed before. As she ran her fingers lightly across the rash the boy moaned and twisted in his sleep. She did it again, with the same reaction, and noted this time that the boy had an erection.

She hurried down to the end of the ward to where Guy was busy with a sunstroke patient.

"Guy, did the boys have rashes when they were admitted?"

"I noticed a small insect bite, but that's all."

"Yet they have rashes now. Look at this."

The two other boys admitted from St. Mary's both had rashes, but in different places. One had it on the side of his neck and across his stomach. The second, and elder of the two, had a rash by his groin.

"Why are they appearing in different places?" Rose

asked, tapping her foot. Absently she rolled up her sleeves again as high as they would go, then pushed them up higher. "Is something biting them, even here in the hospital? An insect or . . . or what?" She frowned, tried to concentrate on what could be the cause of the rashes.

"I haven't seen any insects. With the marshes nearby, though, God knows what sort of fever this could be."

"Yes." The marshes . . . so unhealthy, she thought. Could it really be the miasma of the bogs that created the fevers, or was it something else? Something she—they— didn't understand yet? "The rashes don't seem to be healing."

"But neither are they spreading across the body," Guy pointed out.

"True."

They stared at each other, and not for the first time did she feel so far from the truth.

Guy kissed her sleepily, murmured her name, and slowly his breathing became more and more regular, and Rose listened as he slipped away into sleep. Smiling tenderly, she brushed his lips lightly with her fingertips. He didn't stir.

Arms above her head, she stretched, yawned, and sighed happily. She snuggled closer to the sleeping man, her hip nudging his, and settled down to sleep. While it was still hot despite the late hour of the night, she wanted to be near him. She pulled up the sheet to cover them and closed her eyes.

They'd been up late two nights in a row, and tomorrow they would have to get to work early. Today by now, no doubt. She'd best sleep as much as possible.

She listened to the night insects, the chirping of the crickets, and once or twice the yowling of a lovelorn cat as it wandered under her window. She kept her eyelids shut, but sleep would not come.

Guy continued to sleep peacefully beside her. He should leave soon, she knew. Earlier in the evening he had sneaked into her room at the boarding house to spend a few hours with her, and usually he left long before dawn so that no one would see him. Tonight, though, she didn't have the heart to wake him because she knew how tired he was. She was just as exhausted. She'd wait until much later; at least he could have that much rest.

She brushed back her hair from her flushed face and plumped up the pillow, closed her eyes again, and waited. Still sleep refused to come. The problem, she knew, was that she was thinking too much about that disease. Thoughts tumbled through her mind as she considered one and disregarded another, and her active mind was forbidding sleep to come. So she might as well rise and think some more about this unusual case.

She swung her legs over the bed, reached for her dressing gown, and wrapped it around herself, then went to sit at the small table across the room. She turned on the gaslight on the wall, pulled paper and pen to her, and started writing.

The symptoms were clear: initial loss of appetite, lethargy, a tendency to sleep most of the day and night. Then came an unhealthy paleness, then debilitation, along with a fever which led to death.

Not the most pleasant of diseases, but then not the most unpleasant disease, either, she thought as she recalled the symptoms of smallpox. The new disease left no pustules, nor was there any outward sign of an inner contagion. Except for that strange rash, the bite of some insect. Or animal.

Now that was a possibility she had never considered before. What sort of animal, after all, could it be?

Too, what of the families of those who'd died first? she asked herself. They had not seemed to exhibit any overt symptoms of the disease. She made a note, reminding her to arrange interviews with the families of the victims. Guy would be interested in that.

Then there was the matter of how the disease was passed along. What did the victims have in common, if anything? Most of the victims had been black until the boy at St. Mary's had died. Had they all been to the same place recently? That was fairly doubtful, she suspected.

She retrieved her first report and reread it. When she reached the end, she studied the list of victims of the disease. Her frown deepened as she read the list. She reread it, flipping through the pages, wondering if she'd skipped a name. Was this listing correct? Absolutely.

It seemed almost impossible, and yet . . . yet all of the victims so far had been men; not one had been a woman.

And that, she thought, was very strange indeed.

The ungodly heat continued the next few days, beating relentlessly into the residents of Savannah, sapping their energy, and stilling all but the most necessary work. Men and women peeled off layers of clothing as far as propriety's sake would allow, and most afternoons and evenings were spent idly in hammocks, in swings, on porches, and in whatever shade could be found.

Daniel's nights were spent in torment, not only from the heat, but from his dreams as well. He was ashamed of them, as well as his failure to do something about August in England. Therefore, he had to do something now, had to tell Guy and Rose. But what if, one part of him countered, *she* found out?

He would have to take the chance, he told himself, then shivered, despite the heat, and once more mopped the sweat from his face. He should rise and say his prayers, for he hadn't been to confession in nearly a week, but he couldn't seem to move from the bed. He closed his eyes and sighed deeply, wishing for the relief of sleep.

Ever since the boys had become ill, Daniel had worked harder than usual. Tonight was an exception, though, because of the heat. He rolled onto his side, but that didn't help, and the crumpled sheet bunched beneath him. The faces of past friends paraded through his mind, mingling with the faces he knew now.

He had to tell soon, even if no one believed him. He had to say something.

She was waiting for him at the main gates of Forsyth Park on Bull Street at the hour of twilight. She wore a simple black gown with a low neckline and short sleeves, and she showed no signs of the heat distressing her.

"I don't understand how you can look so cool," he said after greeting her. While it was still hot, it wasn't as unbearable as earlier in the day when the sun had been high overhead.

She laughed. "Simply an ability I have."

"Shall we walk, Mrs. Justinian?"

"Of course, Dr. Maxwell."

They passed the sphinxes guarding the entrance and began strolling down the broad walk. Other couples nodded as they strolled along. In the center of the park was the white fountain, said by some to be a copy of the fountain in the Place de la Concorde in Paris. She stopped at the wrought-iron railing and stared at the broad water lily leaves.

Guy studied her profile and thought how beautiful she was. Her beauty was so great it made him ache, and momentarily he looked away.

One part of him could feel guilty about Rose—if he let himself think about her. But it wasn't, he argued, as if he had proposed to her and then betrayed their engagement.

No, not at all. So there was no reason to feel guilt. They had a friendship, simply that.

There was so much he wanted to ask August Justinian about herself, so much that he wanted to know. But where to start?

She was watching him, her full lips parted, and he could feel desire stirring in him. He wanted her, wanted her right now in this park; it didn't matter that everyone was watching. Involuntarily he took a step forward and half raised his arms.

"Doctor Maxwell?" Her voice was so soft, so beguiling, so inviting.

He shook his head, and the mood passed. "May I take you to dinner?" he asked.

"If you would like," she replied huskily, "although I must warn you that my appetite is small, and with it being so hot, I haven't felt much like eating."

"That's quite all right, Mrs. Justinian, for I would simply like the excuse of your company."

She smiled, and he knew that their acquaintance was bound to grow.

Early the next morning he was still preparing to leave for St. Mary's when someone knocked on his door. Daniel hesitated for a moment, then answered it. He found Guy and Rose outside.

"Come in," he said, smiling.

Once inside the room Guy faced his uncle, and his expression was stern.

"I won't mince words, Daniel," the younger man said at once, "we've come about one thing only."

"Which is?" Daniel knew, even before his nephew spoke again.

"Rose and I want to know everything you know about

the disease that's spreading through the city. You said something about seeing a similar disease a long time ago; we need to hear about it. We have a right to know!"

Daniel dropped his eyes under the intent gaze of his nephew. In one sense he felt relief that they had come to him, and he truly wanted to tell his story, but not to Guy. Not now. There was something in Guy's eyes that hadn't been there before, and while Daniel didn't know what it was, he didn't trust it.

"I will tell," the priest said, his voice low, "but only to Dr. O'Shaunessey."

"What the hell—"

"Guy," Rose said calmly, touching his arm briefly. "It's all right. What does it matter whom he tells as long as someone knows?"

"I suppose you're right." Guy had agreed verbally, but his face was shuttered, as though he didn't want either Rose or Daniel to know his true feelings. He went to the door and paused. "I'll wait for you outside."

She nodded.

"It may take some time," Daniel said hesitantly.

"I'll wait," Guy replied shortly, and left, nearly slamming the door behind him.

Daniel frowned. That wasn't like Guy. Guy was impatient, but not like that. He turned to Rose and smiled sadly. "Please sit down, Doctor." Daniel indicated a chair to Rose, and she drew it around to face him and sat, folding her hands in her lap. Her eyes met his. "I've wanted to tell someone for so long . . . but I haven't been able to." He could feel the relief welling up in him. He cleared his throat and launched into the story he'd kept within him for thirty years. "Many years ago there were three friends who were at their club . . ." He started from the beginning, when he announced to Henry Montchalmers and Wyndham

Terris that Tommy Hamilton had returned to England with a bride, and he left no detail out.

Rose did not speak during his narration. Occasionally she nodded; once, she looked away, an expression of dismay on her face as the horror of his tale mounted. He was aware that tears coursed down his face as he told her about Tommy's death, and then Wyndy's. They were both aware of the passage of time, but time had stopped for them; all that existed for them was Daniel's story. He came to Dr. Napier's death, then Henry's, and he told how he'd realized that the only way he would live would be by going into the priesthood. When he finished, the silence in the room was profound, almost startling.

"Well?" he asked, his voice slightly hoarse.

"It's so incredible," she said, appalled by all that she had heard in the last several hours. "No one could make it up, Father Daniel, not something this terrible."

"No," he said, "I didn't make it up. I couldn't . . . not about my friends."

"Then we must act quickly," Rose said. "She's come to Savannah because of you, and in the end she'll try to take you. We can't let that happen."

They looked at each other.

"But how?" Daniel asked finally.

"I don't know. There must be some way. Some way that we haven't thought of yet. But first we have to figure out what she is in order to find the way."

"We have to kill her," Daniel said at once. "God forgive me, but I cannot think of it as murder, for she's not a woman. Not after all that she's done. All the lives she's ruined." He shook his head as tears filled his eyes. "She destroyed my friends—Tommy, and Henry, Wyndy, others. Destroyed them to satisfy her blood lust. I was such a coward to run." He was openly weeping now.

Rose went to him. Kneeling, she put her arms around him and held the trembling priest, her head resting gently against his. Finally, after some minutes, the priest's sobs subsided, and he cleared his throat somewhat self-consciously. Rose released him and looked at him, compassion in her blue eyes.

"We will find a way," she said, her voice low. "Please don't worry, Father Daniel."

"I wish I wouldn't, but there is no way; no one seems to know how to destroy her. I wish I had faith that a method would be found."

She just nodded and turned to go.

"Dr. O'Shaunessey, one more thing," he said quietly.

"Yes."

"Please, try not to tell Guy."

"Why?"

"Because I fear he may have come under her spell already. If he knew that we planned to destroy her, he would stop us—by having us jailed or committed, or even killed, but he would have us stopped. Her will *is* so strong that she could make him do it, too."

"All right, I won't tell him. But what do I say to him? What can I say you told me?"

"Tell him it really is a disease. I know that places a burden upon you, but if you keep him busy with that, he won't notice anything else—not if he is preoccupied with that woman." He could see the hurt in her eyes, and he wished he hadn't had to tell her about Guy, but there was no other choice.

"All right, I'll think of something. I'd best go now, Father."

"Bless you, Rose."

She smiled and left, but not before he saw the faint glimmer of tears in her eyes.

"A tropical disease?" Guy asked, furrowing his dark brows in a frown. "That's what Daniel was hiding after all this time?"

"I told you," Rose explained patiently, "that he wasn't hiding anything." Before she left Daniel's room, she'd thought about what she would say to Guy when she rejoined him, and she'd decided to use one aspect of Daniel's story. Certainly disease had been suspected thirty years before.

"But he seemed so guilty and furtive."

"Guy, he is an old man, after all, and something from thirty years ago can become easily blurred—or increased in importance."

"True." Guy's frowned deepened. "Tell me more about this disease, Rose."

"Daniel didn't know much. He's not a doctor, after all, but as I said, the doctors thirty years ago thought it was a tropical disease brought in by some of the soldiers returning from foreign outposts. They hadn't traced it to a source, and Daniel thinks it might reoccur in cycles, as do other diseases."

"It could."

She thought he still sounded reluctant. "But isn't this precisely what we had suspected, Guy? And now all we have to do is locate the source. I plan to start doing research on yellow fever," Rose said quickly. "I know it has been prevalent here, and I wonder if this might be related to it."

"He took hours to tell you all this?"

"He broke down several times," she said. "It was hard for him, remembering the horrible deaths of his friends. There were times when he couldn't speak."

Guy's expression softened a little, and he nodded. He glanced down the deserted street, then up at the blazing sun. "God, I'm weary."

"I'll do most of the work, Guy."

"No, that wouldn't be fair."

"It's all right. You continue with the work at the hospital and I'll follow these other leads. Agreed?" She smiled hopefully.

"Agreed," he finally answered, and she breathed a sigh of relief because he'd believed her story.

Later that day, while in between cases, Rose sat down to rest and think over what Father Daniel had told her in confidence that morning.

A woman who could bewitch men, could seduce them unto death..

She had never heard of such a thing, but that didn't mean it couldn't exist. Too well did she remember how engrossed in August Justinian all the men at the party had become. Guy had virtually forgotten about her, although they had arrived together. No, she could believe in a woman who could enchant men. Hadn't Circe done the same? No, she had transformed them into animals, while August killed them. Like animals, one part of her said. Yes, sucked them dry, leaving only a husk, and Rose shuddered at the thought.

She hunted through a desk and found some paper and a pen, then sat down to write a letter to her mother. In the years since Rose had graduated as a physician and had begun practicing, Molly O'Shaunessey had softened in her attitude toward her daughter. Rose knew that her mother, deep in her heart, still desired for her to enter a convent and be a nun, but had recognized that she would most likely never be one. And if her daughter couldn't be a religious and was a doctor—and one of the few women ones—then she would be proud of her.

Once on a trip home Rose had overheard her mother bragging to her friends, and the other women, who had pitied poor Molly O'Shaunessey for her unnatural daughter, now oohed and aahed as Mrs. O'Shaunessey recounted the tales, albeit somewhat exaggerated, of her daughter's blossoming medical career.

Rose considered herself a fairly faithful correspondent, generally sending one to three letters a week to her mother and family, but in the past few weeks she hadn't sent as many letters as usual, due to the amount of work she'd had. The heat, too, had kept her from maintaining her schedule.

After she asked in detail about each of the various family members and apologized for her lapse in correspondence, and after explaining that she was at present busy at the hospital, Rose said she'd like it very much if her mother would relay some of the stories she'd learned in the old country. She was particularly interested in tales of beautiful women who enchanted men.

Rose phrased her request particularly carefully, for she didn't want to elicit too many questions from her parent—questions that she couldn't answer at present—nor alarm her unduly. Her mother, while an extremely faithful member of the Church, was also exceptionally superstitious, two things which, in Rose's mind, seemed to go hand in hand.

When she finished, she reread it, and then nodded, satisfied with it. As she sealed it she smiled. Who knew? Her mother might be able to help with the mystery she and Daniel faced. At this point, she thought a little ruefully, anything would be some help.

It was, at least, a beginning. But she would have to think of something else, some other place to start, too. And as far as she went, she had no ideas whatsoever. Her mind was a blank.

Were they facing a woman possessed by some demonic powers? Rose could well imagine the other doctors at the hospital laughing at her if they knew what she were considering. And yet her mother wouldn't laugh, nor would many others. There were many yet who believed in ghosts and demons and witches.

The question was: Did she?

For the present, she didn't know quite how to answer that.

"Are you alone?" she whispered in the soft cloying darkness.

"Yes," Guy said. "Except for you. She won't come tonight. She had too much work."

"Good."

August Justinian stepped out of the deep shadows into the faint moonlight coming through the open window. He hadn't heard her enter his bedroom. He gazed at her, and could find no words.

She had shed her usual heavy gown, and tonight she wore a shimmering skintight garment, black as night and her eyes, but so sheer the outline of her rounded breasts and the erect cerise nipples were clearly seen, and that only excited him more. The mere thought of her aroused him, and sometimes when he was at the hospital and thought of her briefly—just a second or so was all it took—he would be embarrassed to see how fast—how explicit—was his body's response.

She laughed, a silvery sound that tightened his chest and made him gasp for air, as she saw the expression on his face. She glided toward him, then stopped a scant few inches away. He was so close to her, so close he could smell the perfume she wore, a musky scent that only increased his desire. His groin was growing warmer and warmer, and he thrust it toward her. She laughed and ran a finger down his cheekbone.

"You're so handsome."

"You're so beautiful." His throat was tight with unshed tears. He always felt this way when he saw her, as if he should be worshipping her for her beauty. As if, he thought, she were a goddess.

He reached out, his once-graceful surgeon's hands grown suddenly spadelike, clumsy, and almost hesitantly his thumbs grazed her nipples. She almost seemed to purr as she made a deep sound in her throat and inched closer to him, and he could feel her body against his, could feel his hardness beating against her. She reached down to cup him through his pants.

"If you wait any longer, you'll be a captive of your own clothes."

His cheeks burned red momentarily, then his embarrassment was forgotten as she helped him unfasten his pants. They dropped to his ankles, and quickly he stepped out of them. Somehow in that short time she had shed her diaphanous garment to stand naked before him. Smiling, she threw her head back, her full breasts jutting out. He buried his face in their cool flesh with a strangled sob, and caressed them with his trembling fingers, and lapped the dark aureole with his tongue. Then his lips fastened onto the nipple of the left breast and he sucked, and felt it expand, hardening even more, tasted a cool trickle in his throat, and his hardened manhood throbbed excruciatingly. She pushed him away, and he fell back onto the bed with a soft exclamation. She laughed and kissed his lips, then his chest, even as her hand crept down to the curling hair of his loins. Her hand brushed his engorged member, and he cried out, biting his tongue as he kept from releasing too soon. She inched down his body, kissing and licking him until he thought he could no longer stand it. Her mouth reached his groin, and he could feel the soft feather caress of her eyelashes across his skin, the brief kiss of her lips on his stiff memeber.

Her cool lips excited him as they drew along his length, then her tongue flicked against the pulsing head. He grunted, pressed his hands into the mattress, and thrust his hips up.

She laughed. "Not yet, not yet," she murmured, and even as she spoke, he could feel the tension receding, and then she was drawing her fingers across his testicles, flicking them with her fingernails, and taking his length in her mouth.

The explosion built within him, glowing white-hot, and burned and grew, and there was nothing he could do to restrain it as she worked him, milking every ounce of desire and lust from him, inflaming him as no other woman ever had. And then it burst forward, seeming to fling his soul across the universe, and he screamed full-throatedly as she reared up, and he came, throbbing and pumping and spewing without purpose.

She laughed again, a wild sound that maddened him, as she flung herself upon his sticky body, and they kissed and bit at each other, her lips salty from his seed, and he rolled over and rammed his still-rigid manhood into her coolness, and he rode her roughly, harshly, as he never had before with any woman, and he wanted her to beg for his mercy, wanted her to scream for him to stop, wanted her to acknowledge he was too much man for her, but all she did was laugh and laugh, and the harder he thrust, the deeper he shoved, the more he twisted and strove to cleave her, to break her, the more she laughed and took him in and took from him until finally he was spent and could give no more, for nothing was left, and limp and listless and exhausted into a stunned blackness, he collapsed across her still, cool body and slept.

And in the darkness she smiled as she stroked his wet hair.

Something was wrong. Rose sensed it. In the few days since she'd visited Daniel, she had come to realize that something was wrong between Guy and her. Or more precisely, something was wrong with him. While he acted the same as he always did and spoke the same way and worked just as diligently as before, she knew something was different.

When she asked if something was amiss, he shook his head, saying he was tired from overwork and from the awful heat. No longer did he ask to take her out. Gone were their dinners, their evening strolls, their nights spent together. Instead, when she hinted, he would plead exhaustion. She almost believed it, because she was tired and hot, too, but not so much that she could not hold him in her arms.

Almost believed him, except something didn't ring true with his explanation, and his gaze slid away from hers. Still, she might merely be looking for trouble where none existed. No. It wasn't that. Too, Father Daniel didn't trust

Guy, either, for he'd asked her not to mention what they'd discussed.

All this wrongness. All because of August Justinian. Guy must be meeting with the widow, Rose told herself. He must be going to her, or perhaps she came to him.

The latter, of course, for that explained much—why he never came to visit her at night, why he never invited her to his room. At night the widow visited him. And now he complained of tiredness, and she had to admit that he did look exhausted. But so did she, and so did half the staff of the hospital. Anger welled up within Rose as she thought of what the woman was attempting to do. Not Guy, Rose thought furiously. I won't let you have the man I love! No. She wouldn't let the widow take him away; she'd find a way to stop her. Somehow.

It had been a long day again at the hospital and had proved just as frustrating as the past few days. She was no closer to finding a solution to ending the "disease." The illnesses from the heat continued, and the overcrowded conditions continued in the hospital. Tempers frayed easily, and no relief seemed in sight. The boys hadn't died, but neither were they getting better.

She was home now to stay for the evening, and she knew implicitly that Guy was spending the night in the other woman's arms, and she was angry, and fearful, because she was afraid that August would harm him. No, not now, one part of her said, and she nodded, wishing she could completely believe it. She had finally found a man whom she trusted, whom she loved, and now this woman, this *thing*, dared to tempt him away.

"No!" she cried aloud. "I won't let you! Do you hear me!" Her voice rang through the silent room, echoed against the walls. "Do you hear me, August Justinian? If you want Dr. Guy Maxwell, you'll have to fight me for him!'' She whirled around, her fists balled at her side, and waited, almost as if she believed the woman would appear suddenly. She was breathing heavily, her muscles tensed, and she sensed that the woman—the *creature*—had heard her. Rose frowned. Did she hear faint mocking laughter? "Come to me now, creature, and I'll deal with you. I won't run away like the men have!"

Deal with her? She didn't know if August could be killed or how it could be done, but she'd learn. Somehow. *She* would triumph in the end; the creature would lose. Rose would make sure of that.

Again she paced the room. She was hot and tired, but for the present she didn't care. She wondered if she should write a letter to Guy, informing him of her challenge, and have it sent to his boarding house, but she shook her head. Doubtless he was too far under August's sway by now, and thus he wouldn't come to rescue her—if she needed rescuing.

Time was running out for them, Rose knew, and she and Daniel would have to act soon. It was one thing, she acknowledged quickly, when the widow's victims were unknown to her, but altogether a different case now that Guy had fallen under the woman's influence.

Was he, though? She didn't know for sure, for she hadn't witnessed an assignation between the two. Yet she had only to remember how he had gazed at August Justinian at the garden party or to recall that Father Daniel had reminded her that men found the widow irresistible, and deep down in her heart she knew that through no choice of his own Guy was bewitched by the woman.

That was sufficient. Not a very scientific method, she chided herself a little, but it seemed accurate enough.

There was so much to do, and so soon, as well. She sat

down at the table and began ruffling through her notes and papers.

Her weariness forgotten, she compiled a list of what she must do in the next few days. Finally, when she lifted her head from her work, she saw that darkness had crept into the room. She was surprised, for surely it couldn't be so late. She glanced at the clock on the shelf by her bed. Twelve-thirty. She hadn't even had time for dinner, and now it was time to go to bed. She had an early day tomorrow; she should be at the hospital no later than six. She pushed back her damp hair from her forehead and sighed. If she'd been weary hours ago, she was bone-tired now.

She gathered the papers together, straightened them, and put them in a neat pile. If she had time in the morning before she left for the hospital, she would glance over them. For all she knew, she might have written nothing but page after page of gibberish.

What would Guy think of all this? She undid the numerous tiny buttons on her bodice and shrugged out of it. Would he be sarcastic? Of course, she couldn't tell him, but she did wonder what he would have to say about it.

She eased the skirt off, dancing from one foot to the other, and still in her neatly patched chemise with its trim of white bows she padded across the room to hang her clothes up. She hung them carefully, brushing out their wrinkles. She sent most of what she earned to help her mother, and thus she had to take care of the few clothes she did have. She pulled the chemise off and stared at herself in the mirror over the chiffonier.

Smallish breasts, a tucked-in waist, solid hips tapering into legs made firm by riding and walking, and an Irish skin with a dusting of golden freckles across her arms and upper chest. Nice hands, she admitted, spreading her fingers wide and staring at them and the neatly cut nails. Capable, with long fingers. A surgeon's hand someday, God—and her male bosses—willing. She grinned at herself in the mirror. Even white teeth; eyes filled with humor. An imp's humor, she'd been told on more than one occasion, and chuckled aloud.

Not beautiful like that other woman, certainly not exotic or compelling, but she possessed a certain attractiveness, she thought. She saw it in Guy's eyes when they made love. Or had, before he'd been seduced by the other woman.

"Oh, hell," she muttered out loud, the words sounding harsh in the silence. She pulled her nightgown out, slipped it over her head, and ran her hands through her hair. Normally, she braided it before going to bed, but tonight she was too tired. By morning it would be curly and utterly unruly, but it couldn't be helped.

Rose glanced around the room one more time, checking for anything she absolutely had to do before retiring, and when she satisfied herself there wasn't, she turned off the gas lamp, padded cautiously across the floor in the darkness, and slid into bed.

Listening to the wind soughing through the branches of the oak tree outside, she hoped the room would cool a little by morning. Once the curtains flapped in the breeze, and she started with the unexpected movement; then she chuckled at her raw nerves and closed her eyes. She didn't have long to wait for sleep, for the work and heat had taken its toll.

When she awoke, suddenly, a shaft of moonlight was shining through the window. She was puzzled, for the moon was past fullness, and even while she was trying to figure that mystery out, she heard a whisper of cloth, sensed motion, and in the next moment saw the woman standing in the far corner of the room. Rose sat, pulling the sheet up, and rubbed her eyes.

Neither woman spoke for a few minutes. Rose's heart hammered as she watched the other. What did she want? Why had she come? Why didn't she go away?

"Rose."

The husky voice would no doubt prove beguiling to a man, but to Rose its dark menace frightened her more than anything ever had in her life. She recoiled against the bed's head. "Go away. Get out of here. This is my room, and you have no right being here."

Laughing, the other woman stepped forward, the moonlight bathing her and turning her stream of black hair to starlight. She wore black, the outline of her body clearly visible through her clothing, and the bodice she wore was sewn like a tunic, with one part unbuttoned to reveal a firm breast. Rose was reminded of the Amazons of the Greeks' time, except that this woman had fought no battles beyond the bedroom. Slowly, voluptuously August licked her lips, leaving them glistening.

Rose was disgusted. "Get away, witch!"

"Witch? How quaintly you phrase it! Am I the one with red hair, *Doctor*?" August laughed again, the sound of metal scraping against metal, as Rose gritted her teeth. "You say I have no right to be here, but I distinctly heard you call me. You challenged me, Doctor. And yet now you tell me to go away. You are frightened, and ignorant."

"Perhaps." Rose hoped her voice was firm, but she suspected it held the faintest hint of a quaver. She drew her brows together in sudden anger. She would not allow herself to quail in front of this woman. This creature, she reminded her.

"Creature," August said, her voice amused. "You paint a most unflattering picture, Doctor. Why, you can see that

I am no hulking, slavering monster who rips out the throats of men."

"No," Rose replied slowly, "you're not as honest as that."

There was silence for a moment. "You are a stupid girl, Doctor."

"I don't think so, and I prefer to think of myself as a woman, Mrs. Justinian. Or shall I call you Mrs. Hamilton? What was your name previously? And before that? And even before that?"

"He told you."

"Yes." August Justinian wasn't omniscient, Rose thought with relief. A good sign. My God, it was an *excellent* sign. She tried to quell her rising excitement, for this realization had given her hope. "Yes, he told me. I didn't tell Guy, though."

"Ah, Guy."

Rose disliked the sound of her lover's name on that woman's lips.

"Are we to fight over this one, I wonder?" August mused aloud. "What do you say, Doctor? A fight between two women, one a doctor, the second a *creature*, for the soul and body of this one man? I think this could be quite interesting. Certainly I know the priest would find it so."

"I won't let Guy go." Said almost fiercely, to match her hair.

"We'll see."

"No. I won't release him, not to you, not to anyone," Rose said.

"You know you cannot escape me. Guy cannot escape me, just as his uncle could not."

"He eluded you for thirty years."

August smiled in answer. "Perhaps."

Rose could tolerate the other's presence no longer. "Get out of my room!"

August's expression had changed to a smirk, her beautiful lips curving into a mocking expression. "For now, Doctor, but I promise you I will see you again shortly. Yes, very shortly."

Languorously August raised her hand to her breast and rubbed the firm nipple in a circular motion, with her head lolled back, and her eyelids lowered slowly, provocatively. She moaned with pleasure as she flicked the nipple back and forth between her fingers, and a musky scent wafted through the air.

Acutely embarrassed, Rose dropped her gaze. When she raised her head, the other woman was gone and the strange moonlight had faded with her. She was gone! No! She stared wildly around the now-darkened room, wondering in which corner the woman hid, waiting for her to fall asleep, waiting for her to be lulled so that she could come to her, bend over her, and—

The fear, her companion for hours now, blossomed, almost threatening to overcome her completely, and gasping as if for breath and without thinking, Rose swung her legs over the bed, went to the chiffonier, and pulling out the third drawer, found what she wanted under her spare chemise and a petticoat. In her hand she held an object she had not used in a long time.

Quickly, almost urgently, she returned to the safety of her bed and curled up under the covers. She fingered the carved beads of the rosary, gaining reassurance from its familiarity, and after she had murmured a few prayers, she felt her eyelids begin to droop and soon she was asleep, the rosary entwined comfortingly through her fingers, and she was not further disturbed that night.

Rose found a letter from her mother waiting for her two days later. She opened it with eager hands, nearly tearing the pages in her haste. The first five pages of small neat script were devoted to the most recent news of her father and brothers and their wives and children, her cousins, her aunts and uncles; who had died, who had had to be married quickly, who was lying in childbirth, plus all of the gossip about her mother's neighbors in Boston. Impatiently Rose skimmed those lines, and finally, in the second-to-last paragraph of the letter, she found what she sought.

"I wasn't sure that I understood completely what you meant in your last letter, my dear daughter, and I thought about it long, and the only examples I could think of in the stories I heard as a child were the banshees, of course, and the *leanhaun sidhe*, a beautiful woman who makes men her slaves and is supposedly an inspiration to poets. As to anything more on that subject, I doubt that I can be of any further help."

Her mother ended her letter by sending her love and

hoping that her daughter could come home soon to visit the family. Rose smiled, for whenever she was away for longer than a month, her mother acted as though the absence extended for years.

There was a postscript, and as she read it her expression sobered. "I do not know why you have this interest in these unnatural things, but I warn you, my dear Rose, to be wary, for whenever humans interfere with the spirits, nothing good comes of it."

Rose reread the letter, then carefully folded and tucked it in her desk for later reference.

If she worked quickly this afternoon, she would have time to go to the library and do some research, then perhaps to drop by and see Father Daniel.

Once in the library, Rose conferred with the librarian, explaining that she was interested in legends about women with extraordinary powers. The librarian, a woman with a somewhat pallid complexion, was helpful, although she admitted the library had few books on the subject, for the town itself was not that large. She did, however, refer Rose to a local historian and writer who might be of some assistance. Rose took the slip of paper, thanked her, and left the library.

As she walked away she glanced at the name. S.A. van Cleve. The address was a few miles outside the city. When she returned to the hospital, Rose thumbed through the telephone directory but didn't find the name there, nor did the operator have a number for S.A. van Cleve. Puzzled, Rose decided that she would simply hire a cab and drive out there the next day to talk with the man.

She inquired after Guy, and one of the other doctors replied that Dr. Maxwell was out of the hospital today treating patients. The intense heat had felled numerous older citizens who could not yet be transferred to the hospital, and Guy had volunteered to go and take care of them.

She nodded and returned to her work, and wished that she could be with Guy that night, but she suspected that he would tell her that he was too busy to have dinner with her. For that precise reason she resolved to end the problem of August Justinian as soon as possible.

When she saw Father Daniel later that day, she explained what she had found so far, which only amounted to what her mother had written and the name of the historian which the librarian had given her.

"Don't despair," he said, his tone kindly. "At least you have a place to begin." He patted her hand and gave her a sympathetic smile.

"That's true," she admitted ruefully. "I don't know, though, how I can approach this man and ask him these rather pointed questions."

Daniel shook his head. "Wait; just a minute, Doctor." He stood up and went across to his crowded bookshelves. He selected one, returned to his chair, and thumbed through the book until he found what he wanted. "Here, read this, please."

She glanced at the title of the poem. *"La Belle Dame sans Merci"* by Keats. Her eyebrows drawn together in puzzlement, she looked up at the priest.

"Go on," he said. "Just read it, and then I'll explain."

"All right."

When she was finished, she started to close the book, then stopped and reread the poem. Then she handed the book of poetry to him and waited for the explanation.

"I found that book many years ago in London, and when I read that poem I thought at once of August Hamilton. In some ways your mother might be correct about the *leanhaun sidhe*. It would seem that August was an inspiration—if we can call it that—to Keats for this poem."

"Perhaps it wasn't her; perhaps it was another creature like her," Rose replied gravely.

"Yes, yes, you could be right." Daniel shuddered. "But I cannot conceive of more than one of them."

"There can't have been too many of them, or mankind wouldn't have survived. Or if they were numerous, then their number must have been destroyed. Somehow. Which means that she can be killed."

Daniel sighed. "Yes, somehow. We have returned to that, I see."

Rose shook her head. She didn't know what to say, so she simply sat there.

"I don't know why I had you read this poem," he said slowly, his voice musing, "except that it might help you somehow."

"Thank you for that at least."

They talked for a little while longer; then she excused herself, for she had much to prepare for. She had to return to her room, to her lonely bed, and tomorrow she would visit the historian.

The hour was late, the night dark, and August was abroad. She was restless. She was growing tired of playing this waiting game with Father Daniel. She wanted to claim him now, and yet—yet she wanted to wait, wanted to prolong his fear, for she fed on that, too, as much as the other. She smiled, turned down Bryan Street, and passed Johnson Square with its monument and grave of the Revolutionary War hero Nathaniel Green. She continued, passing Reynolds Square, Warren Square, and Washington Square, then turned onto East Broad Street and headed toward Bay Street and River Street.

She would walk along the river tonight. A fine mist was rising, and no doubt she could find something fairly interesting. Something to pass the time with. She smiled, moistened her lips.

It wouldn't be long before she claimed Guy Maxwell, then the prize she had waited for for so long, and the thought of that gave her much pleasure.

The large rambling plantation mansion sat far back from the road, and as the carriage drove up a straight avenue, willows lining it, and onto the wide sweep paved with tiny white stones and crushed seashells, Rose studied the impressive house.

The once-impressive house, she corrected, for now that she was much closer she could see the small signs of neglect. The white boards were dulled and chipped; one shutter on the first floor hung askew, and on the second floor a piece of board was nailed across a broken pane of glass.

Still, the six columns in front and the ornate wrought-iron grilles on each of the windows were impressive, and over all she was left with a good impression. In front of the house several trees bore late fruit, while autumn flowers of red and golden hues clustered about the porch. Off to the right she could just see the side and roof of a gazebo sitting behind the house.

She paid the driver of the coach she'd hired and instructed him to return for her in about two hours, but she asked if he would first wait until she was sure that Mr. van Cleve was home and that he would receive her. She walked up the steps to the porch, noted the swing there, and the pots of geraniums, and knocked on the heavy wooden door. After a few minutes it opened to reveal a woman who was some ten years older than she and whose dark hair was flecked with grey.

"May I help you?" the woman asked. She had a pleasant resonant voice, and Rose thought she was dressed somewhat extravagantly for a housekeeper. Slightly on the plump side, she looked extremely cheerful.

"Good afternoon," Rose said politely. "My name is Dr. O'Shaunessey, and I would like to see Mr. S.A. van Cleve, if he is at home."

"I am S.A. van Cleve."

"You!" Rose stared. "I thought . . ."

The woman chuckled, a rich humorous sound that put Rose at ease. "That S.A. van Cleve was a man? Everyone does, and to tell you the truth, that's what they're supposed to think. Otherwise, my name wouldn't appear on so many articles. Now, how may I help you?"

"The librarian at the Savannah library gave me your name when I expressed an interest in the occult. I need help on a matter, and I believe—I hope—that you may be able to assist me."

"Ah, won't you come in then, Dr. O'Shaunessey?"

"Thank you." Rose waved to the driver, indicating she would be staying, then followed the woman down a corridor to a door which opened onto a large room where bookcases from floor to ceiling lined two walls, and every shelf was so loaded with books that some were buckling slightly. Books and stacks of papers were scattered across the two mahogany desks there, the numerous small tables sitting about the room, and even the sofa and three easy chairs.

"It's a mess," said Miss van Cleve, airily waving a hand, "but then I work here. I won't let the maid touch a thing, else she'd burn it all, I have no doubt."

"I feel quite at home." Rose sympathized, for she wasn't possessed of a tidy nature, either.

"Sit down, please, Dr. Shaunessey. Would you care for some tea?" Rose nodded, and the woman rang for an elderly black maid, who took her employer's instructions and left. "Now, would you like to tell me about this matter of the occult you think I can help you with?"

Rose took a deep breath. "Yes, but first let me explain, Mrs. . . . Miss?" The other nodded. "Miss van Cleve. Please allow me to present my credentials. I am a physician presently employed at the Savannah Hospital, and have been there for over six months. If you wish to check with my employer for corroboration, please feel free to do so."

"If I should think it necessary, I shall," Miss van Cleve drawled, her eyes showing her amusement, "but you wish me to know you're not an eccentric. Correct?"

"Precisely." At least the woman hadn't thrown her out yet. She considered how best to broach the subject. "It's difficult to explain, Miss van Cleve, although I'll try to be as plain as possible. As for being objective, I doubt I can. If you have any questions, please feel free to ask me." The other woman nodded her head briefly.

Rose took a deep breath and began her narrative. "The number of deaths in Savannah and the surrounding area has risen sharply in the past few weeks, and at first my colleague Dr. Maxwell and I attributed this to the dramatic rise in temperature. But as the deaths continued, we suspected there might be a secondary cause of death as well, an unknown disease perhaps. And we started to work toward identifying the disease. We were convinced we were on the right trail until we talked with Guy's uncle, who is a priest locally. You see, he had heard of a similar condition of victims before; in fact, he had friends die of the same condition—thirty years ago."

At that moment the tea arrived, and they did not speak again until the maid had left the room.

"Please continue, Dr. O'Shaunessey." Miss van Cleve's eyes were half-shut, and Rose wondered how much she had actually heard, but then the woman's eyes opened, and Rose knew she had heard everything.

"We believe the deaths can be traced to one woman."

"I see." Miss van Cleve sipped her tea for a moment, then drew out a small silver flask, uncapped it, and poured a tiny amount into her china cup. She laid a finger across her mouth and looked toward the door, indicating the maid might be listening. "You know, Doctor, women are always blamed for the various ills of mankind—and have been made to suffer for a guilt that was not theirs. The most famous examples, of course, are the witch hunts and subsequent burnings that began in the Middle Ages and continued through the Inquisition and into the last century."

"I've seen this woman with my own eyes," Rose said.

"What did you see?"

"I had called her . . . challenged her aloud one night to come to me and we would fight—" Here Rose hesitated. If she claimed that August had seduced Guy away from her, wouldn't Miss van Cleve simply dismiss her as a jealous woman? "And we would fight for the soul of Guy. Dr. Maxwell," she added quickly.

"I see."

Neutral, she thought. So far. "And she came to me."

"I see nothing unusual about that. There are recorded

cases of people 'sensing' what others have thought. Too, if this woman has taken your friend away, she would doubtless know your mind and know that you wished to confront her face to face."

"No. That's not it at all. She heard me—even though she lives outside the city, and she came to me. Not through the door, either."

"Did you see that?" Miss van Cleve asked with quickening interest.

"No," Rose admitted frankly. "I had been asleep and was awakened by a noise. She was in my room."

"So she might well have entered by the door, or possibly even a window."

"She might have, but she didn't."

"And how do you know?"

"I'm not the first to encounter her in this manner. The priest I mentioned, Father Daniel, has dealt with her before in this way."

"I see."

Rose was growing more and more irritated at this woman's bland expression and her doubting questions. She had half a mind to get up and walk out and—

"Don't leave, Doctor, please," Miss van Cleve said, smiling. "I don't mean to irritate you, but I wish to investigate all possibilities. Because I question you doesn't mean I don't believe you. You say that the priest, Father Daniel, knew this woman before. Thirty years ago?"

"Yes."

"Could he possibly be mistaken about this woman's identity?"

"No, Miss van Cleve. On this Father Daniel is quite adamant."

"So," the other woman said, leaning back, "now we have a woman who appears quickly and without the benefit of using doors and windows, who can hear, or at least sense, the thoughts of others, and who kills men. I assume that all the victims were men."

"Yes, they were. Most of them were young men, and some were boys. From what Father Daniel told me, she did the very same thing in London thirty years ago. Many of his friends died by her hand."

"Yet he lived. Very interesting."

"And she comes to the men in dreams. Father Daniel reported that he's had such dreams—I know Guy has, although he hasn't said anything to me, and Father Daniel also said that his friends reported sensual dreams about a woman—that particular woman—just prior to their deaths."

"Is there anything else you can add? I am interested in everything, no matter how little or trivial you consider it."

"Do you wish to know about the symptoms of the 'disease'?" The historian nodded. "The symptoms—here in Savannah, and in London, as I've gleaned from Father Daniel—include lassitude, a fever sometimes, what looks like a rash or small insect bite marks, with the cause of death being loss of blood."

"Ah, that narrows the field considerably." Miss van Cleve poured more liquor into her teacup and took a solid sip of it. Rose smiled, for by now there could be little tea in the woman's drink. "Now it should be easier to identify what this woman is." She smiled at Rose. "We have a woman who is a seducer of men as well as a killer of men. And a woman who drains them of their blood. Yes, very interesting."

"I wrote to my mother asking about Irish stories, and she mentioned the *leanhaun sidhe*."

"An inspiration to poets."

"Yes, that's just what she said, but Father Daniel and I don't think she is such a thing. Except, of course, he did show me a poem by Keats, *'La Belle Dame sans Merci,'* which seems to have described her quite well.''

"Her type are always without mercy."

" 'Her type'?" Rose asked, frowning slightly. "What type is she?"

The other woman rose and walked across to one of the bookcases and scanned the shelves for a few minutes until she found the book she wanted. She brought the thick volume back, opened it in the middle, and carefully turned the pages. Miss van Cleve tapped an etching with one long finger. "This is what I think you have found, Dr. O'Shaunessey."

Rose studied the picture, which showed a woman of a beautiful countenance with flowing black hair. She was menacing a small child who huddled in a corner. The caption read "Vampyr."

"Vampyr?"

"As in vampire." Miss van Cleve went to another bookcase, returned with a second book, equally thick. "More specifically, I believe this individual you describe may be a lamia."

"Lamia?" Rose asked, looking puzzled. "What's that? I've heard of a vampire, but not a lamia."

"The word was used in the Vulgate Latin to translate the Hebrew Lilith, who was originally a Babylonian night spirit. In Hebrew lore Lilith was the first wife of Adam, and in the Book of *Emek hammelech* she was a spectral whore.

"Numerous writers have mentioned the lamia: Gervais of Tilbury, about 1218, wrote about them; Nicholaus of Jauer, professor of theology at Prague and Heidelberg in the early decades of the fifteenth century, mentioned them in his work; and Johannes Pott in his 1689 study distinguished several kinds of lamiae." Miss van Cleve smiled apologetically. "I'm sorry, Dr. O'Shaunessey. I tend to forget myself and lecture on."

"No apologies are necessary, but I'm still not sure that I really know what a lamia is."

"Succinctly, a lamia is a female vampire. Or nearly so. While she may drink the blood of her victim as does a vampire, she also possesses one singular capability a vampire does not. She draws out—forcefully, I might add—and feeds upon the sexual energy of her victim, and if I deduce correctly from what you've said and have not said, this individual also does the same. In other words, she kills her victims in two ways—both of them dreadful."

Rose nodded, and wished that her hand holding the fragile teacup did not tremble so.

"The Greeks and Romans used the lamia as a phantom to scare children. In classical mythology Lamia was a Libyan queen beloved by Jupiter but robbed of her offspring by Juno, and afterward she vowed vengeance against all children, whom she would entice and subsequently murder. She also had the power to seduce men and suck their blood. I recall that you said some of the victims were male children." Rose nodded, remembering the young boy from St. Mary's. "Keats wrote another poem, this one about a lamia—the poem is of the same name—although the woman in it is much more romanticized than legend portrays her, and she is never blamed for anything."

The historian continued. "Variations exist, of course. Sometimes the lamia is a hideous woman of advanced age—as seen in the image of the old witches—sometimes a beautiful woman; sometimes she becomes ugly only after killing her victim. Unfortunately, less has been written about the lamia through the centuries than about vampires or witches. I suppose scholars did not find her as intriguing, or perhaps they censored their studies because of her highly sensual nature. Still, at least we do have some word of her and her sisters."

"This woman is very beautiful, and Father Daniel said that he has seen her grow even more beautiful at certain times."

"No doubt after she has killed her victims. Their life regenerates her."

"The fountain of youth," Rose said.

"Yes, much like that, although far more ghastly, I would think."

"You think, then, that this woman is a lamia?" Rose asked.

"I am almost one-hundred-percent sure, Dr. O'Shaunessey, particularly if what you've given me is completely factual. Are all men who meet her attracted to her?"

"Yes. When she enters a room, not a man stays away from her."

Miss van Cleve's tone was ironic. "There are women who can do that, and they aren't lamiae."

"I don't think they do it the way she does." Rose finished her tea and set the cup down carefully. "You know, Father Daniel fears that she will come after him."

"Because she didn't thirty years ago?" Rose nodded. "And is Father Daniel attracted to her as well? You say that all men are."

"That's strange, but he isn't drawn to her like the others are. At first he was; then, he said, he began to sense something . . . wrong about her, something about her that put him off. He didn't know why until later. Much later. I must explain, too, that thirty years ago, when he first met her, he wasn't a priest."

"But he became a priest afterward. Most intriguing." Miss van Cleve fell silent for several minutes, then finally stirred, as if she recalled she had a visitor. "I would like to meet this woman if possible, to view her myself, you see."

"I think we could arrange it as she is very active socially. I would have to check with Father Daniel, though, and contact you later in the week. Would that be convenient?"

"Of course. This should prove very informative."

"But she's deadly," Rose blurted out, immediately wishing she'd kept silent.

"Yes, I know. We cannot forget her deadliness at any time, Dr. O'Shaunessey. Too, while lamiae usually choose men as their victims, upon occasion they have shown themselves to women just prior to killing them. This is, I believe, fairly uncommon, though."

With a sudden rush of blood to her cheeks, Rose remembered the night August Justinian came to her. "Yes, I know. She came to me, as I said, and at first I wasn't sure whether it was a dream. I don't think so, not after what Father Daniel told me."

"Be careful, Dr. O'Shaunessey. That shows that she is quite aware of you."

Rose shivered, not liking the sound of that. She rose slowly and shook hands with the other woman. "Thank you for the tea and for the information, and for allowing me to take your time unannounced as I did. I'll be in contact with you by the end of the week, Miss van Cleve."

"Very well."

At the door Rose paused. "By the way, I've heard that to kill a vampire you must drive a wooden stake through its heart, cut off his head, and then stuff its mouth with garlic. What does one do with a lamia? How is it destroyed?"

"That, I'm afraid, not one of the historical sources has

relayed through the centuries to us. I think we'll have to discover that on our own.''

She thanked the historian again, then left the plantation house and walked out to find the carriage waiting for her. She climbed in, and as the carriage rolled away she looked back to see Miss van Cleve wave. She waved in response, then closed her eyes.

She had learned what August Justinian was, but the most crucial information—how to destroy the lamia—no one knew, and suddenly Rose feared that her trip might have been made for nought.

"We have to tell Guy what she is," Rose said quietly. She had returned to the hospital after visiting with S.A. van Cleve, and then she had gone to see Father Daniel. He was looking pale and seemed weak, far weaker than when she last saw him. He denied that August was visiting him at night—except in dreams. Rose didn't know whether to believe him; Guy lied to her, after all.

"Yes, I know. He'll fight the idea, though," the priest said, his voice weary.

"I know, but we have to try to set him right. I'll bring him tonight, along with a few other things," she replied grimly.

Daniel nodded, and she bid him farewell.

When she found Guy at the hospital, they chatted for a few minutes; then she told him that it was very important that she see him at his uncle's later that evening. At first he was reluctant to agree to meet her there, but she kept after him, and finally he gave in. It saddened Rose because months before he would have been suggesting ways to meet her after work. Now he had to be forced to do it. No use thinking about that, she told herself, it would just bring more pain.

"What's this meeting about?" Guy asked.

"You'll see when you arrive," she said, hedging a little.

"Rose, please, I'm very busy . . . I have to know what you want."

"I'm busy, too, Guy. You'll just have to be patient, I'm afraid."

"Oh, all right," he snapped, then turned his back on her.

She pressed her lips together and returned to work. Finally, when she left the hospital by herself, she set about locating the items she needed.

The late afternoon air was hot and damp and motionless. Overhead, dark clouds with a faint greenish cast rolled through the hazy sky as Rose went about her errands. Occasionally lightning glimmered in the sky, followed almost at once by a deep rumble of thunder that seemed to shake the very foundation of the earth.

If only it would rain, she thought, then this terrible heat would break and they would all feel better. The danger would still exist, yes, but they might be better able to handle it. She feared, though, that once more the storm would pass over them.

No rain came, and the heat continued building until she reached Father Daniel's room, and once she stepped over the threshold she found the closeness as unbearable as a blast furnace. Momentarily she swayed, then recovered and greeted the priest. They chatted while they waited for Guy, and much to Rose's surprise they didn't have long to wait before he arrived.

"Now, what's all this nonsense about a secret meeting?" he demanded once he'd sat.

Briefly she outlined her visit to S.A. van Cleve. Father Daniel had heard it earlier and listened quietly again, while Guy frowned as she spoke. When she was finished with her narrative, she leaned back in her chair and studied him.

"I don't understand," Guy said. "What about the disease?"

"There is no disease," Rose said.

"You lied." It was a flat statement. He looked first at Rose, then at Father Daniel. "You both lied to me. Deliberately."

"Yes," she said, although it hurt her to admit it. "We had to. Initially, you wouldn't have believed us, and we had to wait until a good time to tell you."

The priest fingered his rosary as he watched the couple.

"I don't believe you now, Rose. This is absolutely preposterous! Good God, whatever can you be thinking of? A lamia? In the nineteenth century? Come, come. How the hell did you concoct this story?" He tried to laugh, but the attempt failed, and Rose could see that he was nervous and that he believed more of what she'd said than he wanted to admit.

"You know it's true," she said. "That woman has been visiting you. I know it for a fact, even though I've never caught you two." Guy blushed, dropped his eyes, his expression telling her she spoke the truth. "It's not your fault, Guy, for lying to me or for deceiving your uncle and me. You're under her spell. Father, please, tell him what you know."

Father Daniel nodded and launched into the story he had told Rose before. Guy listened, his eyes still downcast, until Daniel had finished.

"And what if I said I thought both of you were simply jealous?" he asked.

"Then you would be wrong," Rose said quietly. "We're concerned about you, Guy. Daniel's friends *died* after they knew that woman."

"Daniel didn't."

"No, but he is a rare case. He doesn't know why, nor do I. I imagine only August does." She looked at him as he raised his eyes. "Will you help us?"

"What do you have in the bag?"

"A few essentials," she replied, "that I thought necessary for this evening. Garlic flowers, and some crosses for Father Daniel to bless, and as for the flowers, well, you'll see."

Without waiting for Guy to answer, she closed the single window tightly, wishing that weren't necessary, for now the heat would rise unbearably inside. While the priest blessed the crosses, she strung the garlands of flowers completely around the window and doorway. Guy sat still, simply watching them, unwilling to involve himself. Rose then set the blessed crosses above the portals, while Daniel followed, sprinkling holy water on the walls and the door and window.

The confined heat and the sickly sweet smell of the flowers made Rose queasy, turning her stomach, and she wanted nothing more than to be outside breathing fresh air, but she doubted they would have long to wait in the close atmosphere. At least she hoped not.

"You're expecting her to come," Guy said. "Why should she?" He was frowning slightly, and she wondered what was going through his mind.

"Because you're going to call her," Rose replied calmly. "I think she'll listen to you. Go ahead, Guy, call her."

He didn't speak, and Rose and Daniel exchanged looks.

She saw the tears in the priest's eyes as he realized to what extent his nephew had fallen under the lamia's influence.

As they waited, they didn't speak, and the minutes dragged by. An hour elapsed, then two, and when it was after eleven, Guy got up.

"I'm going now. I can't wait any longer." He made no effort to conceal his disgust.

"No, wait." Rose put a hand out to restrain him. "Just a few minutes more. Please.

"All right." His tone was somewhat petulant, and she felt the pain inside her chest, for he had never used that tone with her before. But he did sit down.

Daniel hadn't stirred much during their vigil as he found it almost impossible to respond to anything, and the blessing of the crosses and sprinkling of the holy water had sapped his emotional reserves. He lay back on the bed, the heat constricting his chest, making it difficult for him to breathe. Sweat trickled down the sides of his face, and he wondered that in his youth he had not minded heat half as much as he did now.

The air grew closer, hotter, and Rose dozed, her head nodding forward. Abruptly she sat up in her chair. The room was different—darker now, and warmer, with something else. A scent of musk.

August was there.

Somehow she had entered the room, getting past the crosses, the garlic flowers, the holy water. Numbly Rose stared at her. It shouldn't have happened! Crosses and garlic and holy water kept vampires away. Why hadn't it worked? Why?

August laughed. "How kind of you all to assemble to greet me. Why, my poor dear Guy, you aren't looking very robust."

He mumbled something about the heat.

"Well," said the priest impatiently, "what do you want here?"

"How brusque you are now, Daniel." He shuddered visibly at her use of his name. "May I remind you that Guy called me. Was it simply to test me? How delightful!" She draped one of the flower strands around her neck, and inclining her head slightly, she sniffed a blossom. "How delicate is the scent. I really must commend you on selecting such an attractive flower—one of my favorites, by the way. Did you know that?" she asked, gazing directly at Rose.

Rose shook her head sluggishly. She found it difficult to reply, to even think of an answer in the face of the other's mockery, and too, she felt defeated. Hoping against hope, she'd wanted to believe that the crosses and holy water and garlic would work, and they hadn't. Finally, Rose's words struggled out. "At least we've found out what won't kill you now," Rose said, mustering a practical tone. "Now we'll set about finding what will."

August laughed again and arched a delicate brow. "I wish you luck."

"We *will* find a way to destroy you, and we won't rest until we find it."

Again laughter greeted her challenge. "You are such a determined woman. Is that why you . . . admire her, Daniel? I see it in your eyes. Some would call it admiration; I would call it something else, something baser. And poor Guy, who doesn't want the good doctor any longer, and she hates him for it. My, what an interesting trio you are." She laughed, amused with some private joke. "Is it rest you want? Sleep, my children."

Her eyelids drooping, Rose felt the heat of the closed room rise to an unbearable temperature, and then it was swirling around her, blanketing her, smothering her until she couldn't draw in any air, and then she was yawning and yawning, wishing she could go to bed because of the late hour.

Darkness descended, and she had only one last glimpse of Daniel falling asleep and Guy asleep on the floor, and by them the lamia smiling and smiling.

She struggled through miles of cloying greyness that wanted to smother her, broke through, and finally awakened. The light was out, and she turned it on again to discover she had slept for some time, as had Guy and Daniel. A few minutes later the two men stirred, then gradually awakened. Rose searched the room, but she could not find the lamia. They were alone.

"She's gone," Guy said somewhat unnecessarily as he peered about the shadowed room. He sounded vaguely disappointed.

"Yes, she's gone," Rose snapped more sharply than she'd intended. She was irritated that Guy was acting so dreamy and befuddled, and yet, she reminded herself, he was bewitched and couldn't help it. Another part of her, far deeper, muttered darkly that if he really loved her, he wouldn't have fallen under the other woman's spell. She ignored that voice.

"What now, Rose?" Father Daniel's voice was filled with weariness. Deep lines were etched in his face, and unceasingly he fingered his rosary, and she thought he looked closer to his age than ever before.

"I don't know, Father," she admitted. She was drained from the events of the day and night, and from her failure. "Maybe we should just go home." She wanted to return to her boarding house and lock herself in her room and go to bed and sleep a dreamless sleep.

"I'll walk you there, Rose," Guy said quietly, and she

was surprised by the offer, although she quickly accepted.

Not long after that they left together, walking some distance apart, and it was almost as though they were strangers; certainly it appeared as though they had never been intimate. She'd never felt so separated from him, and dismay filled her because she knew she couldn't compete against the lamia.

The night air was cool and fresh after the closeness of Father Daniel's room, and as she breathed deeply, filling her lungs with the good air, she was beginning to feel less tired. Just before the couple rounded the corner to go to her boarding house, she stopped.

"I've changed my mind, Guy. Would you mind walking with me to the hospital? I know it's rather late, but I don't think I could sleep now. Besides, I have a lot of work to do."

He didn't protest; in fact, he said nothing, but merely nodded, and they turned and set out in the direction of the hospital. The air was growing lighter as dawn approached, though it was still a few hours away. In a tree behind them a bird sang, the notes fluting through the still air.

It would be a scorcher today, Rose thought, and she wondered how many other men and women and children would be brought in, dying victims of the cruel heat. How long would this continue? Until all of Savannah was dead or deserted?

She sighed and pushed back the wet hair from her forehead, and they continued in silence toward the hospital. Once in a while she glanced at Guy; his face was set in hard lines, as though he were deeply engrossed in thought, and she did not disturb him.

The sky was tinged a charcoal grey as they approached the hospital, and they could see someone sitting on the steps, as though waiting for them.

An old bum, she thought, who had no other place to go. Certainly it wouldn't be the first time.

But as the couple drew closer, she realized she was wrong. They stopped only a few feet away from the steps, and with horror Rose recognized the woman sitting on the bottom step.

It was Miss van Cleve, and her throat had been torn out.

Several days had elapsed since Rose and Guy had found the body of the historian, and in that numbing time Rose had realized that August had killed the scholar simply to taunt them. She had no reason other than to prove how easily she could kill them, whereas they didn't know how to destroy her. And her point had been made.

Rose could have wept with frustration. She did not have to be shown how easily August could kill; she knew that. Too, she felt somewhat responsible for the amiable historian's death; if she hadn't gone to van Cleve, then August would not have known about her, and thus the woman would still be alive. Yet she couldn't wholly blame herself, for she'd only consulted van Cleve for information on what sort of creature August was. After all, it wasn't as though van Cleve had given her a way of destroying the lamia.

Or had she? Rose wondered on the third day after the woman's death. During that brief visit had there been something inadvertently said? Something they didn't realize, but which the lamia feared Rose knew, or would remember?

She said nothing of her thoughts to Guy, who had immersed himself in his work. They hadn't spoken in days, and she wondered how long the silence would stretch between them.

When she had time that day, Rose paid a visit to Father Daniel and found he was still in bed.

"I'm tired, Rose," he offered feebly as his excuse. "I didn't sleep much last night. It was the heat, you know." He closed his eyes, apparently too weary to keep them open.

Rose suspected that the reason for his being in bed was the he'd simply given up. He didn't think he could defeat August, and so he was retreating within himself, retreating from the world and the ugly horrors of it. Guy had isolated himself as well from her, and Rose found herself very much alone.

When it came time to destroy the lamia, she knew she would have to act alone. Daniel was much too weak, too tired to be of any help, while Guy wouldn't lift a hand to help her.

If that time ever came, she told herself.

She sighed and fanned herself with a folded piece of paper. "I think I have what might be good news, Father." He tried to sit up in bed, and was too weak, so she reached over to help him. "I don't know why it's been happening, but in the last two days we haven't had any unusual deaths. There have been the usual number of victims of the heat, but none, as far as I can tell, from August."

"What?" Frowning, Daniel struggled to a more upright position, leaned forward. "What are you saying, Rose?"

She repeated what she said.

"None?"

"Just from the heat."

"But I don't understand. She has killed steadily since she arrived in Savannah. If those deaths have stopped, then . . ." He paused.

"Then what?"

His face seemed to brighten as she watched. "Then I have to conclude that she's left Savannah."

Rose remained more cautious. "She might have left, Father, or she might wish us to think so, Father, so she can fool us."

Daniel shook his head adamantly and his voice grew excited. "I don't think so, Rose. I truly don't. She is a deceptive creature, but not in that manner. That's far too complicated for even her webs. No, no, I think that for some reason she's left, left Savannah for good, left for a brief time. However long—she's left. And now I can have time to heal, and even Guy will be free of her spell and will return to you."

Rose still could gain no enthusiasm about the idea. "I hope so, Father. For all of our sakes, I hope she's gone, but somehow I doubt it."

Daniel smiled blissfully, almost as if he hadn't heard Rose's words. "She's gone, and already I'm feeling much, much better."

Rose decided it was best not to argue with him and left shortly thereafter.

Daniel tried to sleep after his visitor left, but he was too excited, and so he ventured out of bed in the early afternoon. That night his sleep was blessed with no dreams. The following night was spent the same way, and the next day even the heat shrouding the city eased.

Daniel could have wept with joy. She was gone. The lamia had left. His life was free once more.

Why had she left, though? Certainly neither he nor Rose had done anything to banish her. That was the only thing that puzzled him now. But as his strength returned, so did his resolve. If August had truly left, that meant that she was somewhere else, perhaps waiting, waiting for him to become weak again. So now he must do something; he must destroy the lamia before she returned to destroy him. He couldn't let poor Dr. O'Shaunessey act on her own. He had to be the one to do it. After all, hadn't August come to Savannah because of him.

But where could August have gone?

A week after his dreams of August had stopped, he went to bed feeling better than he had in months. He fell asleep almost instantly and woke to find himself standing in an immense marble-walled foyer. It was a foyer he didn't recognize; perhaps a theater.

Across from him was a full-length mirror; he glanced into it and saw that he was young once more, his hair dark, his skin unlined, and he was dressed impeccably in the fashion of the day. There was a jaunty smile on his lips. He crossed the parquet floor to double doors that swung open as he approached, and he found himself not in the interior of a theater, as he'd expected, but rather in an immense ballroom. Mirrors lined the four walls, and the ceiling was opened to the starry skies.

Light from thousands of candles and stars blazed and dazzled so that he held up his hand to shade his eyes while he gazed longingly at the couple waltzing to the strains of music by Johann Strauss. The music darkened, went into the minor key, and grew discordant, ugly, threatening, and as one each one of the women on the dance floor turned in a graceful sweep toward him. It was August and she was smiling. And she was reflected in the mirrors a hundred times over, and as she began laughing, a thousand laughing Augusts advancing on him, he woke again, screaming.

But he knew then where August had gone.

London.

Without a word to Rose or Guy, the next day he slipped away from St. Mary's and left for London. On the voyage over he tried not to think about what he was doing, about what would happen when he came face to face with the lamia. That was for later. He was sorry, too, that he could not confide in the couple, but he knew they would try to stop him. Rose would, he knew; as for Guy, he didn't know what his nephew would do anymore.

When Daniel arrived in London, he was weary from traveling and rested for some time in his inexpensive hotel. This was the first time he'd visited London since he'd left three decades ago. The memories of a lifetime long ago and of friends long gone crowded him, threatening to crush his senses, and he closed his eyes, seeking sleep. For now, the other matters would keep.

When he awoke later in the day, he felt much refreshed. He went to dinner, and as the hours passed, he could feel the years of his life being stripped away, and he felt as he had thirty years before, and he was strong and more determined than ever to find the lamia and destroy her as he should have done before.

The first day proved frustrating because he learned nothing, but he reassured himself by reminding himself that she was a wily creature; the second day Daniel learned that a number of young men had just recently died, all from a peculiar blood disease.

August is here, he told himself with mounting excitement. Here and waiting, and I *will* find her. I will destroy her.

The following day he located the families of the recent victims and went to talk to them, but although Daniel questioned them to the point of his own exhaustion, the anguished family members provided little information to him. None of them reported their sons and brothers as having been seen with a beautiful black-haired woman prior to their deaths.

This isn't right, Daniel told himself when he returned wearily to his hotel room after he'd talked to the families. Not right, because there had to be a connection with August. He would not even consider the possibility that another lamia, or even a vampire, existed and was preying on the young men of London. It *had* to be August. He *felt* it. Hadn't the dream led him here?

But if she was in London, she wasn't making her presence known, for no one he talked with seemed to have seen this particular woman, and he knew that once she had been seen, she would be remembered. Too, since his second day here no further deaths from the strange "blood disease" had been reported.

What could that mean? She had no reason not to kill, did she? Unless . . . unless she had left. Again. Again, to where?

But he couldn't believe that, so he stayed on and looked for her, searching through the slums of London, through the great bustling streets, wandering all hours of the day and night; he was jeered at, shouted at, and once someone threw a rotten apple at him. He stopped everyone he met, asked them if they had seen a beautiful woman with black hair and compelling eyes. Some laughed at him, some avoided him; but no one said they had seen her.

He walked by the club and stopped outside and thought about how it had been three decades ago. The warmth and friendship of Montchalmers and Terris. The good times they had had, the long hours of companionship and conversation, all gone because of August. She had destroyed his friends as she had destroyed poor Tommy Hamilton day by day, as she had tried to destroy him. But she hadn't. Not yet. He left the club and found himself walking in no particular direction, but when he looked up again, he was standing outside *her* house. The house where he had last seen Henry Montchalmers.

Tears blurred his eyesight, and he put his hands up to his eyes.

He went slowly up the steps and rang the bell. The door swung open, and a middle-aged servant stood there.

"Yes, sir?"

"Is . . . Mrs. Hamilton . . . in?" he asked.

"You have the wrong house, sir," the man replied politely.

"Mrs. Justinian, then," he said, his voice eager, his eyes desperate.

"I'm afraid, sir, that no one by that name lives here. My mistress is a woman of advanced years." The man stared at him as if he had lost his mind, and Daniel began to wonder if he had. He looked down at his clothes and saw that they were wrinkled, as if he had slept in them for days.

"Thank you," he whispered, and turned and walked away, without glancing back.

She had gone. She had left the town.

He could feel the void, feel the emptiness at her departure, and so he fell across his bed into an exhausted sleep, and when he woke, he knew where she had gone. Wearily he packed his bags.

Rose walked into the office and sat without waiting for an invitation. After a moment Guy looked up from the book he was studying.

"Father Daniel has been gone for over two weeks now," she said. "I'm worried, Guy."

"I'm worried too," Guy admitted, closing the book, but marking his place with his finger, "but what can we do?" His tone sounded almost flippant.

"We could start searching for him," she replied, trying to keep her tone even. "You know I've wanted to do that, but I can't do it completely by myself. What if he's lying out in some marsh, injured or perhaps dead?"

His face darkened. "Then we probably won't find him, will we?" Guy snapped.

Wordlessly she stared at him, unable to believe she was hearing this from him; then she glanced away. In the past two weeks she had greatly missed the priest and worried about him, apparently more than his own nephew had. Father Daniel had thought that August had left; perhaps she had, but her influence was still with Guy. Of course, it had lessened somewhat, but he still seemed caught in some unknown dream. She found him from time to time staring out the window, looking at nothing, murmuring something she couldn't distinguish, and seeing him like that brought a deep-felt pang, and the tears would start to well up, and she would force them away. Tears wouldn't solve anything, she told herself.

Guy passed a hand over his face. His expression had changed to one of pained embarrassment. He shook his head. "I'm sorry, Rose; I really am. I shouldn't take that tone with you. I know you're worried. God knows, I'm worried too, and I don't want him found dead. But I just don't know what to do."

She ignored his backhanded apology. "I've talked with the other priest at St. Mary's, and Daniel didn't tell him where he was going. No one knows. Except—" She stopped, not wanting to say it.

"Except August," Guy finished for her. She nodded. They did not speak about the lamia. Ever. "But she's no longer here."

"Perhaps not, but that doesn't mean she didn't lure him away and kill him."

"But wouldn't she have left his body where it could be found? Wouldn't she want to frighten us?"

"Why, Guy? She would have had what she wanted all along. What she had come to Savannah for would have been completed." She had to go on, had to say it to him, even though it might be cruel, even though she might hurt him. Her face was sympathetic, her voice earnest. "It wasn't you she wanted, Guy. The only reason she seduced you was to get to your uncle. She's always wanted him."

"No." It was an anguished sound.

"Yes. Why do you think she came to Savannah after thirty years? She'd found Daniel, and she came to claim him."

"No." He shook his head over and over, as if by his denying it he would make it so. "He's old, and a priest. He's—"

"Yes, he is older than you, and yes, he is a priest, but

somehow he's special to her. I don't know why; he doesn't know why. But she spared him for thirty years for whatever reason." As Rose gazed at him she felt sorry for him. She hadn't wanted to say that to him, but he had to know the truth, and perhaps now the last lingering remnants of August's enchantment would be broken.

Guy turned his head away and did not speak again for several minutes. Rose continued watching him. He put his head in his hands and his shoulders shook, almost as if he were weeping. He was fighting with himself, she knew. Fighting to come back. Perhaps not to her, but at least to come back. Finally he looked at her.

"I was a fool." His tone was bitter, his voice flat, emotionless.

"You were under a spell," she corrected.

"The same. What does it matter?"

She felt like shaking him. "Guy! You couldn't help it! I've told you that before. No man could resist August. You know that."

"No man except my uncle."

"Yes, and perhaps that's the reason August wanted him more than any other man. Perhaps she had to know why he could resist her, or perhaps she already knew. I don't know. The important thing is she's gone, and you're you again."

"For what that's worth."

"I think it's worth a lot, Guy, and I really wish you'd stop the self-pity." Her tone was sharp, but she didn't care.

"Self-pity!" He turned angrily to her. "Why, I—" He stopped, seeing her ironic smile. Slowly he grinned. "Self-pity, my foot, woman."

"Yes, self-pity, your foot."

"I haven't been good to you," he said.

"No," she agreed softly, "but that can change."

"Yes," he said with a wry twist of his lips. "I imagine it can." He bent over and kissed her gently on the lips. "Friends again?"

"If not more," she whispered.

"An excellent suggestion, Doctor."

"I thought so, Doctor," and they kissed again.

Weary, bone-tired, he arrived in India three weeks after booking passage on a Peninsula and Oriental steamship in Southampton, England. The ship had sailed down the English Channel to the Bay of Biscay, had made its first stop at Gibraltar, then gone on to Malta and Alexandria, then through the Suez Canal to the Red Sea, and finally to India. Then he made his way overland to Delhi. He had seen all of this without seeing; he had stared out at the distant shore, and his mind had been a blank.

Now that he was in Delhi at last, Daniel stood stock-still and stared around with wonder at the bustle of the Indian city. He had never been this far east before, had never seen anything to compare with it, and his interest in it could almost lead him to forget why he was there. Almost.

After a short search he located an inexpensive but clean hotel, and once he was settled in, he rested. He slept longer than he'd wanted, but then, he was exhausted. He had traveled more in the last month than he had for thirty years, and he, he had to remind himself ruefully, was no longer young.

He washed up, then stared into the mirror as he toweled his face dry. He saw new lines that hadn't been there the day before, saw that his eyes were red, saw that his hand shook. He breathed deeply, murmured a prayer, and changed into fresh clothing.

Later he went out to stroll around, nominally to see the sights, specifically to see if he could learn anything about August.

Here, he mused, all of his trouble with the lamia had begun so many years ago, and here it would end. How strange it would have been, he thought, if August had not selected Tommy Hamilton, but one of the other English officers. Would he have never known her, then? No. He thought he would have met her, no matter what officer she had selected long ago.

Was it not their fate to be brought together? He shuddered at the thought.

Sweating already from the heat, his clothes sticking wetly to him, Daniel walked through the hot and dusty streets, thinking about what it must have been like over thirty years before, during that time before the Sepoy Munity.

Oblivious now to the sour smell of unwashed bodies and rotting animal offal, to the harsh cries of the child beggars who scampered after him, whining piteously, to the babble of foreign tongues that washed around him, he wandered through the dusty lanes and streets. Tommy Hamilton had come here long ago to visit August Parrish; here he had fallen in love with her; here they had talked and walked and dallied; and here she had begun to murder him ever so slowly.

He stared at the exotic flowers and trees, watched as a

sacred cow lumbered across the road, watched as all traffic halted while the beast ambled away from him.

Here he felt Tommy's presence, even more than he had in London. It was almost as though he could talk with that Tommy of long ago, as if he could say to his friend: "Beware, beware, Tommy; don't lose your heart."

Despite the high temperature Daniel shivered, and he looked up to see that a dark cloud had momentarily obscured the sun. Again he shivered, then continued walking through the winding noisy streets until afternoon when he turned around to return to his hotel. He bought several of the English newspapers, and after a light dinner of curried chicken with rice and raisins he retreated to the coolness of his room to read them.

And buried in the back pages of one newspaper he found what he wanted: evidence of August's presence in the Indian capital.

A brief article reported a young man's death; the cause being suspected was a strange blood disease similar to the others reported a few days ago. Like the others, the youth had been European and in perfect health prior to his death.

This was her calling card; this was it, Daniel told himself triumphantly, and he carefully noted the attending doctor's name.

Tomorrow he would pay a call upon the physician, then the family; tomorrow he would be that much closer to finding August.

"He's dead," Guy announced, then dropped into the chair. "He has to be. It's been over two months now since we last saw him. God knows what happened." He closed his eyes, and for the first time Rose saw the lines around his eyes; it was almost as if he were aging in front of her.

That was August's work, she thought angrily, and knew it was one more thing she had to settle with the lamia.

"Maybe not," she said. She spoke with more enthusiasm than she felt; she was no longer confident that Daniel might still be alive.

"After so long? Surely, if he were alive, he would have written us before this. A letter, a note . . . just something. But he hasn't. He's dead. And we didn't do anything to prevent it."

"Because we haven't heard from Daniel doesn't mean he's dead," she insisted. "Maybe he's been sick or—"

"Or what?" Guy's tone was sarcastic, as was his glance toward her. He took out a handkerchief and rubbed it across his face. "Could he have lost his memory? He might as well be dead, then."

Neither one spoke for a few minutes. Guy crumpled the handkerchief and tossed it away from himself.

"I don't think he is dead, Guy. I really don't. I did before, but the more I think about it . . . I'm not so sure that's what's happened. I think he must have a reason for not writing to us. Maybe he's been busy; maybe he's pursuing something . . . or someone."

"Maybe."

"We'll just have to wait and see."

"How long?"

"I don't know," Rose admitted. "I don't know how long to wait, but we can't give up on him." She wished that she could reassure Guy or herself, but somehow she couldn't. She felt empty. She stretched out her hand to Guy, and he took it in his, and they sat, without words.

The physician knew nothing. In fact, the man knew less than Guy and Rose, Father Daniel told himself, and disgusted at the man's ignorance, he left.

He walked through the city, read more newspapers to see what new accounts could be found, and in the evening, when it was much cooler, he briefly visited the families of the dead men. The three mothers he spoke to reported seeing their sons in the company of a black-haired European woman, but not one of them knew her name, or where she lived, or where she had come from.

They didn't have to tell him; he knew who it was.

That night, and every night for the next week, Daniel exhaustively prowled the narrow, dark streets of Delhi, looking for her, hoping he might stumble by accident—or by something else—across her. Had he not realized that nothing in his life was coincidence? He was fated to meet her again; he knew that.

When he returned to his hotel early in the dark hours of the mornings, he would climb wearily and fully clothed into his bed, and he would call out to her, call for her to come to him.

Since he had come to India no dreams had haunted his sleep, and as the days passed, he grew more puzzled. He was ready for her. He was waiting. He had gone out to the market the day before and had made purchases. He had read about vampires before he left England, and he would treat her as one. He had the stake to drive through her heart, the holy water to sprinkle over her remains. And yet she did not come to him.

The long days passed slowly, and all the leads that he thought he had withered away, and still he had no word from her.

Daniel was so exhausted and weakened now that he could scarcely pull himself out of bed each morning, but somehow he did. And he managed to dress himself in fresh clothes, although the process grew progressively slower. He had stopped eating three meals a day, and now ate only when the pangs of hunger reminded him of his empty stomach. As if in a daze, he wandered through the streets, and the faces around him blurred into a brown smoothness that seemed to hypnotize him even more. Unseeing, he stumbled on, the hot midday sun burning him.

A lost soul, he walked through the city, walked and walked, until he finally found himself outside the city on the bank of the Jumna River, not far from the Bridge of Boats. Wildly, feeling so numb he wondered if he still lived, he stared down into the muddy depths of the water and saw himself: red-faced from the sun, his eyes blank, his hair long and disheveled.

There was a ripple across the surface, as if a fish had swum by, and then, there reflected, he saw another face hovering behind his shoulder. The lush red lips were drawn back in laughter. And the dark eyes sparked with malicious humor.

August. Laughing at him for making him look like a fool.

For she had.

He was a fool.

A damned fool.

She wasn't in Delhi. She probably hadn't been there since the first day he arrived.

She had tricked him. Again. Once more the lamia had been just a step ahead of him. He should have known in the first few days of the hunt that further searching would prove futile. While he'd confidently believed he was chasing her from continent to continent in preparation for killing her, the truth was altogether different. August was toying with him, leading him on, controlling his every action.

Why? He tried to laugh, saw his lips pull back in a grotesque expression, and a rusty sound rumbled in his throat. Why had she done this? Simply: because. She was cruel, without feelings, and she had wanted to break him, to wear him down, to batter her opponent's reserves, and she had chosen this wild goose chase as her way of doing just that.

And she had succeeded.

He was broken, defeated.

He was a shadow of his former self, a mockery of a man, and he wanted to go home. He wanted to be back in Savannah, back there so he could die in peace.

But he was too tired right now. First he had to rest. Just a little. Sick at heart, he stumbled around and somehow found his way back into Delhi and to the cool retreat of his hotel room, where he fell into bed and slept, without dreams, without thought.

Rose woke.

Gradually she grew aware that the man lying next to her was sweating as though he were suffering a high fever. She managed to wake completely and propped herself up on one elbow to glance at Guy. Still asleep, he moaned, arched his body, and stretched out his arms as though someone were there. His body was aroused, and he thrust and thrust, until Rose could not bear to look. He was crying out, and Rose touched him once, but he flung her hand off. Over and over he repeated one name.

August.

She could no longer bear hearing his moans and grunts, the sounds of his pleasure. Wearily she rolled out of the bed and dressed, her numb fingers fumbling with the many buttons.

That Guy was having those dreams again could mean only one thing to Rose: the lamia had returned to Savannah. Thus, if Father Daniel had left to destroy August, as Rose had suspected, then he had failed in his mission, and God only knew what had happened to him. Now the lamia had returned and was renewing her enchantment of Guy, and Rose's time with Guy was ending all too abruptly.

As she glanced at Guy, she saw he was once more soundly asleep. Saddened, she left. She didn't want to stay there any longer.

In the weeks of Daniel's absence she had thought about what she would do if she saw the lamia again; she still didn't know how to destroy the creature, but she was determined to.

In the meantime she had checked and found August still owned the Justinian estate outside Savannah. If the lamia had returned to Savannah, then it was only logical that she was living there. Rose vowed she would go there and take care of the woman—the *lamia*, she corrected—once and for all.

The first light of dawn was streaking the grey sky, and she encountered some trouble hiring a carriage to take her to the docks. She knew it looked strange: an unaccompanied woman by herself at this early hour. But she had brought her medical bag along, and she explained that she must visit a sick patient.

Along the docks she rented a boat to take her down the river to the island where August lived.

Rose asked the boatman to wait until she returned, and he nodded and immediately pulled his cap over his eyes and began dozing.

She got out and looked around the island. She knew it wasn't large, so it shouldn't be too hard to find the lamia's house. The beach was narrow and crescent-shaped, and the dock, where the boat was tied up, was old. There was no other boat there. A few yards from the beach woods rose up out of the sandy soil: green and dark and strangely silent.

She had no weapons, but then she didn't know what to use.

She set off briskly in the direction of the house. Around her gnarled live oaks, grey Spanish moss dripping from their twisted limbs, formed a dark avenue through which she had to go. She paused in the cool darkness with its scent of moss and decaying flowers, and to her left something scurried through the thick underbrush.

She remembered the many times she and Guy had gone to the seaside parks to picnic, and sadly, she knew those days were finished. She continued walking and caught the flicker of some motion out of the tail of her eye. An animal. A cat, or squirrel, something, she told herself, and breathed in deeply to calm herself. She mustn't suffer from nerves now.

The air was motionless, almost as if something or someone were waiting, and she heard no sounds. No birds were trilling their songs, and she couldn't even hear any noises from the river. It was truly isolated here; August had chosen her husband well.

The path she followed meandered, and when she came around a huge tree, the house seemed to loom up suddenly. She stopped, surprised to have found it so quickly, and she had the disquieting thought that it had just appeared to her. The sun was burning off the mist that clung to the trees and the house.

It was huge and old and dark. A colonial mansion from long-ago days, of a past century, of a family that had been prosperous. Of a family now dead. A long porch fronted the house, and two narrow windows flanked the double doors, once a polished wood, but now scarred from neglect and weather. Some of the windows on the second and third floors had been boarded up.

The bushes in front of it were nearly dead, and the lack

of activity anywhere bothered her. She hesitated, then licked her lips and told herself not to be a coward. She had faced the lamia before.

But not on her own ground, she thought, and despite the heat of the morning she shivered.

Holding her head high, she walked up to the double doors. When she lifted the brass knocker and let it drop, the sound echoed through the house. Minutes passed as she waited, and no one came. Once more she knocked; still no answer. She peered through a window adjacent to the door, but it was too dark inside for her to see. She tried the doorknob, found it locked.

Easily remedied, Rose told herself, and bending down, she ripped off the hem of her petticoat, wrapped it securely around her hand, then thrust the protected hand through the glass of one of the windows. She flicked the remaining shards out of the frame, pushed the curtain aside, and crawled through the window. She looked around the dark room.

Mustiness and a sharp odor she couldn't place choked her momentarily. She coughed, then took a deep breath. She could still see little because of the curtains, so she flung some of them back. A layer of dust coated everything in the old-fashioned room, as though it hadn't been used in some time. As though it hadn't been used since the death of Mr. Justinian, Rose thought.

She glanced around for a gas lamp, but there was none, and so she settled for several long white tapers she found in a drawer. She stuck them in a three-pronged candelabrum, lit them with matches from the drawer, then began her search for the lamia.

She went through the downstairs parlor, a library containing many dusty volumes, another parlor, the dining room, kitchen, and servants' quarters, and found no sign of August. As Rose walked, dust was stirred and billowed upward in clouds. She sneezed several times and listened as the sound echoed. Well, if anyone was here, they knew she was as well, she thought ruefully.

She went up to the second floor and found the bedrooms and sitting rooms there empty. The third floor was vacant and even dustier than the two below. The attic contained a handful of rooms used for storage, and here Rose poked through bundles and boxes, but found nothing more sinister than old clothes and books and memorabilia of several generations of Justinians.

She realized she didn't really know what to look for, except that she had read in one of Miss van Cleve's books that vampires needed to stay out of the light during the day. Thus, Rose reasoned, so would a lamia. After all, she knew of no one who had been attacked in the daytime by August. Thus she must sleep by day. The lamia would need an enclosed place in which she could sleep and hide and which could be carried easily.

A box or trunk, then.

In the basement Rose found more boxes and managed to pry open the tops of some, but they were filled with packed dishes. She was about to give up when she saw another crate tucked into a shadowy corner. She walked toward it and held the candelabrum aloft, the light revealing a carved sandalwood box, a chest such as those found in India. Trembling slightly, she set the candelabrum down so she could use both hands, and traced the carving with her fingertips. Then she slowly raised the lid.

The box was empty.

Disappointed, and yet slightly relieved, she dropped the lid with a resounding crash, and in the silence that followed she thought she heard a high laugh. It had to be in her head, she reasoned.

Damn. Defeated again. Defeated at every turn. She knew the carved chest had been the lamia's sleeping place, and she knew August must have feared discovery and so had moved her bed elsewhere. God knew where; certainly she couldn't search all of Savannah and the surrounding countryside. Damn. Hot tears of frustration and anger filled Rose's eyes.

She grabbed the candelabrum, nearly flinging it into the pile of boxes on the floor. It would serve them all right if she burned the damned place down.

Burned. She stared thoughtfully at the flames of the candles. Something stirred in her mind, a half-forgotten memory. Something from the day she had talked with Miss van Cleve. She concentrated. They had talked about the occult, about witches, and about—

Wait. The crosses and holy water that she and Father Daniel had tried to use against the lamia which had proved ineffective were used against vampires. Could it be that the lamia, being older than Christianity, was not at all affected by the trappings of that young religion, but by something more basic.

Such as . . . fire?

Miss van Cleve had mentioned the trials of witches in Europe in past centuries, trials where the witches had been burned.

Fire was a basic element, and even though lamias weren't witches, it might work. What else was basic? Earth, fire, air, water. The four elements. Obviously, earth and air could do the lamia no harm, and Rose could hardly tie the lamia up, then toss her into water. So all that was left was fire.

Fire . . . the all-consuming element. Fire, which destroyed all and everything.

Fire, which was one of mankind's oldest weapons against the darkness.

"It's worth trying," she murmured aloud.

First, though, she must see if Father Daniel had returned. She had to know what happened to him, and if he wasn't there, she would go to Guy and have him call to the lamia.

As Rose came out of the house she saw the sun had shifted considerably since she'd gone in. It was afternoon by now. She couldn't have spent all those hours in there, but somehow she had.

She had to hurry now. She knew she had little time left.

That morning Daniel had returned to Savannah, and he had slept since that time. Sometime in the afternoon he heard someone pounding on his door. Then someone called his name repeatedly.

Rose, he thought sleepily. He tried to call out to her, but he could only murmur. After a while the pounding stopped, and he drifted off to sleep again.

And the dream, always the same, came to him over and over, and tormented him, taunting him with its sensuality. Finally, Daniel could stand it no longer. He forced himself to wake up, to sit up, and he stared, wild-eyed, around the room.

"Stop it! Stop it!" His entire body trembled, and acid tears burned his eyes; he felt as though he hadn't slept in weeks. The return trip from India had been rough, the seas choppy; he had been ill the entire time, and he had dreaded the return to Savannah, the return to the place where he would die.

But he had no choice. He had come straight home,

hadn't even gone to St. Mary's; he had spoken to no one, cared to speak to no one. He was glad Rose was gone; then she couldn't bother him. He hoped she wouldn't return because he had to wait.

The afternoon had given way to evening; darkness had fallen now. A shaft of white moonlight thrust its way through a break in the curtains and pierced the dark air. He hadn't changed clothes, and now they were damp from his sweat, musty from travel. He pushed back his tangled hair and settled back in the bed. Dimly he was aware of hunger pangs. He couldn't remember when he'd last eaten, but he didn't care, and so he pushed the hunger away. He knew he should try to go back to sleep, but the dream, bringing with it his exquisite torment, would return.

He couldn't fight any longer, he told himself wearily. Not at all. He was too old, too tired to fight anymore. He couldn't even pray any longer. God would not help him, hadn't helped him yet, hadn't helped ease the torments he felt. He had prayed these past weeks, had prayed, and felt empty of God's grace.

"Come to me," Daniel said aloud. "August, come to me, please. End it all. I admit defeat."

Rich laughter bubbled forth from the opposite corner as August stepped from the shadows. He stared at her. She had never been more beautiful with her glittering red lips, her dark mocking eyes, and the cascade of midnight hair with its musky scent.

He had never seen her more vibrant, more *alive*, than she was now, he thought dully. Nor less human.

Unable to respond beyond watching, he waited as she swayed gracefully across the wooden floor to stand by the bed. She stared down into his dulled eyes.

"You admit defeat, Daniel?" He nodded almost mechanically. "This is what I have waited for so very long, my dear." She flicked a pink tongue across her full lips; they glistened in the moonlight. Her voice was almost merry. "I wanted not only you, Daniel, but the desertion of your God. I have waited, seeking to seduce you away from your false faith." She brushed his cheek with the tips of her fingers and laughed as he recoiled. She whirled away from him, sat in a chair by the bed. "In the beginning you were strong, and yes, your will matched mine. I was intrigued, very much so, and then you grew afraid and fled to the Church. That, Daniel, was your downfall."

"My faith, the Church . . . it was the only way I . . ." His voice faltered, and he tried to look away.

"You were never safe there," she said, a half-smile curving her lips. "I could have come for you there at any time. Any time." She laughed at his expression. "But, you see, I preferred the game, and so I waited, bided my time, and I permitted you to grow complacent. Now"—she rose and stepped closer to the bed—"you cannot resist me, Daniel. You see, your God, a false one, has sapped your manhood."

Numbly he recognized the truth in her words. These past thirty years he had deluded himself into thinking he was safe from her. He had tried to hide, had only succeeded in hiding the truth. He shook his head, hotness stinging his eyes.

"Why me?" he whispered. "Why did you want me so badly?"

"I wanted you more than any because you did not desire me as the others did. And because you were very special to me."

"You said that before . . . that I was special to you. I don't understand." Each word was agony for him to speak. The nearness of her body was overpowering, and he could feel himself breaking. "Why?"

"Don't you know?"

He shook his head. He could think no more.

"You might call this visit tonight a somewhat overdue homecoming."

"What?" Her words made no sense to him.

"A homecoming," August repeated as she draped her lithe arms around his neck. "Yes. I have left you twice, Daniel, not once. Did you know that?" He stared at her. "Can you not think back, back to when you were a child?"

The scent of musk. The laugh. Merest scraps of memory. Something struggled in his mind, struggled to free itself, and he shook his head, feeling the pounding of his temples, the pain shooting through his brain.

"No. No, no, no." That wasn't what she meant. It. Couldn't. Be.

"Yes. My son."

He screamed.

"No!" he shrieked. "It isn't true! It's not!"

But he knew it was. He screamed again as she bent and kissed his lips, and a shock jolted throughout his body. He tried to struggle, tried to push her away, but he couldn't move. She placed her hands on his shoulders and pushed him, unresisting, back onto the bed. He kept shaking his head, denying. It couldn't be so; it couldn't, for his mother had died; his father had told him so.

"Died? No, I left for I had become bored with your father, a rather pale, uninteresting creature." She chuckled. "I don't always kill my husbands, Daniel. Not always. And as you will find, I can be a very loving and tender mother."

He recoiled as she kissed him again, forcing his lips apart with her tongue. It traced his lips, explored the cavity of his mouth, and he felt the nausea rise up in him, even as the desire did, and he was ashamed. Her hands fluttered across his body, undressing him swiftly, touching him deftly, moving away, returning to tantalize, and he closed his eyes against the inner pain. He tried to pray, but no words passed his dry lips nor came from his deadened brain. When he was finally unclothed, she laid her hands upon his chest and dragged her nails down his skin.

His body shook with new tremors, and slowly his eyes opened, and he stared, unblinking, at her as she eased out of her gown; she wore nothing underneath.

Naked, she paraded before him. She cupped her ripe breasts in her hands; then she bent over him, brushing the crimson tips against his face, thrusting them into his pliant lips, against his clenched teeth. He tried to move his head, tried to look away, but couldn't. She stood up, yet stood so close to him, and she stroked her breasts, then trailed her fingers down to rub her hips, her thighs. Slowly she spread her legs, thrust her hips forward, and fondled herself, then laughed. She slipped onto the bed and crouched above him. Her damp flesh pressed against his, and he burned as though he'd been branded with a hot iron.

God will damn me, he thought; God will damn my soul to hell for my sins. All my sins. Lying and lust and . . . and . . . and now this.

God doesn't hear you, mocked a voice in his mind.

She rained burning kisses upon his face, his neck, chest, thighs, nipping at his flesh, seizing a fold of skin between her strong teeth and worrying it. Pain and pleasure mingled with his terrible shame, producing an answering effect Daniel had never before experienced. It was fire and ice, comfort and agony, and he knew he couldn't stop, not even if he wanted to. That was the last damning bit, that he could do nothing, could not keep himself from liking it. And yet he knew this unnatural lassitude was what her other victims had experienced. The thought did not console him. Other victims. And now he was one, he even more than the others.

She stroked his manhood, laughed when he would not become firm. "Do you need more coaxing, my love?" she whispered into his ear. She stuck her tongue into his ear, and he twitched as the liquid sensations coursed through his body. She kissed the tip of his manhood, licked it languorously, maddeningly slowly, and slowly brought him to arousal.

Humiliated, he lay with his hands clenched into fists at his side. Even his body had betrayed him. He was dying. He had failed again, failed as he had with everything in his life. Bitterness filled him because of his empty life, a life devoid of any reason.

Devoid of anything except sin, he told himself.

August kneaded the muscles of his arms and chest, licked his lips, and gripped his testicles in her fingers. She stroked them, and he cried out. Carefully she positioned herself above his groin, then lowered herself until she was just brushing the tip of his throbbing manhood. Groaning, he arched upward to meet her.

Suddenly the door crashed open.

"No!" he heard a woman scream, and then August was wrenched off him. Startled, Daniel looked, but his head moved so slowly, as if he were suspended in time. He saw that it was Rose who had come into the room. She had dropped a small keg onto the floor.

She slammed August, still startled at the interruption, against the wall, and before the lamia could recover, Rose grabbed the keg, uncorked it, and began flinging a clear liquid on the other woman. The smell of kerosene filled the room. Rose dropped the keg, then stumbled back a few feet, ignited a match, and tossed it onto the drenched lamia, who was trying to rub the kerosene off.

With a roaring sound flames engulfed August, and screaming, she reeled away, falling against another wall and setting fire to the draperies. Rose backed away as sparks flew off the lamia's body and landed on the carpet, setting it afire. The sound of inhuman cries, the snapping of the blaze, the smell of kerosene and burning flesh filled the room, gagging Rose and Daniel. Rose doubled over as black greasy smoke billowed upward, enveloping everything in the room. Daniel tried to sit up, but couldn't.

Suddenly, there was a shout, and Guy rushed in just as the walls ignited. He saw his uncle, still lying stunned on the bed. He threw a robe around the naked man's shoulders, and lifting the old man easily in his arms, he ran outside. He set him down carefully, then ran back to the building.

"Fire! Fire!" Guy called and ran to help the other residents of the burning building.

In the distance Daniel could hear the clanging of a fire bell and the sound of shouting, and in the fresh night air he blinked as he slowly recovered from his semiconscious stupor.

With great difficulty Daniel eased himself into a sitting position and stared at the burning spectacle in horror, and the memory of what had been about to happen returned. He would have committed . . . if it hadn't been for Rose—Rose. He looked around, but didn't see her anywhere outside. A crowd had gathered to watch the fire, and he couldn't see too clearly, but he knew she wasn't here. She must be inside, only Guy hadn't seen her.

Daniel knew he couldn't wait for his nephew to return and then go back inside. It would be too late for Rose. His own anguish forgotten, he stood, pulled his robe around him more securely, gathered his strength, took a deep breath, and rushed back inside the burning building. He found a handkerchief in the pocket of his robe and tied it over his mouth and nose, and he beat at the flames licking along the door frame with a rug he found. Then he dashed into his room.

Flames were everywhere, and in the midst of the fire he saw the two women. They were locked together in a grappling embrace as they fought one another. To his horror, one of the women burned like a candle. The clothes of the other smouldered. He peered through the blinding smoke and flame, and saw that it was Rose. They struggled soundlessly, the one trying to pull the other into the flames with her, and they twisted, battling, the flames shooting upward, and as they turned, he saw the strain on Rose's face.

With a cry of rage Daniel raced toward the women, but at that moment Rose kicked her opponent's foot out from under her, and August fell to the floor, and there, with an unearthly shriek that chilled him, August suddenly vanished. The flames died down, and the smoke evaporated, and though he couldn't see any burns on Rose, she collapsed. Sobbing with relief, Daniel caught her before she hit the floor and carried her outside. Guy rushed toward him.

"My God, what's happened?" Guy asked as the priest carefully laid Rose under a tree. Guy dropped to his knees and began to check her for burns.

Daniel shook his head and wiped the soot from her sweating face. He coughed a little as he spoke from the smoke that had almost suffocated him. "I came around and didn't see her outside, and knew she had to be inside yet. When I got in there, they were fighting. August was completely on fire. As I started to get Rose, August disappeared." He wiped a hand across his forehead, and soot smeared his fingers. "Thank God, you and Rose came tonight."

"Don't thank me, Daniel." Guy's tone was chagrined. "You have only Rose to thank for your life. This afternoon she came to me and told me that if I ever wanted to see you alive, I'd best come to see you this evening; then she ran off before I could say another word. I didn't see her again until now."

"For whatever reason you came, I'm glad you did." Uncle and nephew smiled at each other, close again, after months of separation. "How is she?" he asked, his voice anxious, as he watched Guy examine Rose.

"I can find only a few slight burns on her hands, and one on her arm that's a little more serious, but overall they don't look too bad. We'll take good care of them, and I doubt if they'll take long to heal. They shouldn't be disfiguring, either."

"Thank God," Daniel said, and the words were like ashes in his mouth.

Guy stroked her hair back from her forehead and laid a wet cloth against her skin. "Rose, darling, can you hear me? The lamia is gone." He laughed a little. "Rose, you were so strong, so wonderful. You saved Daniel." He wrapped cloths around her hands and laid them across her stomach, then smiled reassuringly as he stroked her cheek. "You won! We've all won!"

By her side Daniel watched as she slowly regained consciousness. Behind them the house collapsed in a fury of flames, and in that momentarily bright, hellish light Father Daniel saw that Guy was wrong.

It was Rose who lay upon the ground.

It was August who smiled up at him.

BESTSELLING BOOKS FROM TOR

- [ ] 58725-1 *Gardens of Stone* by Nicholas Proffitt $3.95
  58726-X Canada $4.50

- [ ] 51650-8 *Incarnate* by Ramsey Campbell $3.95
  51651-6 Canada $4.50

- [ ] 51050-X *Kahawa* by Donald E. Westlake $3.95
  51051-8 Canada $4.50

- [ ] 52750-X *A Manhattan Ghost Story* by T.M. Wright $3.95
  52751-8 Canada $4.50

- [ ] 52191-9 *Ikon* by Graham Masterton $3.95
  52192-7 Canada $4.50

- [ ] 54550-8 *Prince Ombra* by Roderick MacLeish $3.50
  54551-6 Canada $3.95

- [ ] 50284-1 *The Vietnam Legacy* by Brian Freemantle $3.50
  50285-X Canada $3.95

- [ ] 50487-9 *Siskiyou* by Richard Hoyt $3.50
  50488-7 Canada $3.95

Buy them at your local bookstore or use this handy coupon:
Clip and mail this page with your order

TOR BOOKS—Reader Service Dept.
P.O. Box 690, Rockville Centre, N.Y. 11571

Please send me the book(s) I have checked above. I am enclosing $_____ (please add $1.00 to cover postage and handling). Send check or money order only—no cash or C.O.D.'s.

Mr./Mrs./Miss _____
Address _____.
City _____ State/Zip _____
Please allow six weeks for delivery. Prices subject to change without notice.

MORE BESTSELLERS FROM TOR

- [ ] 58827-4 *Cry Havoc* by Barry Sadler — $3.50
  58828-2 — Canada $3.95
- [ ] 51025-9 *Designated Hitter* by Walter Wager — $3.50
  51026-7 — Canada $3.95
- [ ] 51600-1 *The Inheritor* by Marion Zimmer Bradley — $3.50
  51601-X — Canada $3.95
- [ ] 50282-5 *The Kremlin Connection* by Jonathan Evans — $3.95
  50283-3 — Canada $4.50
- [ ] 58250-0 *The Lost American* by Brian Freemantle — $3.50
  58251-9 — Canada $3.95
- [ ] 58825-8 *Phu Nham* by Barry Sadler — $3.50
  58826-6 — Canada $3.95
- [ ] 58552-6 *Wake in Darkness* by Donald E. McQuinn — $3.95
  58553-4 — Canada $4.50
- [ ] 50279-5 *The Solitary Man* by Jonathan Evans — $3.95
  50280-9 — Canada $4.50
- [ ] 51858-6 *Shadoweyes* by Kathryn Ptacek — $3.50
  51859-4 — Canada $3.95
- [ ] 52543-4 *Cast a Cold Eye* by Alan Ryan — $3.95
  52544-2 — Canada $4.50
- [ ] 52193-5 *The Pariah* by Graham Masterton — $3.50
  52194-3 — Canada $3.95

Buy them at your local bookstore or use this handy coupon:
Clip and mail this page with your order

TOR BOOKS—Reader Service Dept.
P.O. Box 690, Rockville Centre, N.Y. 11571

Please send me the book(s) I have checked above. I am enclosing $_____ (please add $1.00 to cover postage and handling). Send check or money order only—no cash or C.O.D.'s.

Mr./Mrs./Miss _____
Address _____
City _____ State/Zip _____
Please allow six weeks for delivery. Prices subject to change without notice.